Michelle Duff

A mad8 Publication

Other Books by Michelle Duff

Make Haste, Slowly - 1st Edition published 1996
Make Haste, Slowly - 2nd Edition published 2011

Serial Number 6218 - published 2005

Mikita, A Legacy Earned - published 2009

The Secret Meadow - unpublished

Five Cats, One Dog, A Motorcycle, and A Lady in a Hot Pink
Jacket - unpublished

Books in the Wolf Series

Book 1, Jennifer's Boots - published 2009

Book 2, The Black Wolf - published 2010

Running Fawn's Legacy

Michelle Duff

A mad8 Publication

Canadian Cataloguing in Publication Data.

Duff, Michelle - Running Fawn's Legacy.

ISBN: 978-0-9685706-5-4

1. Duff, Michelle, 2.Young Adult - Canada - Fiction, 3. Fantasy, 4. Wolves,
5. Ojibwa First Nations, 6. Ojibwa Mythology, 7. Manitoulin Island.

mad8 Publishing
1810 Island Road
R.R.#1,
Coldwater, ON L0K 1E0
Canada

Tel: (705) 686-3167
Email: mad8@amtelecom.net
Web Site: www.michelle-duff.ca

FRONT COVER: The Ghost Village of Daniel's search nestled within the trees by a lake, in a time long, long ago.

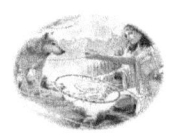

CONTENTS

For my love of wolves, especially black wolves, and for my two dogs, Sara and Nikkita, who resemble wolves in so many ways. May they forever be man's (or woman's) "Best Friend". They are mine.

Michelle Duff

Prologue

A green, fibre glass canoe glides swiftly towards shore. The stern paddler expertly guides the small craft parallel to the dock. He holds the canoe steady while the bow paddler steps out onto the dock, and then she helps a young girl to get out who'd been sitting in the middle.

"Mom, listen, I can hear the falls from here," the young girl shouts excitedly.

"Come on you two, steady the canoe so I can get out too," says the man.

"Oh Daddy, can we go up and have a look now?" asks the young girl as she holds the canoe for her father.

"We will go as soon as we make our campsite ready," replies her father. "You two get our stuff out onto the dock, and I'll go up and get our camp-pass. Pull the canoe up onto the beach when you finish unloading it."

"Aw," complains the daughter as she pulls the tent out of the canoe.

"It won't take long, Sweetheart if we all help then we can walk up the river bank together," consoles her mother.

A warm wind courses through the camp site and stirs dust up from the car park and blows in the father's face while he walks along the path to the office. Sunlight beams through the early autumn colours of the trees lining the edge of the path. The man's sharp beak-like nose protrudes out just above his hair-line lips. Bushy eyebrows give his face a permanent scowl, framed by long black hair that's pulled back and braided in a single fall down his back and tied with a length of rawhide. A small white feather, fastened into the long braid by a length of rawhide, flutters in the breeze.

At the camp store the man waits patiently while the clerk deals with two American visitors who have pulled up in their long motor-home. When no one else is in the office the clerk asks, "Can I help you, Chief?"

"I would like a camp pass for the night," the father replies, "a site by the river for my tent."

"Not sure I have a site available," replies the clerk viewing the camp schedule.

"I phoned. I have a reservation."

"Oh. Um, well, okay," stutters the clerk. "How many are there of you? Yer not going to cause any trouble are yuh? An' no drinkin's allowed."

"There is only my wife, my young daughter and me. We cause no trouble. It is just for one night."

They stood looking at each other for a few moments, then the clerk says, "That'll be $18.00," and hands over a receipt. "Pin this here notice on the post by site 46. It's down in the far corner by the river."

"Thank you," replies the father.

The clerk says nothing, just nods curtly.

Their camp made ready, the three travellers walk the short distance along the path to the base of the falls.

"Many times I have come here," comments the father. "And I always feel humbled by this place. You know the water drops nearly twenty metres in the centre? And, sometimes, when the sun is just right you can see a rainbow right there in the mist. It is one of the most beautiful sights in the area and said to be a holy place held in great esteem by our ancestors. Just above the falls, the river separates into two rivers, one river falls here," he points to the falls. "And the other tumbles down the rapids over that cliff," he says pointing to the high wall of solid rock that diminishes in height to the right along the far edge of the river. "The rivers join again just above our camp site before rushing into the Big Water."

While her parents rest on a wood bench under the cool shade of a tree on the river bank the young girl wades through the shallows at the base of the falls picking up pretty stones and shells. "Daddy, look. What's this?" she asks, holding an odd shaped stone.

"Bring it over, Sweetheart and let me see." He tells her it is an old flint arrow head. "There should be lots of them around," he says. "Our elders tell stories of a battle that took place here many, many years ago, long before the white man came. Little is known about the battle, but what is told is that our early peoples were victorious."

"Wow," replies the young girl. She looks down at the arrowhead in her palm. With a finger nail she scrapes away a bit of dirt. "Oh, look. What's this bit of white stuff here?"

"I don't know," replies her father. "It could just be a bit of white stone. It's too old to be sure."

"Maybe it's a bit of bone."

"Such an imagination," smiles her mother.

"I'm going to see if I can find more." The young girl runs back to the

shallows and continues to look beside a large rock lying flat on the ground.

Totally consumed by her search the young girl suddenly feels someone is watching her. "What?" she asks and turns, thinking she also hears voices crying out. She looks around for an animal perhaps that accidentally plunged over the falls, but there is nothing. Her parents are still sitting on the bench, and seem not to have heard anything. She turns and continues to look for more arrowheads, but she is once again plagued by that same feeling of being watched and is sure she hears voices crying out. She again looks around, but like the time before, sees nothing. But, just there within the swirling mists of the falls is a large fading image of a young Indian woman, waving.

"Mommy, Daddy. Look!" she shouts, turns to get her parents attention and points towards the falls.

"What is it Holly?" asks her mother. Both parents look in the direction their daughter is pointing.

"It's in the mist at the bottom of the falls." Holly turns and looks again at the swirling mist. "It's a girl's face, oh, ah, no. It's gone now, but it was there a moment ago, and she was smiling at me."

Chapter 1
The Ghost Village

A vast array of stars spread across the sky like diamonds casually thrown onto black velvet. Daniel stood on the end of the dock and looked up, as he often did in the predawn, and felt overwhelmed. To the east, in preparations for the arrival of the morning sun, the celestial display above the distant trees had begun to fade, the sky there a royal blue.

We've got about half an hour, thought Daniel.

Ebony had already climbed aboard the canoe. He turned and looked towards Daniel, his black coat shone in the diffused light. He pricked up his ears and cocked his head to one side with a questioning expression.

"Oh, sorry," said Daniel. He pictured the sun rising above the trees in the east. In response, Ebony transmitted a feeling of anxiety in suggestion of the need to hurry.

"Okay!" said Daniel, aloud. This the black wolf understood. Ebony's understanding of spoken language was little more than a few dozen words, the word 'okay', one of them. Like most canines, Ebony's mind formed thoughts in picture format, not a collection of words, like his human counterparts.

Daniel zipped up his jacket to keep away the chill of the morning damp and had a last look up the road. "I guess she's not coming," he whispered to himself, turned and pushed the canoe away from the dock. Climbing aboard the stern end, he settled into the seat. A "V" shaped ripple flowed out onto the mirror smooth lake waters and disrupted the perfect reflection of the trees and rocks on the far shore. He'd taken no more than a couple of strokes with his paddle when a horn blared from behind and a black pickup truck skidded around the corner and came to a sliding stop in the gravel.

A female voice shouted, "Daniel Santos! Wait for me."

"Running Fawn you came." Daniel paddled backwards, bringing the canoe parallel with the dock once more. "Grab the other paddle," he said, pointing to the end of the dock. "I'm so pleased you came. I'll steady the canoe while you climb aboard. What changed your mind?"

"It's such a lovely morning I couldn't refuse your invitation to explore the old village. Sorry I'm late."

"No problem." Daniel was clearly pleased Running Fawn had come.

Holly Kanipiswet was her common name, but Daniel preferred Running Fawn, the name given to her by her grandfather, one of the village elders.

Ebony moved to the middle of the canoe, and Holly stepped in at the bow end.

"It's so lovely and quiet, Daniel," commented Holly, then added. "I need my morning smoke." She pulled out her lighter and lit a cigarette.

Daniel agreed it was a lovely morning. "Hey," he grumbled and faking a cough he said "the wind's coming in my direction."

"Oh, sorry." Holly took one long drag, then with her fingers separated the burning ash from the cigarette and dropped the red ember into the water. "I'll save the rest till later." She put the unused butt back in her cigarette package.

"Thank you," Daniel said, and he smiled looking at the back of Holly's head.

Puppy love, he thought. *That's what she thinks it is.* But, he knew better. Holly had just turned nineteen, which made her eight and a half years older. *Eight years may be a lot right now,* thought Daniel. *But it won't mean much in ten or fifteen years.* He sighed, remembering when he first met Holly at his father's and step-mother's wedding about five years ago. She looked so beautiful in her native Indian dress, he fell instantly in love. She had just begun to blossom into a young woman back then, her female characteristics clearly visible inside her Native dress. He'd kept his feelings secret though, even from his new mother. He was just four at the time, and who at that age could talk about love. A few months ago, he'd finally told Holly how he felt. She just smiled that knowing smile that young women get when they have the upper hand in matters of romance.

"Oh, Daniel," she had said. "I do really appreciate your feelings, but don't you think I'm a bit old for you? Some day, when you're a bit older, you'll meet a young woman your own age and fall madly in love. But, I'll always be your friend."

And that's the way it had been left. Daniel was happy to have Holly as his friend, but he always knew their relationship one day would blossom, and Ojibwa elders would tell stories about their love over lodge campfires at night.

Few sounds filtered across the water from the surrounding countryside. The air smelled fresh, with the scent of pine all around, and a hint of lingering skunk carried with it. Two bats darted just in front of the canoe sending out rhythmic sonic beeps as they skimmed the water's surface for an early morning breakfast of bugs. Periodically they swooped down to scoop a small quantity of water into their mouths and left telltale ripples in the still water's surface just in front of the new bow wave created by the canoe.

A small cluster of five or six cottage-type homes crowded the west shore of the lake. Much of this land had been cleared to accommodate man's motorized toys and modern necessities. A gravel road bent around the corner of the lake, and gave access for the few families that vacationed or lived permanently in the area. Beside the dock, a public boat-launch gave local visitors access to the lake, but no one used it because the majority of the lake would not accept anything much bigger than a canoe, row-boat or personal water-craft.

The waters at the western end were up to five metres in depth, but the eastern end was shallow and filled with an abundance of lily-pads and underwater grasses making navigation by motorized boats difficult, but acceptable for a craft without a propeller. Except for a three-acre clearing of solid ground at the extreme eastern end of the lake, the entire shoreline of the lake harboured a dense marsh of bull-rushes and reeds. This clearing at the eastern end, completely surrounded by the marsh, had been a favoured area for archaeologists digging for Native artifacts. According to the local government, long before the arrival of the white man, a First Nations Indian village occupied these lands and flourished. Whatever happened to this village remained a mystery. Because of the site's age, few of the expected artifacts were ever found. Financial restraints had prevented proper study programs to properly date the sight or establish its importance in aboriginal prehistory. The site was thought to be thousands of years old. Just beyond the clearing and the protective marsh, in the woods and adjacent hill an old Indian ossuary bore witness to a substantial Indian population at one time. Few items found at the site had ever been carbon dated, and those that had been created many doubts among the acknowledged archaeologists who had spent time at the site. So, its true age remained speculative, and a point of contention. Indian concerns for the safe keeping of the site, prevented any excavation of the area, and local governments had prohibited any development of surrounding lands mainly because of the dense marsh.

The village site had been well chosen by those who occupied it all those years ago. Three sides were protected by the dense marsh; on the fourth side, the lake afforded comfortable access to invited guests, but gave the land dwellers a distinct advantage in defence against their enemies.

About fifteen years ago, the clearing had been declared a national heritage site otherwise human encroachment would surely have developed the lands. For the moment, at least, the village clearing, and the grave-yard beyond, were safe from developers.

It was this clearing that Daniel, Holly and Ebony planned to visit this early morning. The three adventurers had often explored the clearing, Daniel for the sense of adventure possessed by most nine-year-old boys, for Holly because of her own personal interests to learn more about her native heritage, and for Ebony, just to be with Daniel.

"Look," declared Holly, pointing skyward.

Two Great Blue Herons flew overhead in lazy flight silhouetted against the dark blue of the growing morning sky; the rush of air their great wings displaced could be felt more than heard in the morning quiet.

Daniel paddled on for many moments; he and Ebony were both deep in their own thoughts.

"Over there, Daniel," said Holly pointing to a large rock on their left that appeared sewn to the surrounding land by bull rushes and marsh grasses. Two otters played on the rock. They ran in and out of the water, and jumped over each other. Daniel watched and laughed at the otters' antics, and envisioned young children beaching canoes on this rock in days gone by to swim and play with parents and friends. Ebony transmitted his own thoughts of long gone wolf packs resting from a morning hunt across the frozen expanse of the lake in a winter scene void of colour.

A log appeared in front being pushed by a beaver, only the top half of the beaver's head visible above the water's surface at the far end of the log. A sudden slap of his tail against the water's surface warned others of his kind that apparent danger approached before he disappeared below the surface, just as the canoe bumped into the abandoned log.

Above, two mated Kingfishers flew together in circles swooping in and out in spiralling figure eight loops. Occasionally one dropped down to the water's surface to scoop up an unsuspecting fish then they were gone, lost in the light of the sun whose orange rim had suddenly peaked above the distant trees. The moment possessed tranquillity and a promise of greatness not felt at any other time of day. Daniel stopped paddling and let their craft coast. He took a deep breath soaking in the added warmth of the sun's rays. Ebony nodded in agreement to Daniel's feeling of peace, for he too felt it.

"Hey," shouted Holly. "Leaving me to do all the paddling? Oh, sorry, you two transmitting thoughts are you? Come on you guys; don't leave me out of it."

After all the years she had known about the mysterious mental link between Daniel and Ebony, and their ability to transmit thoughts to each other, it never ceased to amaze her. At first she didn't believe it, but in time it became so obvious, she couldn't disbelieve it anymore.

Daniel explained what he and Ebony had been thinking when they watched the otter at play. The trio went silent again and paddled on.

"I love it this time of the morning," said Daniel to Holly momentarily. "It's so quiet and peaceful. I wonder how different it is now compared to when the village was full of people. Don't you?"

"Yeah, me too, but as interested as I am in the history of my people, I do like lots of stuff about the modern world too. You know all the convenienc-

es. I couldn't imagine not having proper toilets, running water or electricity. I go to university next year, and I'm really looking forward to that, anything to get away from small town Manitoulin. Sudbury's not that big a city compared to Toronto, but at least it's a city with lots of people and a night life. I can't wait to experience some of it. And, thanks to your grandfather, the grant I've been awarded will allow me to get some higher education, when the time comes."

A light mist drifted up from the cool waters as they drifted into the eastern bay that was the far end of the lake. The warmth of the rising sun's rays suddenly burst upon the waters and the mists grew in intensity like a white blanket being dropped upon them. Their canoe coasted quietly into it. A clammy dampness surrounded them, and Holly shivered. "Wish I'd brought a warmer jacket."

"Yeah, I've never seen mist like this before," replied Daniel. "This is not normal."

Now totally engulfed in white, Daniel could no longer see Holly sitting a few metres in front of him. Even Ebony, sitting within arm's reach, was little more than a vague dark image. All around was nothing but a world of white, the sound of the water being displaced by the bow of the canoe, their only link with reality.

A pinpoint of light appeared in front and became brighter and grew in intensity. Within the light, a space about the size and shape of a garage door began to shimmer and swirl like milk poured into water. All around the large square of swirling light the mists began to rotate and formed a tunnel until everything around them, including the canoe, seemed engulfed in one huge vortex of rotating mist. A sucking wind came from the light and pulled at their damp clothes and hair. Daniel had trouble holding onto his paddle as their little craft was pulled towards the light with surprising force. The square of shimmering light quite suddenly shot rearward forming a reverse cone and from within the cone a deep humming noise drowned out all other sounds, followed by a shrill scream, like an animal caught in the death jaws of a large predator. Daniel could feel a strange tingling caressing his skin as they were jerked forward into the reverse cone and pushed out from within the mists into bright sunshine and blue waters to the sounds of children laughing.

Four or five children, all topless and wearing only light beige breechcloths and leggings, played near the water's edge about fifty metres in front of them. In front of the children, pulled up on the sandy banks, sat a number of canoes. To the right of the canoes, a couple of women, clothed in light beige dresses, fringed leggings and moccasins, were laying pieces of something on racks in the sun. A sweet scent of burning aspen came from smoke drifting up from simmering ashes below the racks. It drifted across the clearing and out onto the lake bringing with it the smell of food cooking. Beyond them, a cluster of bark wigwams crowded the open land. A sparse palisade of wooden

poles rimmed three sides of the clearing. The flimsy fence did not extended along the shoreline, but left a large opening to the water.

A short distance to the right of Holly and Daniel, a large canoe travelled in the same direction at great speed paddled by four men, all with feathers in their long braided black hair.

Daniel felt an instant anxiety in Ebony long before he had time to react to his own emotions at what he saw. The intensity of the black wolf's anxiety startled him, but there was something else about Ebony that was even stranger. A barrier had been put up in his thoughts and Ebony seemed distant and strangely different. What thoughts Daniel could read were vastly more complex than anything he'd experienced before from his canine buddy. So confused was Daniel with the sight of the village and the possible peril in all its reality, he had little time to consider the situation with Ebony.

"Daniel!" shouted Holly, the panic in her voice echoing his own fears.

"Holly, paddle back, quickly. Paddle!" They both pulled back hard on their paddles in an effort to turn the canoe. It swung around slowly and they headed back towards the mist. In the heat of the moment, time seemed to slow, their minds raced ahead both wanting desperately to return to a more familiar situation.

A young boy playing near the water was the first to notice the strange craft that came from the mists. He shouted the alarm. A woman turned from her labours to tend to the boy's needs and seeing the strange canoe cried out. Other people emerged from the wigwams to see what was happening. A momentary silence hung on the air. Everyone turned to look at the strange canoe and its occupants.

The canoe with the four warriors began to turn and head towards the three adventurers. The men began whooping and shouting. Daniel and Holly paddled hard to return to the mist.

Daniel could feel more than see the other canoe getting closer. "Go, Holly. Go!" he shouted in a final outburst of desperation. *Just a bit more,* he thought.

At that instant a sudden pain shot through his head and he slumped forward into unconsciousness.

Chapter 2
Biizhaan, Awi Jiimaan

Holly reached over as best she could with her tied feet and gently nudged Daniel's legs. "Wake up damn you."

Daniel, still unconscious, gave no response to Holly's prodding.

"Come on Daniel," she again nudged his legs to no avail.

In his unconscious state, Daniel mumbled an occasional slurred word and struggled to lie down within the confines of his bindings. He cried out and his body jerked violently as the dark image of a truck came towards them, rolling over and over. Sparks from grating metal on tarmac flew in all directions, and the grotesquely beautiful lights, bright white lights and red lights, spinning around in picturesque patterns, and suddenly, the terrifying crunch of metal. He gasped heavily at the envisioned moment of impact, the darkness surrounded his dream, and the empty feeling left by the absence of his mother and twin sister from his life.

The black of the night was replaced by the ghostly white of a room, and all the blurred people in it all dressed in white. This image faded, replaced by someone singing. His father appeared, holding his stepmother's hand in the meadow with trees all around. His father was singing to her as she lay sleeping on the stretcher. And the little black wolf puppy, Ebony, was there too. Daniel began to mimic his father's operatic voice, a poor facsimile in his confused state, he sighed and his body relaxed. He opened his eyes. "Oh, where am I," he groaned, shaking his head.

"Daniel, Daniel, I thought you'd never wake up," whimpered Holly. "Daniel, please; I'm so scared."

"Oh," he moaned. Daniel tried to move, but could not. He was propped up against a stake in the ground. His wrists were tied, and similar heavy vines were wrapped around his waist and around the stake to hold him in position. Beside him was Holly, tied in the same fashion to another stake.

"What happened?" Daniel asked. "Where are we?"

"We're inside one of the little wooden huts. After one of the Indians hit you over the head with a club, they grabbed hold of our canoe, and pulled it back to the village. Then they dragged us in here. How are we going to get out of here, Daniel?" whimpered Holly, and she began to cry.

"My head hurts too much to think right now. Give me a minute. I feel

rotten." Daniel turned as best he could and wretched what little substance remained in his stomach.

"Oh, that feels better," he said clearing his throat. He took a deep breath and had a good look at the insides of the wigwam they were in and could see some things outside through the doorway. "Yuh know, what we are seeing here's pretty crazy. This stuff looks ancient. Do you think we're still in the 21st Century?" Daniel struggled with the bindings. "Oh, I know," he suddenly said. "They're making a movie, and we're being held here to keep us out of the way."

"I don't think so," replied Holly, in control of her emotions again. "I didn't see any equipment around, and these people look like the real thing."

Daniel focused more closely on the structure they were in. It looked like he imagined the inside of an Inuit igloo would look, except this hut was not made from snow. Small tree trunks had been stuck in the ground in a circle and were bent over to the centre and held together with leather cord to form a hemispherical shape. Additional branches spanned horizontally between the vertical tree trunks in circular rows for added support. Large chunks of tree bark were strapped to the horizontal branches and layered in overlapping rows similar to modern day roof shingles. The structure stood about two metres high in the centre and maybe twice that in diameter. In the middle was a small fire surrounded by field stones laid in a circle. The smoke left the structure through a small soot covered hole in the roof above the fire where the tree trucks met in the middle. Immediately behind him was a platform raised knee high above the ground. Underneath he could see an intricate weave of what looked like thin strips of bark, and laid on top were animal furs. A sleeping platform he assumed.

Corn husks, braided together, and cobs of corn, squash and beans were strung from the hut support frames. Small pumpkins or what looked like pumpkins lined one corner of the hut, along with more squash and other food products. An animal hide, stretched tight on a wood frame, hung from the bed chamber support poles. It was a beautifully constructed building made totally of natural products, efficient, brutal in its aesthetic crude elegance. *And, if this really is the village for real, this house is even more amazing,* he thought.

He shook his head to clear his thoughts. "Where's Ebony?" he asked. "Is he all right?"

"I don't know, Daniel. When the Indians grabbed our canoe, Ebony jumped overboard and swam to shore. The last I saw him he was running for the forest."

"You mean he just abandoned us? That doesn't sound like Ebony. Didn't the Indians go after him?"

"No they just let him go. They were more concerned with us than him." Holly began to relax with the conversation, but still she was afraid, more

frightened of what she didn't understand. "They weren't speaking English," she said. "Their language was really weird. There were a few words of Ojibwa I think, but other words made no sense to me at all, and a dialect I've never heard before. I don't know enough Ojibwa to understand much of what they were saying even if they were speaking Ojibwa. Some guy was here a little while ago shouting orders and everyone was running around like crazy. He must have been the head elder or holy man or maybe the chief or something. Everyone jumped when he spoke. And the head guy was overly careful of anyone hurting you."

"Yeah? What do you mean?"

"Like they really handled you with care, but it was more than just being careful. The chief or holy man seemed afraid of you. He was in here with a funny rattle, and he sang a strange chant over you, and danced around a bit while shaking his rattle."

"Maybe they think we're gods or something. We could say untie us or we'll get you," replied Daniel.

"Yeah, sure, and if we were gods we could untie ourselves. And how are you gonna talk to them. They don't speak English, remember."

"Oh, yeah, forgot, and you don't know much Ojibwa, do you?"

"Hardly," sighed Holly. "And how they speak isn't at all how the elders back home speak. Come on Daniel, think. How are we going to get out of here?"

At that moment, a group of women and children appeared at the doorway. Four or five at a time entered the building and each group stood gawking at the two alien visitors.

"Look at that little boy's clothing," whispered Holly. "It all looks hand made, not a single machine stitch anywhere. I love his fringed leggings, and his breechcloth and leather moccasins. They'd cost a fortune in a souvenir shop. And that feather in his black hair looks like a real eagle feather."

The young boy cautiously approached Daniel and extended a finger; he gently touched Daniel's face, pulled back and giggled. The other children giggled too. A young girl hiding behind a smaller boy reached out and ran her fingers through Daniel's dark blonde hair then turned towards a woman as if to ask for permission to do what she was doing. The woman, wearing a three quarter length leather dress and high leather moccasins, smiled. The

other women dressed in a similar style seemed most interested in the jeans and jackets Holly and Daniel wore. None were violent or showed any disrespect, but without exception, they all ran their fingers down the fabric of Holly's clothing.

Within a few minutes everyone had entered, had their look, touched and laughed a little, and left. "I wonder what that was all about?" asked Daniel. "The way they all looked at me, you'd think they'd never seen a blond headed white person before."

"Maybe they haven't, replied Holly.

"At least you look like one of them, except for your clothes."

"If this is the real village that was on this bit of land, it was here long before any white people came. Do you think this is what's happened to us? What we came through in the mist was certainly a tunnel to something."

"I don't know, Holly. Wouldn't that be cool. A time tunnel. Wow."

"This is no joke Daniel. Time tunnels aren't real; they don't exist, except in make believe stories. Get real will you. Whatever it was we came through, I just hope we can find it again to get home."

It was then Daniel noticed the legs of a young woman standing in the shadows by the door. "Look over there," Daniel nodded with his head. Both he and Holly turned to look at the young woman when she stooped to enter the wigwam.

"Look at her dress, Daniel. It's beautiful."

An elegant design of porcupine quills and sea shells filled the front bodice and lower arms of her dress. The skirt came to nearly her ankles. An intricate pattern of animal designs that seemed burnt into the deerskin covered the bottom portion of her skirt. An ornate belt cinched her tiny waist and accentuated her rounded hips. On her feet were leather moccasins with more multi-coloured sea shells and porcupine quills. She came over to Daniel and knelt down in front of him, bowed to him and spoke quietly into her hands looking at the ground while she did so and seemed to be praying. Her voice was soft almost musical; she seemed to be singing or chanting. She got up, sprinkled some flower petals on him and bowed again, then stood and walked slowly backwards out the door.

"Did you understand anything she said?" asked Daniel after she left.

"Not much. I could hardly hear her. I thought she said something like, 'gii-mamaa ningozis' which I think means something is missing, but I'm not sure. That's what my grandmother used to shout at me all the time when I stole

hot biscuits fresh out of the oven. I didn't understand anything else, though."

"I wonder what she was up to."

"Beats me," replied Holly.

An older woman came into the wigwam carrying two clay pots; the legs of a male warrior could be seen standing outside. Hanging down from the warrior's waist was a wooden handle with a baseball size stone attached to the end. Small feathers decorated the carved handle. On his other side hung a length of white bone shaped and carved to a fine point.

The woman untied Holly's hands, but she left her feet tied, and left the vine wrapped around her waist. Then she did the same to Daniel. She turned to Daniel and said, 'Giwii-wiisin ino' and moved her hand to her mouth.

Both Holly and Daniel just stared at her. The woman repeated the words, this time rubbing her own stomach.

"She's asking if we're hungry, I think," suggested Holly.

Getting no response from the two captives, the woman went to the fire, knelt down with the pots beside her. With two sticks, she picked up one of the hot stones ringing the fire and carefully dropped it into the larger of the two pots. The pot's contents steamed and bubbled. She turned and did the same to the second pot. A few minutes later she reaching into the biggest pot with a wooden spoon and scooped out some of its contents onto two wooden plates. She brought the steaming plates to Holly and Daniel then went back and filled two clay cups with the liquid from the smaller pot.

On the plate were chunks of meat in thick gravy mixed with a combination of wild berries, like cranberries, and roots like sweet potatoes, and bits of square yellow cubes that looked like squash. Corn kernels were scattered throughout the gravy. The meat had a gamey taste to it, and Holly thought it was probably venison or moose. In the cups, was a tea that tasted strong of peppermint and sweet herbs, and was quite delicious, but they both had more pressing matters on their minds than feeding their stomachs - how to escape. Out of respect for the woman who brought the food they ate some of it.

"I could use a cigarette rather than food," said Holly.

"You and your smoking, you'll not get any cigarettes here," remarked Daniel, and he laughed.

When they'd finished eating, the woman took the plates, the empty cups, re-tied their hands and left.

Daniel and Holly sat in silence for quite some time before either spoke.

"I wonder what time it is?" asked Holly.

"I don't know. I was wondering that myself. Judging by the length of the shadows outside, it's probably late in the afternoon." Suddenly the vine holding Daniel to the stack dropped to the ground.

"Sssshhh," whispered a voice from behind. It was the young woman in

the beautiful dress who had sprinkled flowers on Daniel and had spoken to him earlier in the afternoon. She cut the bindings holding both Daniel's and Holly's hands. Daniel had untied his feet and tried to stand. He rubbed his hands and ankles to quicken circulation again. In the meantime, Holly also untied her legs and stood.

The young woman pointed to a small hole underneath the sleeping platform. "Biizhaan," she whispered, and motioned for them to follower her. She crawled underneath the sleeping platform and through the small hole, shortly followed by Holly and Daniel.

"Awi," the woman whispered, and motioned with her hands for them to leave. "Jiimaan," she said and pointed towards the canoes at the water's edge.

Daniel and Holly skirted around the back of the wigwam over to another wigwam getting as close to the canoes as they could. "We're close here," said Daniel. "It's not far to that first canoe. There're even a couple of paddles inside. You can see the top of them. Think we can make it?"

"We won't know until we try," replied Holly.

Daniel turned to thank the young woman who had set them free, but she had already gone. At that moment, another woman walked around the back of the wigwam and nearly bumped into them. Daniel shoved her away, and he and Holly took off, headed for the nearest canoe. The woman yelled a warning. The warrior standing guard at the entrance came running. Holly was pulled to the ground. Daniel hesitated.

"Run, Daniel, run," shouted Holly. "Go, get help."

Daniel ran the short distance to the nearest canoe, pushed it into the water and jumped in. He quickly grabbed one of the paddles and began paddling for the mist. The large birch-bark canoe lumbered slowly forward. He pulled hard on the paddle, stroke after stroke. His muscles ached. He could feel the presence of someone close. Afraid to look behind until the bow entered the mist, he then turned and saw Holly being dragged back into the wigwam, and immediately behind him, just beyond reach, stopped in the water, another canoe sat with two warriors watching him. They appeared afraid to come closer.

The white mist closed around Daniel and his canoe.

Chapter 3
Reminiscing

It had been a long winter. The warmth of the early April sun gave promise to a coming season of change.

For the first time in many months, Jennifer Santos was able to stand on the front porch of their home without a winter jacket and heavy boots. In the far distance ice crystals twinkled in the early morning sun reflecting off the still frozen North Channel. *Another month and the ice will be gone and there'll be so many boats I won't be able to see the water,* she thought, and smiled.

Looking down into the valley she ran her fingers through her shoulder length blond hair. "I wonder if the wolves have moved into the summer den yet?" she asked herself, then rubbed her bulging tummy. She spoke softly to the new life within. "A new spring litter should be coming along soon, little baby. I wonder if you'll be able to feel the wolves and talk to them the same as your brother, Daniel, and me. My how the pack has grown in the last few years," she continued, still rubbing her stomach. "When Big Black was the alpha leader, the pack's future didn't look good. You know there are nearly a dozen healthy wolves in the pack now, thanks to Boots." Jennifer sighed, looked down at her tummy and continued to talk. "You remember me telling you about Boots the new Alpha leader of the pack? Lots of people would like to see the wolves gone, but here on Grandpa's property they are protected from hunters. Local authorities are always worried that the wolves will attack livestock in neighbouring farms. You remember Big Black? He was Boot's dad, and since the incident a few years ago when he raided Mr. Lafave's chicken farm, local people were really angry about the pack's protection. The wolves don't usually leave the property. They've got the 1,000 acres of Grandpa's farm to run in, but once in a while I guess one of them does wander a bit, and when that happened it has no protection. Not many people like wolves around here. We're trying to change that attitude, and it is happening, but it's an uphill battle. We've had a few incidents when the authorities received complaints from neighbouring homesteads. Once in a while one of the wolves is shot. People are so ignorant, Little One," continued Jennifer, still rubbing her tummy. "They don't think of all the good the wolf does in the balance of things."

A tear trickled down her cheek when she thought about the wolves, and Daniel. "Where are you, Daniel?" she asked through eyes filling to overflowing at the memory of him running with the wolves. "If only I hadn't let you

go exploring the old village site that morning, you'd still be here. You were so strong and confident, far older and wiser than your nine years. You'd be almost eleven now. If only we had found something, anything, some evidence of foul play, or your body, it would have been easier to accept. There would have been some resolution to the mystery of your whereabouts. Are you still out there, Daniel, somewhere struggling to find your way, searching for home, suffering from amnesia or kidnapped? Will we ever know what happened to you?"

Jennifer Santos had been born three years after her parents Jason and Heidi Davis had married. She was an only child. Her parents had wanted more children, but Jennifer's birth had been difficult, and the doctors had told Heidi she might never be able to have another, which to date had been true.

The Davis family had come from Toronto and moved to Manitoulin Island a year or so after her father received a sizeable inheritance from his Aunt Myrtle's estate following her death. Jennifer had hated Manitoulin at first and threatened to run away which in fact she did the first summer they had lived on the Island. That was six years ago. She had rescued a little wolf puppy, the puppy she named Boots, one of Big Black's, the black wolf's, puppies. The pup had fallen down onto a ledge on the rock wall beyond the meadow, and when she'd brought him home she tried to convince her parents he was a dog given to her by her Ojibwa school friend, Sharon Goodchild. Jennifer's defiance and subsequent arguments with her mother, mainly about the puppy, added to her growing reluctance to conform to her parent's wishes. The turmoil with her mother compelled her to run away, not wanting to give up the little wolf. The ensuing adventure in Toronto with her friend Ashley with whom she lived for a summer, and the difficulties of raising a wild wolf on the streets of downtown Toronto, taught her much about wolf society and life in general. The girls had many adventures, the most serious included police charges for suspicion of cocaine possession. Late summer Ashley's mother had an accident from which she died. This had left Ashley orphaned, and in the care of the Catholic Children's Aid Society.

Jason had flown to the rescue and brought Jennifer back to Manitoulin, but she was a solemn and morose reflection of the former daughter the Davis' remembered. Ashley had arrived on their Manitoulin doorstep, a runaway from the Catholic Children's Aid Society and the Canadian justice system. With no living relatives in Canada and no family will, the courts wanted to return Ashley to an aunt and uncle in Ireland, but she was subsequently adopted by the Davis family and became Jennifer's sister. The adoption renewed Jennifer's relationship with her mother, but time needed to heal previous wounds, time that now had done just that.

Ashley and Sharon had become great friends on Manitoulin, and at times Jennifer had felt left out of their plans. Her studies of veterinary medicine had taken her in a vastly different direction from her two friends, both of

whom had joined forces to work together on a major agricultural project initiated by Jennifer's father.

It had been Sharon's long-time wish to renew some of her people's lost pride in themselves and to return much of their forgotten culture and self respect. Her grandfather, a respected elder of the Ojibwa First Nations Peoples, had predicted a leadership role for his granddaughter within the tribal hierarchy, a prediction that had begun to come true, for Sharon was now one of the respected leaders and clan matron of the local band of Ojibwa peoples. From high school, Sharon had gone on to study agri-business, biochemistry and earth sciences at Laurentian University in Sudbury, an hour and forty-five minutes drive north east of Manitoulin. Ashley had followed Sharon and became her keen supporter and classmate. Jennifer's father had invested a large sum of money with the proceeds going to the local high school scholarship fund to assist outstanding Ojibwa students to further their education. And, Sharon had been one of the first to receive the benefits of this scholarship. Jason had also allocated a five acre plot of rich farmland on the corner of the Davis property for Sharon and Ashley to experiment with different seeds and grains in an attempt to develop a new strain that would grow faster and under more extreme weather conditions, like those found on Manitoulin Island. The Island's growing season had limitations. A late spring or early fall cold spell could mean total crop failure for the few farms that persevered on the Island. Developing these new strains could rejuvenate the farming community on Manitoulin, and with Sharon's people at the forefront of its development, it could go a long way towards re-establishing her native community and bring much needed government support to the struggling economy of the Island. Some favourable results from Ashley's and Sharon's experiments had been achieved. However, University studies had taken precedence over their own activities, and progress had been slow, but with the discovery and development of the patented Dafave Formula, success had been imminent.

The Dafave Formula had been created by a neighbour of the Davis', Jean LaFave, who used it as a preservative for slaughtered chicken meat. With the help of a local veterinarian doctor, and Jennifer, the Dafave Formula was found to be a natural preservative for severed human limbs to keep them healthy over a long term for reattachment and/or transplants. But along with the Dafave Formula, an old Ojibwa medicinal paste made from rare poppy seeds was also necessary to cure the constant problem of rejection previously associated with organ transplants.

During her third year of studies at Guelph Veterinary College, 250 kilometres to the south of Manitoulin Island, Jennifer had been able to experiment more with her greatest interest: natural Ojibwa herbs and medicinal remedies, many long forgotten, except by a few remaining First Nations elders. Sharon's grandfather had been one of the elders who had agreed to teach

Jennifer as much as he could remember about ancient medicines, but the few sessions she'd had with him were difficult because his memory, good on many days, faltered and ceased to function on as many other days.

While at home during Christmas break, Big Black had caught his lower leg in an old leg hold trap and had chewed off his paw to escape from the saw-tooth jaws. She'd found him near death in the frozen wilderness not far from her parent's home, brought him back to the house and nursed him back to health, albeit a tenuous existence with only three full legs. She left him in the hands of the pack and Nature and returned to her studies.

During her second term at the Guelph Veterinary College, she'd befriended a fellow student, Doug Holder, and with his help and computer skills, she researched the possibilities of a prosthetic replacement limb for Big Black's missing paw before the discovery of the severed paw and subsequent controversial surgery to reattach it three months after the fact.

Jennifer's friendship with Doug had introduced Doug to her sister, Ashley, and the two of them developed their own relationship.

Anthony Santos, Jennifer's husband and Daniel's father, was employed with the Ontario Ministry of Natural Resources as a Conservation Officer. Following the death of his first wife, Barbara, and Daniel's twin sister, Stephanie, in an automobile accident near Kapuskasing, Anthony had requested and was granted a transfer away for the memories of the horrible accident and moved to the Espanola office of the MNR. He had been given Manitoulin Island as his territory and this brought him into contact with Jennifer. Following a sometimes rocky first few meetings, the two fell in love and subsequently married in a double ceremony along with Ashley and Doug. Anthony and little Daniel could not have been happier about the union.

During the summer before Jennifer's and Anthony's wedding, Big Black had been killed by a disgruntled hunter, but when little Ebony had been born shortly after Big Black's death, and possessed so many of Big Black's personality and the same mental link, it was suggested he was a reincarnation of Big Black.

Dressed in his government-issue dark brown uniform, Anthony opened the front door and stepped out onto the porch. "I wondered where you were," he stopped in mid sentence. "Oh dear," was all he could say when she turned around and he saw her tears. He engulfed her in his arms. "I know, Sweetheart."

Jennifer always found great solace in her husband's arms. His personal air of confidence and strength gave her much needed emotional comfort. "I was just remembering back to the first summer you two were here. Daniel was so fragile and vulnerable, so innocent. Oh, Anthony, I can still feel him in my arms. He was so warm and, and........ It seems like only yesterday. Do

you think he and Holly are safe somewhere curled up asleep and will come home?"

"You mean like Rip Van Winkle?"

"Like who?" asked Jennifer between sobs.

"Oh, it's just an old fairy tale. We can only hope at this point, Sweetheart." He nuzzled his cheek into the top of Jennifer's head and smelled the fresh fragrance of lilacs that always lingered in her freshly washed golden locks. He could feel the warmth and love he felt for this woman rise within him. "I think about him all the time too. I miss him so much, but we have to accept reality. It is doubtful he is ever coming ho..." Anthony's voice began to crack. He took a deep breath. They had been over this a dozen times. "Someday we will learn the truth." He released his hold on his wife and held her at arm's length. "Take care of yourself. Try not to think about him. It's important for the baby. We've been trying for so long. I'd hate to lose him now that it's so close."

"Her," said Jennifer, through tear stained cheeks and a little smirk. "And her name's Brittany."

"What?" Now it was Anthony's turn to smile. "As long as he's healthy; it doesn't matter if he's a boy or a girl." He kissed her on the forehead and ran his hand down the back of her hair and gently massaged her shoulder muscles. "I'll call you from the office later. Don't dwell on Daniel too long. You know how it upsets you." He stood looking at his wife and her tear-filled eyes. "You've gotta stop blaming yourself, Jennifer. It wasn't your fault."

She sniffled and wiped her cheeks on the sleeve of his uniform.

"Gees, thanks, this was clean this morning," he said, and smiled. "I'll see yuh later. Sure you'll be okay?"

She nodded yes.

"Love you."

Jennifer smiled, mouthing back the same words to him, and waved as Anthony climbed aboard his Ministry truck. He turned and blew her a kiss from the driver's seat and drove out the drive.

Jennifer sat down in the big rocker at the corner of the porch after Anthony left and gazed out over the valley in the direction of the wolves' den. Letting her mind wander back six years to Daniel and his first interaction with the wolves when she found him in the den curled up with all the puppies. Misty visions came to her in the unusually warmth of the morning sun.

"Daniel, Daniel. Are you in here? Everyone's so worried about you, Little Guy. Half the world's out looking for you."

"Jen-fer. Jen-fer, me Dan'l."

"Is that you Daniel? We have been looking all over for you. You had

us so worried."

"Ni'e puppy Jen-fer. Ni'e puppy."

She remembered her sudden surprise when she realized that Daniel had spoken the first words she's ever heard him say.

One vision faded replaced by another. It was the first winter that she had known Daniel and Anthony. She had been left in charge of Daniel while Anthony went off to work. She, Sharon and Ashley had been busy in the greenhouse researching the poppy seeds, and Jennifer had half forgotten about her charge playing outside in the snow. When she'd finally thought about him, it had snapped her back to reality. "Daniel!" she had declared aloud, and ran outside. But, Daniel was no where to be seen. She'd searched frantically for him without success. "Feet leave tracks in the snow," she'd said to herself aloud, and began looking more closely at markings in the snow. On the perimeter of the play area, a set of little foot prints headed down the trail in the direction of the wolves' den, which had not surprised her. Half-way to the meadow and the den, she'd found large feline tracks in the snow walking parallel to Daniel's little prints. They were far too big for a house cat. Jennifer began to run, frantic with fear of what might already have happen.

Two hundred metres farther along the trail, numerous large canine tracks joined the parade of prints, and a few metres more there was evidence of a skirmish. Bits of grey and black fur littered the trampled snow and the feline tracks ran off in the other direction. When she eventually found Daniel, he was curled up in his familiar spot in the den with the nearly full-grown puppies, none the wiser for the near contact he'd had with either a bobcat, a lynx, or maybe even an elusive cougar, all of which could have been fatal for the young boy, and just because she had been 'too busy'. Her shame had so subdued her, she told no one, not even Daniel, how close he had come to harm, or how profoundly it had affected her.

She had just begun the roll of a mother and had found the responsibility a bit overwhelming compared to the total freedom she'd previously known. But now she could not imagine not having those responsibilities. "And soon, Daniel," she whispered. "You are going to have a little brother or little sister. Oh, Daniel! I miss you. Where are you?"

She shook her head to clear the sadness she felt, and let her mind return to the day she and Anthony had decided developing a wolf education and research centre was what they wanted to do. This decision had needed to be made quickly; plans for the house construction were being finalized. They wanted to include a new wing in the house for a large meeting room that would double as a classroom. They had to get a variance to a local by-law to allow them to develop the lands as an educational area, but local authorities had been cooperative, saying they didn't worry too much in an area as remote as their's.

Following construction of the house, a viewing platform overlooking the meadow was one of the first projects to be scheduled. It was needed to allow visitors to observe the wolves' activities in the meadow below without causing them any interference. And then during late summer when the wolves had moved to the winter den up near her parent's house, construction had begun on a tunnel in behind the birthing den. A one-way sheet of glass had been installed so people in the tunnel could see into the den without the wolves being able to see them. Construction had been difficult, but the idea had worked well. A small night-light had been installed in the den that illuminated its dark extremities enough that people could see what was happening in the den. Jennifer worried that the wolves might reject the summer den now because of the construction and the little light, but they moved back in without a complaint.

Occasionally, a person behind the glass wall would break the imposed silence and disturb the wolves, but in time the wily canines grew to accept the close proximity of the odd human sound. Jennifer wanted some sound-proofing installed, but there really was little that could be done in the confines of the tunnel dug in the earth. In general, though, the entire idea worked well. The Ministry of Natural Resources approved the Centre as an official wolf research station and had found Jennifer a generous government grant to help her fund the operation. Many government biologists and naturalists had visited, and used the viewing chamber spending countless days making notes and observing the intimate lives of the wolves in their own living space and environment.

Jennifer had made contracts with many local schools to teach first hand the merits of wolves in the balance of Nature. Everyone had left with a greater understanding of the importance of the wolf in the scheme of things. Jennifer was pleased that finally she seemed to be getting her idea out to the masses. But, what had pleased her most were the changes in government legislation towards the wolf. The provincial bounty on wolves had been lifted. No longer could anyone kill a wolf and collect money for doing so. And indiscriminate killing of wolves was no longer tolerated. If a farmer or landowner killed a wolf, the killing had to be substantiated, or they would face stiff fines and/or penalties. But still, the hatred was there, and many farmers shot, dug a burial hole, and kept quiet about it.

That first year of Anthony's and Jennifer's marriage had been so hectic for all the family, especially Jennifer. Major demands had been placed on her to appear at various functions, with both Daniel and Ebony in tow, events she always enjoyed. But, now with development of the Wolf Education and Research Centre as well, it seemed she had little time to do anything else. And yes, they even had a sign out on the main road. 'Come Dance with the Wolves' it read, and a large arrow pointing in towards the house. Business had been so good that at certain times of the year it was necessary to restrict visitors to

appointments only, but generally, anyone coming at any time would be accommodated.

A couple from Minnesota had stopped by one day and asked to see the Santos Wolf Pack. It seems the name given to Jennifer's wolves by the local school children had spread. During the American couple's visit in the tunnel, young Daniel had been asleep in the den curled up with five of the new pups born earlier that spring. The surprise look on the American couple's faces when they realized a live young boy was actually in the den with the wolves, and in no apparent danger, was worth the disruption they initially caused by arriving without an appointment. Daniel had awakened and pressed his face against the glass making a face as he did so. His actions had been copied by two of the puppies, and everyone laughed.

Jennifer smiled at the memory. The image of five-year-old Daniel asleep in the den faded, replaced by an impish face of eight year old Daniel. His self assurance and maturity in this image were clearly evident. It was the day after summer holidays had begun when he came to her and said, "I want to live with Ebony, just for the summer," as if saying, just for the summer, would make it all right.

The idea seemed preposterous at the time. Initially, both Jennifer and Anthony had said no.

"I don't know, Daniel," Jennifer had argued. "I don't know how your presence with the wolves would affect the Research Centre? Or how visitors would react to you being with the wolves all the time?"

Daniel didn't like it. He initially honoured their decision not to let him live with the wolves. However, as the summer progressed, he often sneaked out of the house after everyone had gone to bed. In the morning, his parents would find him in the den curled up asleep with the wolves, or playing with them in the meadow. In the end, Anthony and Jennifer had relented and allowed Daniel to follow his dream a few nights a week.

His frequent presence with the wolves had given visitors to the Centre a false impression of the status of the pack. Many suggested that these wolves were not really wild, and that the entire operation was based on a misconception. Then one day, the pack had killed a deer and dragged it into the centre of the clearing in plain view of visitors who watched from the platform above. The gruesome details had been too much for many. Some turned away, but the incident had dispelled any suggestions that the wolves were tame stooges.

It was during this first summer living with the wolves that Daniel's and Holly Kanipiswet's friendship had developed. Running Fawn was her Indian name, which Daniel preferred. She was Sharon Goodchild's niece, the same niece who was the flower girl at Jennifer's and Anthony's wedding. Holly was attracted by Daniel's reversal back to the wild.

"That's really cool," she had said. She'd made an Indian breechcloth for Daniel, a pair of genuine Indian leggings, moccasins and a beaded sheaf for his knife to match the headband Sharon had given him the previous year. Holly had also obtained from one of the village elders, an awful smelling ointment for Daniel to smear on his skin to protect him from the sun. Holly could then smell Daniel, long before he came into view. Fortunately, the wolves did not find the smell repulsive, but whiffs of it occasionally permeated from the den into the viewing tunnel.

Jennifer remembered back to when she and Daniel had sat in these very chairs a few days before he was to return to school and talked about his summer and his relationship with the wolves. He'd seemed so different than the young boy who'd come to her a few months before with the idea of living with the wolves.

"Ebony kept asking me why I had to go back to school," Daniel had said. "But I think in the end he understood a little. I thought about the pack on a hunt, with Ebony being trained by one of the adult wolves. I'm sure he knew what I was trying to tell him, but the message Ebony sent back to me was really strange. He thought that I spent too much time learning, and not enough time using my knowledge. It was funny. He thought I must be either a slow learner, or that there was too much to learn. That's the message I got Mom, honest. To him, it was strange, you know, what I was doing, living with him sometimes, and living with you the rest of the time. I guess he thought I should be one or the other, and suggested that one day I would have to choose. He gave me a really weird feeling about that, Mom. I felt a lot of confusion in him about what would become of him when I had to make that choice. It was like he was a person, or something, and then a wolf again. I've never felt him so upset. He didn't want me to leave. I'm sure of that. It was like he needed me to take him somewhere, and he was afraid I wouldn't be around to show him the way. I don't know. It was really weird."

Jennifer remembered that she found his explanations of the mental thought transfers between himself and Ebony to be unbelievable. She had come to accept that Daniel's link with Ebony was much stronger than hers had been with either Ebony or Big Black. *Was I too old,* she thought, *to think that mental telepathy was possible? Did my common sense prevent me from developing the link with Big Black the way Daniel had with Ebony? Probably!*

A cold nose was pushed into Jennifer's arm. Standing beside her on the porch was Boots.

"Boots, what is it?" she asked as she reached out to pet the side of his head. "What's that in your mouth?" she asked.

Boots dropped a small bundle into her lap then turned and romped back into the bush. The bundle began to squirm in the bowl of her house coat between her thighs. "Oh dear. It's one of the puppies."

Its breath was shallow and every once in a while it shuddered and then tried to cough. She got up and took the little wolf inside into her examining room where she could more closely inspect the small canine under the lights. The wolf pup couldn't have been more than four or five weeks old. It reminded her of Boots when he was a young pup. This puppy was the first sign she had that a new litter had been born. The puppy seemed healthy enough, but was experiencing breathing troubles. She opened its mouth and peered inside. Under closer examination, she saw the problem. A small stone with a sharp edge had lodged in its throat. With a pair of long tweezers, she carefully removed it. The little wolf took a couple of deep breaths, got up and transformed into a normal busy little canine. He promptly piddled on the examining table. "True to form," said Jennifer. "A chip off the old man's block, eh?" She placed the puppy inside one of the small cages for safe keeping. "Gotta take you home, little guy." She left the room and went upstairs and dressed.

Down in the meadow the air was fresh. Lots of snow still clung to shaded areas under evergreens and north facing rocks. Part of the stairs and walkway to the birthing den just below the visitor viewing platform had been replaced at the end of the summer. Construction had not been finished with the onset of winter. The cleared ground, soggy from a heavy snow, felt spongy under foot. *I gotta be careful not to fall on the slippery snow*, thought Jennifer. "Anthony would not be pleased with me coming down to the meadow by myself in my condition," she whispered to the little wolf.

Nearing the den opening, the little puppy got a fresh scent of his siblings, struggled to be free and jumped down from her arms. Jennifer stumbled sideways trying to hold him and slipped on the icy snow landing seat first in a small puddle of muddy slush.

"Oh, damn," she said.

Suddenly she had an uncontrollable urge to pee. A gush of water soaked her entire genital area, far too much liquid to have been a normal urination. "What is that?" she asked out loud,

31

then realized that her water bag had just broken.

Boots appeared at the den opening shortly after the little puppy ran inside and when he saw Jennifer lying on the ground, he ran over to her and began licking her face as if to ask if she was okay.

"Oh, Boots, give me a hand up. I've gotta get back to the house." With one hand on the back of the wolf she struggled to stand. "Ouch, damn that hurts." Clutching her stomach she fell back onto the ground. The pain subsided. "I've got to at least get out of this muck." Crawling on her hands and knees over to the den opening, again she tried to stand. The pain returned. "That was about four minutes," she said when the pain subsided again. "Those have to be labour pains." She felt down inside her track-pants between her legs, and the baby's head was at the opening of her birth canal. The contractions were coming quicker now, about two minutes apart. Sweat furrowed her brow and she thought for sure she would hyperventilate. Boots remained beside her offering his body for support. She struggled to pull down her sweat pants and underwear. Within minutes, and two more contractions, the baby's head had emerged out into the world. *Damn, I thought these things took more time. I've gotta get it all out. It could strangle in that position.* Another contraction started. "Push, Jennifer, push," she said aloud. She pushed and pushed, but nothing happened. "Damn, this hurts. Think girl, relax. Oh, Boots. I'm so glad you're here. I'd hate to be doing this alone. Oh, here it comes again, another contraction, so soon?" Jennifer took a deep breath, tried to relax and pushed again. This time, the baby began to move, and she pushed again and its head emerged from the opening. Another contraction and Jennifer gave one huge push and suddenly its entire little body dropped down onto her track pants. She quickly picked up the baby and checked for movement of some kind to ensure the baby lived. Not a sound came from the tiny infant. Jennifer was confused and she began to panic. "No, no," she cried. She struggled to hold the baby, but her discomfort was intense and the tiny body slipped from her arms and fell to the ground.

Boots moved to the front of Jennifer and began licking the tiny infant, pushing his nose into the baby's tummy as he licked. There was a rush of fresh air as the infant took its first breath and began to cry.

Jennifer looked down and smiled. "Hi", she said, trying to pick up the struggling little body again, but then grabbed her stomach, instead. The placenta dropped down onto the ground. Boots began gnawing on the umbilical cord. One of the other wolves, who had been watching the birth from inside the den, reached out and grabbed the placenta just as Boots severed the cord.

Jennifer took a deep breath and tried to relax as she once again tried to pick up the tiny infant, this time successfully. She wrapped the baby inside her jacket and held the struggling body close to her. Tears of joy streamed down

her face as she looked towards the alpha wolf. "Boots, you're an uncle. Thank you. You brought my baby to life. It might have died had you not known what to do." Jennifer sat down on the ground. "I am so tired. Don't know how I'll get back to the house. Maybe I can lie here for a moment and get some strength back." Squirming partially into the den opening she lay down to rest with her head just outside.

Jennifer awoke with a start; she felt cold. "My baby," she whispered. But it was no where to be seen. A little human cry, more a gurgle than a cry, came from inside the den.

It took a few moments for her eyes to adjust to the low light, but a metre beyond her feet, there was her new baby in amongst half a dozen little wolf puppies all licking crazily all over its little body. Jennifer reached out and pulled the baby towards her. Crawling backwards she emerging into the daylight and with the help of Boots, she was able to stand.

At the bottom of the steps they ran into Anthony, his face mixed with anger and relief.

At the sight of Anthony, Boots turned and trotted back to the den.

"I was so worried. I called twice and got no answer either time," Anthony said as he took Jennifer's weight in his arms. "What are you doing down here? You said you wouldn't do anything stupid."

"I know, I know, but I had good ...." She let her sentence trail off then giggled.

"I don't see what you find so funny. You might have fallen, and then what? You could have done yourself, and the baby, serious injury."

"Anthony?" she said, in her best little-girl voice.

"What!" he snapped at her.

"I'd like you to meet Brittany, our new daughter." She opened her jacket to show him.

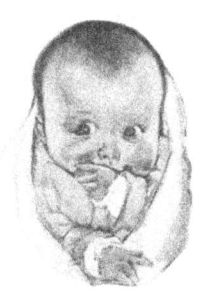

Chapter 4
Help

Daniel burst into the house, shouting. "Dad, Jennifer, help."
Jennifer was in the kitchen. "Daniel," she whispered and turned to look. "Daniel! It is you." She burst into tears, ran to him and flung her arms around her young son. "Daniel, it's really you. I can't believe it. Where have you been?"

"Where's Dad? Holly and Ebony are being held by the Indians at the village. We gotta help them."

"Daniel, slow down. What village?"

"The village at the end of the lake."

"Daniel, you've been gone over a year and a half. Where have you been," her relief turning to anger.

"What do you mean? We only left this morning," replied Daniel.

"Where have you been, Sweetheart?" Jennifer asked again, her anger abated. Still with her hands on his shoulders, she said. "You don't know how we searched for you. Your father and I, and Holly's parents too, we searched for weeks. Tom, from the police station, had the entire force out looking too, but we found nothing. We'd almost given up hope. What happened?"

"But, we only left this morning. Honest." There was a little cry from the front room. "Who's here?" asked Daniel.

"It's Brittany, your baby sister."

"Sister, I don't have a sister." Daniel walked into the front room to see the baby.

"You didn't when you left, but you do now," replied Jennifer as she picked Brittany up and cuddled her. "There's today's newspaper over there on the table. Have a look at the date."

"Where's Dad?" was all he could say, dropping the paper back onto the table.

"He's working today. I'll call him on his cell phone, and Tom, too." She made the calls.

"Come sit down and tell me what happened."

Sitting down, he began. "Well, Holly met me and Ebony at the dock early this morning like we planned. We got in the canoe and paddled to the far end of the lake. There was lots of really thick mist. It got dark, then there was this little light up in front of the canoe and then the mist began turning around us and the light. It was crazy all the screaming wind. It was like a huge tunnel, and we got sucked into it. When we came out the other side it was bright daylight, and the Indian village was there. No kidding. The village was there."

"The Indian village has always been there, Daniel. How was it different?"

"I mean the village had real Indians. The wooden walls were around the village. There were women cleaning fish and wigwams all around the clearing. Four big Indians came after us in their canoe. We were really scared. We tried to get away, get back to the mist, but the Indians caught up to us and one of them hit me over the head with something. See." He touched the back of his head. "I have this lump to prove it. I don't remember what happened after that, not until I woke up inside one of their wigwams. We were both tied up. The village was like it was a long time ago. The Indians kept touching my skin like they'd never seen a white person before."

"How'd you get away, and what happened to Holly?" asked Jennifer.

"There was a young Indian girl who dug a hole under the wall of the wigwam. She untied us. We tried to get to one of the canoes, but Holly got caught again. She yelled for me to go and get help. I got to the nearest canoe while the Indians were busy with Holly. I made it to the mist before they could catch me. When the mist cleared, the village wasn't there anymore. I mean, it was gone. It had just disappeared. I came straight here to get help. That's what happened, honest. And it all happened this morning, not last year or the year before. You gotta believe me." Daniel paused for a moment. "We gotta go back, Jennifer."

Jennifer looked at Daniel. She had never seen him so desperate. Carefully examined his features, he had not changed since she last saw him that fateful morning, so long ago. He had on the same clothing he'd worn that morning, and his hair had not changed, either. She checked his height against the mark on the wall made a week before he disappeared. It too was exactly the same. As strange as it was, she had no reason to doubt his story.

"Daniel," shouted Anthony as he came in the door. "Oh, god, it's true. You are home." He put his arms around his son and hugged him.

"Dad," said Daniel, pulling away from his father. "We gotta get help. Holly and Ebony are still at the village. We gotta go, now."

"Anthony, you have to hear this story," interrupted Jennifer.

There was a knock at the door. "That'll be Tom, from the police station," said Jennifer to her husband. "I called him too."

Jennifer let Tom in; they all sat down and Daniel retold his story.

"Wow," said Tom when Daniel had finished. "Do you believe him?" he asked Jennifer.

"Well, he's wearing the same clothes he wore when he left. Look at his head. He has a lump the size of an egg where he said the Indians clubbed him. All the evidence indicates he is telling the truth, as strange as that may be."

"You have a point, Jennifer," replied the officer. "And did you see that canoe down at the dock? It looks like somethin' out of a museum." Tom thought for a moment. "We should call Holly's parents and the elders at the reservation. Maybe they can tell us what's goin' on. I don't disbelieve anything in connection with them Indians anymore."

A search party was formed. A thorough investigation of the lake revealed nothing. The mist had gone; the remains of the village were as they had been for as long as anyone could remember.

Darkness began to fall; the search party dispersed except for Anthony and Daniel. Anthony was walking back from the far end of the clearing. Daniel stood alone in exactly the same spot where he had last seen Holly.

"Holly, Ebony, where are you?" he hollered to the trees. "You gotta be here somewhere. I was here only a few hours ago, and you were here then. I can still feel you here." A tear trickled down his cheek as he bowed his head and looked at the ground. He had never felt such despair. His sorrow quickly turned to anger. He clenched his fists and shouted again to the trees beyond the marsh. "If it takes me forever, I will find you, wherever you are. Ebony, Holly." but his cries were absorbed by the trees beyond, from which came no response.

"Come on Daniel," said Anthony, placing his hands on his son's shoulders. "It's getting late. The light will be gone soon. We better get back to the house. Mom will be worried." They pushed off their canoe and paddled back to the dock at the western end of the lake. Anthony stood for many moments examining the birch-bark canoe Daniel had brought back earlier in the day. As strange as Daniel's story was, this canoe had to come from somewhere, and it was clear evidence of the truth to his tale.

Daniel's concern for the loss of Holly and Ebony went deeper than just losing his best friends. Even though Holly was nine years older, Daniel loved her, or he thought he did. She had ignored his suggestions of love saying it was just youthful infatuation. She'd said he would understand better when he was older.

And Ebony, he couldn't remember a day without Ebony being with

him. Ebony was as much a part of his very being as was his arm or his leg. To be separated, perhaps forever, from his friend was intolerable. What confused him most was that the link he always felt with Ebony, he could still feel. This alone gave him the strength and courage to carry on against all adversity, knowing Ebony still existed in both body and mind, somewhere, some time.

For days, Daniel searched the far end of the lake. The days stretched into weeks, then months. He never found anything that collaborate his story, but he never gave up his quest to find his friends.

"We know nothing about a disappearing village, Daniel," said Black Sky, Sharon Goodchild's grandfather. "I do not remember any songs, or any stories that tell of what you say happened to you. But, if you have the time, I can tell you what we know about the beginning of light from darkness, and how our world was created."

"Yes, please," replied Daniel.

"Come outside by the counsel fire." Outside, Black Sky motioned for Daniel to sit across the fire from him.

"Corn Husk," he shouted. "Bring us some tea,,,,,,, please. And hurry." Black Sky winked at Daniel. "Women like to be ordered. It gives them direction in life." He smiled.

Corn Husk brought the tea. She too winked and smiled at Daniel. She turned and gave her husband a gentle kick, touching him on his shoulder as she returned to the house.

Black Sky began.

"Kitchi-Manitou, the Great Mystery, is the creator of all things. He first created the earth, then the sun to light the sky during the day, and then the moon to reflect sunlight onto the earth at night. The grasses of the fields, the trees of the forests, and all the variety of flowers, are his creation. But, no living creatures roamed the great forests he had created. It should be so, said Kitchi-Manitou to himself. There must be life that can benefit and enjoy the beauty and the bounty of these rich, new lands. Casting his hand to the ground, a great well opened, and from out of that well he brought forth the great bison, the prairie dog, and the antelope to roam the prairies in the west. Then out came the moose, the fox, the bear, the raccoon and the deer for the eastern forests. The mountain lion, Grizzly bear, the big horned sheep and the elk for the western mountains came next, then, the rabbit and the ground hog, the skunk, the muskrat, the squirrel, and all the many varieties of animals one by one came forth from the depths of the well. Eagles and osprey, hawks, owls, chickadees, robins and herons, too, and other varieties of birds flew from the well to fill the skies with colour and grace, and to sing their songs. They all went far and wide and soon filled the forests, the plains, and the great moun-

tains with living creatures. He then filled the oceans with fish and mammals of such variety.

To all the creatures, his greatest gift was the ability to evolve and multiply according to natural laws of selection.

Each creature he created for a special purpose, to be part of the whole, dependent to all others, yet unique. For many summers everything was in balance and all creatures lived in peace and harmony. But, each summer the trees grew and began to block the sunlight from reaching the soil. The deer were the first to suffer and many began to die. Over time they had become many, and the many could no longer find enough fresh grasses and saplings to eat. So the Great Kitchi-Manitou brought up from the well, the beaver. And, to the beaver he gave sharp teeth like those of a vast cutting machine, and a passion for work along with an unusual level of awareness and sense of family. The beaver cut down many trees surrounding the rivers and opened up large areas of land to the sun. He built his lodges at the river's edge and constructed dams of sticks and mud across the rivers to hold back the mighty river waters to create gentle flowing pools behind the dams. Sunshine poured in, and so began the growth of new saplings and grasses to feed the deer and many other animals too. And all was once again in balance.

In times of plenty, all creatures share in their reproduction. The weak breed equally with the strong planting imperfect seeds. Again it was the deer that first showed signs of imperfection, and they began to die in large numbers. Kitchi-Manitou was puzzled by their deaths until he realized a key predator was needed to keep the herds strong. He once more reached into the great well for yet another creature. He made this creature a cunning hunter, with a high level of intelligence, strength and endurance to run long distances. Strong family ties he imbued within this creature, for it was the family as a unit that culled the deer, elk and bison herds of the old, the sick and the dying and would leave the strong to breed. And so Kitch-Manitou brought forth the wolf and in time once again, all was in balance.

As his new world grew, the responsibilities of his new world increased. To share these responsibilities, Kitchi-Manitou created other lesser Manitou beings, in his own image, to dwell just beyond the earth. He gave them immortality, virtue, wisdom and responsibilities to watch over different aspects of his new world.

He was pleased, but something still seemed missing. He thought for many moons before realizing the problem was that creatures in his own image were nowhere upon the land to look after and police all that he had created. Turning again to the great well, he pulled out a man and a woman. He gave them a large brain and the ability for a complex language, and hands with a sensitivity not possessed by any other creature upon the land. He called these creatures, Human Beings. "Everything you need to sustain life can be found

upon the land," he said to them. "Go forth and multiply."

They did as they were commanded. A great population of Human Beings inhabited the lands. However, the Human Beings began exploiting the land of its many riches, and cared little for other creatures. They left only destruction. A great evil spread across the land and a greed for material wealth. Angered by the actions of the Human Beings, Kitch-Manitou condemned all the creatures living upon the land. "I have made a grave mistake in creating these creatures," he said to himself. He therefore called upon the great clouds to build, and the winds to blow, and the rains to fall in sheets of running water. It rained for two moon cycles, and soon all the land was covered by a big sea, except for a few islands of higher ground. All Human Beings perished, as did most of the animals, but a few creatures managed to find shelter on a few islands which had been the tops of the highest mountains. More and more survivors crowded onto these islands, and soon the islands became too small for all the creatures seeking refuge.

Kitchi-Manitou would not listen to the cries of the suffering animals, so, the giant turtle called up to one of the lesser Manitous, Geezhigo-Quae, (Sky Woman) and begged her to come down from her place to see the suffering that was taking place on the world below. Turtle offered his back as refuge for Sky Woman to rest upon. Accepting Turtle's invitation, Sky Woman descended from above and settled on Turtle's back to see for herself the suffering. Her heart went out to all the animals and she immediately asked for a quantity of rich soil available only from the deepest depths of the flood waters. Many animals tried to dive deep enough to do Sky Woman's bidding, but none succeeded. The rich soil she required was too deep, they all said. Then, lowly Muskrat asked if he could try. All the other animals laughed at lowly Muskrat calling him dim-witted and slow, but Sky Woman granted him his wish. "It is his right to try," she proclaimed.

Muskrat was under the water for a very long time, and everyone thought he must have drowned. Loon saw him first deep down in the water as he rose to the surface. She dove down to assist Muskrat to help bring him to the surface. When finally he was brought to Sky Woman, all saw that he was dead. Sky Woman gave thanks to Muskrat for his attempt to save all the animals then she looked closely. There clutched in Muskrat's front paws was a small ball of the rich soil she required. Muskrat had given his life to save the earth and all those creatures that remained, and by doing so, forever fulfilled the destinies of all Muskrats for all time. The female Manitou took the soil from Muskrat's paw and sprinkled it around the outside of Turtle's back. All the animals watched what she was doing. She then called upon the four winds, to breath upon the soil and give it the qualities of life, kindness, love, compassion and creativity, the qualities Kitchi-Manitou had not given to the Human Beings he had created before the great flood. Sky Woman caused the land she

had created on Turtle's back to grow, and it became an island which she called Manitou Land. All the animals scampered onto the island and were grateful and gave thanks to Sky Woman for listening to their plight.

Still within the soil on Turtles back were the seeds of life so created by Kitchi-Manitou. Sky Woman impregnated herself with these seeds and soon gave birth to twin boys, who she named Tijus-Keha, and Tawis-Karong.

Sky Woman's two first-born children called themselves Anishnaubaek, which means The Good People. Tijus-Keha was a gentle spirit, tall and muscular with a kind and understanding enthusiasm towards all creatures, a gifted artistic person with a love of life. He grew tall and of strong body.

Tawis-Karong also possessed great height and strength and was just as clever and gifted as his brother, but he was an angry child, and never seemed to find happiness. In time he grew to hate his brother and said that Tijus-Keha was given all the favours and that none were given to him. But, even though he inwardly despised his brother, he was clever at keeping his feelings hidden.

When the two first-born had grown and matured, Sky Woman commanded them to go forth and multiply upon the land she had created. They did as their mother commanded, and brought forth man and woman in their own image, known as The Good People. They created two separate villages for The Good People on Manitou Land, but soon The Good People became many. Manitou Land became too small for the great number of the first-borns' creations. Sky Woman commanded the shores of Manitou Land to grow, and the land to spread across the open water. These new lands became a great Continent and were known as The Land of the Great Turtle, in honour of Turtle who had offered his back to Sky Woman to rest upon.

Everything all The Good People and all the animals would need for survival - materials for shelter, food, clothing, warmth and prosperity - could be found on the Land of the Great Turtle. Many of the first-borns' offspring spread forth and populated parts of the great continent. There they developed their own traditions and cultures.

Kitchi-Manitou had observed the work of Sky Woman and he was pleased with Sky Woman's work. He saw that The Good People became masters of creativity, and developed tools for cultivation, spears and bows and arrows to assist in the hunting of food, and medicines to defend themselves against ills that came their way. They cared for the land given to them, taking only what they needed for survival, and were always conscious to leave the land in balance. Now, Kitchi-Manitou's work on the lands he had created was complete; he felt fulfilled. He, therefore, granted all the men and women, and their descendants, guardianship of all the lands, and the creatures within. He vowed to take no further part in mankind's affairs.

The Good People were grateful for all the things given to them by Kit-

chi–Manitou. They wished to bestow upon him their gratitude for all of these gifts.

"Thank you my children," were his parting words. "I need nothing of you, other than for you to watch over the lands and the creatures within. Learn and be just, for you have been given all the tools you will need to prosper and grow. Within you lies the future of all things. Your gift to me is to keep the air pure, the waters clean, and all the animals healthy. Do not disappoint me in this one gift of which I ask. Go and do my bidding, for I leave you now. But fear not my children, I am always near."

"And that is the end of the story as told to me by my father and his father to him. So you see Daniel, The Great Mystery, Kitchi-Manitou, is with us always."

"Thank you for telling me the story, Black Sky, but I don't see how it will help me in my search for the village."

"Do not despair, Daniel. You did what you could, but these things are beyond both of us. Keep searching you must, but remember, Kitchi-Manitou, will reveal all in his good time. Be patient, my son."

Daniel appreciated hearing the story and respected the elder's remarks. He believed very strongly in Ojibwa beliefs. It had always been easy for him, but his beliefs were now being tested when the concerns were so close to home. He couldn't wait for Kitchi-Manitou to do whatever it was he was going to do, or whatever the elder had said was going to happen.

On a subsequent visit with Black Sky, the aging elder seemed to ignore Daniel for many moments and in fact appeared to be asleep.

"I'll come back another time," Daniel commented to Corn Husk.

"Just wait a moment, Daniel," she said. "He's not sleeping; just thinking. Give him a moment."

Daniel settled back into the cushions of his chair.

"Daniel," said Black Sky, momentarily. "You once asked about the two first-born children of Kitchi-Manitou and what happened to them. I have another story to tell. I don't know if it will help with your search, but if you have a minute, I will tell you."

Daniel agreed, but remembered that Black Sky's minutes were often very long.

"Corn Husk, more te........."

Corn Husk had already prepared the tea and placed the tray on the table in front of them. She turned and again winked and smiled at Daniel.

"Oh thank you my wife."

Black Sky began:

"Unobserved by Kitchi-Manitou, one of the first-born sons, Tawis-Karong, had become very greedy and cruel and he ruled his people with an evil hand if anyone displeased him. His people greatly feared him, his quick temper and brutal recourse.

He had built his village at the far end of a beautiful lake on Manitou Land on a small clearing with marsh land on three sides. Around the clearing he had built a palisade wall of wood to give The People security. He also created many large and ugly animals that roamed the lands a short distance out side his village beyond the marsh. He ruled his People with force and punished those who tried to oppose him. The Good People he punished were first banished from the village then cast out beyond the marsh. Once beyond a certain distance from the palisade, they would be devoured by the giant beasts that lived there.

Tijus-Keha had heard about the wrong doings of his brother and went to visit him one day. On his journey to Tawis-Karong's village he saw the giant oversized animals so created by his brother and he made them all a normal size so they would benefit the land and The People.

Before reaching his brother's village, Tijus-Keha changed himself into a wolf so he could watch his brother and his brother's village from a distance without himself being observed. But, Tawis-Karong was waiting for him and the two brothers had a great battle. Tijus-Keha, was struck down and nearly destroyed by his evil brother. He lay unconscious on the ground. Tawis-Karong picked up his brother's body and threw him far out onto the lake beyond the village where his body was swallowed up by the mist and he was never heard from again."

Black Sky finished his story and then appeared to fall asleep again. Daniel sat is silence awed by what he'd just heard. "Thank you, Black Sky," he mumbled. *This is very interesting,* he thought, and wondered if it had any relevance to his search. He had been deeply moved by the story and felt certain it did.

Chapter 5
Endless Research

Eight years had past since Daniel returned home. During that time, between school and homework, and between a series of part time or full time jobs, he studied all available material he could find on Ojibwa mythology and religious beliefs. His research had become an all consuming obsession; despair was his constant companion. He continually mourned the loss of his first love, Holly, and of his buddy, Ebony. His depression was so intense at times, he felt his life useless, and without a future. He even convinced himself, at one point that his few hours in a distant time, hadn't happened at all. To remind himself of the reality, he just had to feel Ebony's presence. The black wolf still existed, somewhere, sometime, but where and when he constantly asked himself. His love for Holly had certainly been real, even though she considered it mere infatuation. His need to discover the truth drove him.

All his close friends had deserted him suggesting he needed more professional help than they could offer. He'd had his share of "shrinks" but all he talked to had one common result, a total disbelief about his story. In the end, as it always was, he went his not so merry way, and continued his research.

During these times, he was his happiest paddling the far end of the lake searching for the portal, the portal that refused to reveal itself. Here too, the link with Ebony felt the strongest.

One particular library in Toronto had a special section devoted to books and articles by and about Indian writers and local native customs and mythology. With a small recent photo of Holly playing with Ebony always in his possession, and which he would prop up against a book while reading, Daniel felt a special connection in this library, a oneness with Indian ways, and it was here he reaped the most benefit from his research. He felt sure the information he needed would reveal itself somewhere in the confines of these walls. If he just kept looking, he knew he would eventually find something.

One book on Ojibwa myths and legends mentioned Sky Woman's two first-born children and a fight between them. Daniel found it particularly interesting, because it was almost identical to the story told to him by Black Sky. The only difference was that the evil son Tawis-Karong lost this fight and it was he who was banished from his village.

Daniel sat in silence after reading this story and the reversal ending compared to Black Sky's story. *Hum*, he thought. *I wonder if there were maybe*

two fights. At first he didn't think it meant anything, but the more he thought about it, the more this village could easily have been the village of his search. Daniel photocopied the story and placed it in his portfolio for future reference.

Daniel found several stories in other books about different nations that told of the battle between the two first-born twins of Sky Woman, where the evil twin killed his good brother. Some versions in other cultural nation's writings, mentioned a curse, but none gave enough details to be specific. And information concerning the first-born twins, though sketchy at best, varied from nation to nation, and often from book to book, depending on the era. In some stories, the good son died in the fight, but in most, the details were not clear about the outcome of the battle between the two first-born. However, it was clear that in all the stories the two first-born did have a great battle, or perhaps it was that they were going to have a great battle the outcome of which was yet to be determined.

On the suggestion of one of the librarians who had been helping Daniel, a Mohawk woman, Daniel journeyed to Brantford, a small city on the Grand River in southern Ontario, to speak with an elder from the Six Nations Iroquois Reservation. Daniel and the elder talked for many hours, but the elder could not offer much help in Daniel's quest, except that he vaguely remembered a song sung to him by his great grandfather many years ago.

"It is only a song," he said. "I cannot remember much about it except I remember that the Eagle flew up to tell The Great Mystery that Tawis-Karong and Tijus-Keha were fighting. The Great Mystery was very angry and when he heard that one of his sons was dead at the hand of his brother he became so angry he made a village disappear. I remember my great grandfather saying, poof and it was gone. That's all I remember. I do not know what happened during the fight or what happened to the village."

Was it just a song, distorted by time and frequent recounting of the details, or was there some truth to it? None of the Ojibwa elders on Manitoulin Island heard of the village or of a curse in their stories that the Iroquois Elder had mentioned.

While in Brantford, Daniel visited a local Mohawk museum that had some literature written in the Mohawk language. Mohawk was one of the first native languages to be given an alphabet, which allowed the Mohawk peoples to record events in their own words. One book in particular, that had been translated into English, written by a descendant of Joseph Brant, a famous Mohawk leader from the 18th Century, mentioned a ghost village that could be seen on misty lakes, but otherwise gave few details. Was this the village of Daniel's search, or some other village in another song or story?

For every morsel of evidence found, Daniel searched hundreds of documents. And often some answers to questions created a dozen more questions.

It had been a long day, his eyes were tired after eight hours of reading; he was about to leave. He almost missed it, a brief news clipping from a

Manitoulin newspaper dated in the mid-thirties, yellow with age and badly torn, and now recorded digitally. A reporter had related the adventure of a young Ojibwa warrior who had disappeared from the reservation only to reappear, many years later. This, in itself, was not unusual because many warriors "escaped" from the reservations that were under much heavier white restrictions then than they are in today's society. What struck the reporter as strange, though, was that this warrior had apparently not aged since the day he left. His story was never believed, even though no one could explain why the warrior appeared unchanged since he had disappeared for so many years. Here was the first clue that followed, with some degree of similarity, what happened to Daniel.

Daniel's search for this man took almost a year. He had begun to fear he had died, not remembered by family and friends, but eventually his whereabouts Daniel discovered.

Torn by decades of guilt and tribal distrust, this man lay rotting away his few remaining years in an institution for the mentally disturbed, deserted by all. The first time Daniel visited him, his mind was vague and unclear, and he babbled and shouted incoherent statements, and constantly chanted ancient Indian songs.

"The ramblings of an old man," had said an attendant at the home. But, on a subsequent visit the old warrior spoke clearly with detailed and vivid memories.

"You are the only person who has ever believed me," he had said. "Thank you for coming. You have given me hope that I am really not as crazy as the people around this place say I am."

This man's story was very similar to his own, with the same vortex of spinning mist, and the same village in all its ancient glory, exactly as Daniel had experienced. Whereas Daniel spent only a few hours in the village, this man stayed overnight before escaping, and returning to his previous life through the portal of swirling mist.

Daniel now had a clearer picture of what might have happened. With little else for support, he believed the old warrior. If it wasn't for the strange birch-bark canoe he had brought back with him, the same canoe that now lay housed in the Royal Ontario Museum in Toronto, he too might believe he only dreamed it. And then there was the mental link with Ebony, the link that he and his mother had developed, when the wolf was a young pup. That link was still strong with Daniel. It was a constant reminder that Ebony still existed, somewhere in time, but, where, and more precisely, when?

Was the portal at the village end constantly open just off the coast of the village in the mist in their time? Or did it appear only briefly every once in a while? How often did it appear in Daniel's time? Was its re-appearance always the same time frame? And, did it always open at the same place on this side? It seemed to have been about ten years for the warrior in the institution.

But, what troubled Daniel is that the warrior had said that the portal he'd found was not on Manitoulin Island.

The more Daniel read the more confusing and vague were the fragmented answers to these questions. Calculating his own time on the other side, the ten year per day time frame seemed to fit, or was at least close. Did the warrior stay exactly 24 hours? If it had been an hour less or an hour more, it could make the difference on this side of six or eight months.

Daniel frequently walked through the old village, and envisioned what he remembered, and always wondered where the village was now. He paddled the small bay so often he knew every ripple, every outcrop of rock, every beaver and every heron. He welcomed the misty mornings, but none revealed the portal to the village.

During his time researching, Daniel learned the Ojibwa language. It was easier for the elders of the village to remember events of the past in their own language; many of them had only a limited knowledge of English. And, many Ojibwa words had no direct translation into English. In learning the language, he also learned a great deal about Ojibwa cultural beliefs, and came to appreciate a way of life that was timeless in nature, and true to itself, a oneness with the natural world.

Daniel's quest had struck a sympathetic chord with the elders of the village with whom he spent much of his time tapping into almost forgotten memories hidden in the recesses of aging minds. His reclusive nature was respected by the People, and they allowed him to live in a small cabin at the eastern corner of the reservation overlooking the lake of his quest. He spent endless hours consulting his many notes and files created over the years, since that fateful day so long ago. He seldom saw friends, and visited his parents only occasionally, usually on Sundays. By all accounts he had become a very disturbed and distant young man.

Daniel frequently visited with the wolves on his family's property. It's where he found some peace, but without Ebony as his mentor and go-between, his status within the pack hierarchy had changed. Boots, the alpha leader still respected Daniel's presence and always welcomed him. New pack members had no knowledge of either Ebony or Daniel and they shied away from the young man, not accepting him as did the older wolves.

Six months before the tenth anniversary of his original disappearance, Daniel set-up a camp in the old village site, and every spare moment he paddled his canoe around the small bay in search of the portal. Much to his disappointment the portal remained elusive. He never gave up though, never wavered in his quest to find it. The days passed with agonizing monotony, and quickly turned into weeks, still with no success in finding the portal. The ten year anniversary had come, and gone, as did the summer and then the fall. The glorious colours of the autumn leaves as usual were breathtaking, but they too had faded and now lay scattered on the ground in different stages of decay

returning their nutrients to the soil. The weather had turned decidedly cold. Still he searched. He worried that maybe he'd somehow missed the moment the portal was available? This thought became an ever increasing obsession. And the concern that perhaps the portal did not always open at the same spot in his time, ate at his very being. Convinced the portal would open here on this particular lake, and fearful of missing the moment, he spent all his time in his canoe, paddling the small bay.

Daniel was tired, more tired than he could ever remember. He came ashore for a moment's rest and a bite to eat. The air possessed crispness this late in the day. The last remnants of sun cast a bronze glow on the frost-covered marsh reeds and grass. Daniel felt cold. It had been days since he'd had a solid night's sleep, and even longer since his last hot meal. He tried in vain to re-kindle the cold, damp embers of his camp-fire, but without success. He crawled into his tent and lay across his sleeping bag, too tired to even slide inside. Visions of Holly and Ebony raced through his mind, robbing him of any chance to sleep. He sat up sobbing their names. "They are here, exactly where I am now. Why can I not find them?" Daniel wiped the tears from his eyes, and breathed in a big sigh, but sleep would not come. Fearful of missing the moment of the portal's arrival, he returned to his canoe, and the familiar lake waters.

Long shadows closed around him as the sun sank below the trees at the far end of the lake. Daniel shivered in the sudden dampness and pulled his jacket zipper up higher to retain what little body heat his emaciated body generated. *Strange*, he thought, *how sleep always comes so easily when I'm in the canoe. Why couldn't I sleep in the tent?* Daniel paddled aimlessly letting the canoe glide until it nearly stopped, and then paddled another stroke. Minutes passed; his mind numb and empty of thought. He slumped forward, and quickly jerked himself upright again. Twice more he slumped forward and twice more he jerked upright in a vain attempt to remain awake. In his enforced stupor, he again slumped forward. His exhausted body relaxed, including his grip on his paddle. It quietly slid into the water, and slowly drifted away, unnoticed by the sleeping body slumped over in the canoe.

A heavy mist rose from the waters of the bay, and soon engulfed the small craft suspending it in a whitewash world. Still Daniel slept. The mists thickened, and began to spin, slowly at first, then with increasing speed, pulling the canoe and its sleeping occupant forward into the spiral vortex of mist, water and reeds towards a glowing light. Unheard winds screamed as the canoe shot out into quiet waters bathed in warm moonlight.

Chapter 6
Lost Again

It had been nearly a month since anyone had heard from Daniel. Ice had begun to form on the edges of the lake waters, and a light dusting of snow had already covered much of the marsh land around.

"I am worried Jennifer. I have been up to Daniel's cabin overlooking the lake a couple of times," said Sharon when she telephoned her friend one day. "I had some food for him and I wanted to see how he was doing, but he was not there. In fact, there were no signs that he had been there recently."

"It's not unusual for Daniel to be away from home for periods of time, but it was always days, not weeks," replied Jennifer. "You'd think at least someone would have seen him coming or going. He usually stopped by on Sundays, but I must admit we've not seen him for at least a month. I'm a bit worried too. Maybe he found the vortex again. If so, I wonder if it will be another year and a half before he comes home again."

"I do not know, Jennifer. My grandfather said Daniel believed that for every day in the village, about ten years passed in our time. If Daniel did find the portal again, maybe he will find what he has been looking for all these years. If that is what has happened, maybe that is what is meant to be."

"Whatever, I hope he has found some peace. He has been so troubled the last few years, I feared for his well being. He went so strange there for a while. His father was so worried about him, but Anthony didn't know what to do other than to leave him to pursue his desires, and to be here for him if he needed anything."

"Should I go to the end of the lake and see if he's at the old village? He was spending so much time on the water. He may have a camp there."

"Would you mind, Sharon? I'd really appreciate it if you did."

"I will go tomorrow," she said. "But, now I have things to do. Talk more, later."

"Okay, thank you, Sharon. I do appreciate your concern and help."

The next morning, as promised, Sharon paddled off towards the eastern end of the lake. Ashley came with her to keep her company and to be an-

other pair of eyes.

"When the temperature gets colder, and the heat is gone from the water, it is not wise to be on the water alone," said Sharon.

"You know, in all the years I've been here, I've never been to this end of the lake," commented Ashley. "I see now why Daniel enjoyed it so much. It's so beautiful, and quiet."

They paddled in silence for a few minutes, then Ashley asked if Sharon believed Daniel's story?

Sharon was silent for a moment. "I," she hesitated. "To be honest, I do not know, Ashley. I want to, but you have to admit, it does sound impossible in this day and age. A portal in time to another day and age sounds too difficult to believe."

"Yeah, I was thinking, and I don't mean to be disrespectful," giggled Ashley. "Daniel so totally embraced the Indian way the last few years; in many respects he is more Ojibwa than many of those born to it."

"Yes, he is isn't he," laughed Sharon. "He speaks the language fluently now and that makes him one of only a couple of hundred people on the island that do. Very few of the young people have much interest in learning it. But what I worry about is if what Daniel says is true, I wonder how it will change my people's beliefs?"

"I wouldn't think it would change anything," replied Ashley. "Surely it would confirm so many of them."

"If Daniel's village is real, the way he described things is different than what The People believe it was like in our history," remarked Sharon. "And if he's gone back there now, and he stays for any length of time, I worry how his influence will effect history today."

"I've never thought of that. You think he might change the past which will change our world?"

"Yes, for sure it is possible," confirmed Sharon. "It is a question we may never know the answer to."

"Yeah, that's for sure."

"As you know, I am a strong believer in traditional Ojibwa customs, but I worry that the truth may be too difficult for The People to accept if it is a lot different than what we now believe. They could lose all faith in all our traditions, if some are proven to be false. I know that we must integrate ourselves with white ways in order to survive, but I worry new generations will want less and less to do with Ojibwa beliefs. I hate to see my People so dependent on welfare cheques, and government hand-outs. I want my People to be independent; I want each member of the band to stand tall and proud to proclaim

their native heritage. It is also important for each person to know their heritage and to honour it. But if everything we presently believe is questioned because of Daniel and his village, it could change so much of our way of life. We believe it was then a world in total balance with Nature, but somehow I think that thought is too perfect to be true. I do not know what I believe and I have no idea what will happen. Maybe if Daniel's world really exists I will get the opportunity to visit it some day."

"That would be some experience wouldn't it." said Ashley.

"That is for certain."

They paddled on both deep in their own thoughts.

"Do you miss the old days when we had so much freedom?" asked Ashley. "You know when we were doing all the development work on the Dafave Formula?"

"Yes and no. What I miss is the excitement of new discoveries when we were doing all that research especially the tests with the poppy seeds. Every day it was like something new to try. And then your father and Mr. Lafave sold the Formula to the Canadian government, and it was all over. At least we were able to keep the fertilizer part of it for The People. That has been very good for all native peoples on Manitoulin Island. It has built schools and created jobs for us all. I am very happy with that."

"Can I ask you something personal, Sharon?"

"Yes of course, anything."

"Why did you never get married, or have any kids of your own?"

"I wonder that too, I never met the right man I guess, but I did so want to have children. I am sorry I have been so busy that I have not done so. I was happy for Jennifer when Brittany was born. When she asked me to be Brittany's godmother, it was a little bit like having a family of my own, and I was very happy for that. But it was not the same as having my own baby. I think Jennifer sensed this, and she allowed me to participate so much in Brittany's early days. She's such a nice little girl, although not so little anymore."

"Yeah, you can say that again. I think she's taller than me now. She's a good kid, though, most of the time. Like all kids, she has her good days and her bad days."

The two were approaching the clearing and the ancient Indian village site.

"If we beach the canoe over there," Sharon pointed with her paddle, "we can get out without getting our feet wet."

A cool north-east breeze blew through the trees at the edge of the

marsh and brought with it ice crystals of snow dust from the tree branches and whipped it into the faces of the two women. They stepped out onto the soft sand and stood gazing over the desolate scene void of colour except for the few green fur trees visible through the light mist condensed from the last remnants of warmth in the soil.

At the far end of the clearing they found the remains of a make-shift camp.

"It is definitely Daniel's," commented Sharon. "These are his things. But the ashes in the fire pit are cold and there are no prints in the snow. When did we get the snow?"

"Yesterday morning, I think," replied Ashley.

"So it has been at least two days then since Daniel was here. And I can not see anything that tells me where he might have gone. I wish we had better news to tell Jennifer. She will be upset."

Ashley agreed. "What should we do now?" she asked.

"We have no reason to look more here. Maybe he has returned to his cabin. We should go there and look before seeing Jennifer."

The two women returned to their canoe and pushed off to return to the western end of the lake. They weren't more than a few metres from shore when Sharon spotted something. "What is that over there?"

"Where?" asked Ashley, looking around.

"There, on top of that beaver lodge." Sharon pointed her paddle towards the shore on their right.

Chapter 7
Daniel's Return

Daniel's first sensation was that of warmth. He opened his eyes and tried to focus on the fire in front of him. Again, he was inside a wigwam, perhaps the same wigwam as before, and again he was tied to a stake in the ground. He shook his head to clear his stupor and turned in the other direction. There was Holly, also tied to a stake as she had been the last time he saw her over ten years ago.

"Running Fawn," he sputtered. He smiled at her and was visibly pleased to see her. He licked his lips to relieve the dryness. "It is good to see you. You look exactly as I remember you, the same hair, the same clothing and the same lovely smile."

"You know me?" she asked, her expression turning to one of surprise. "Who are you?"

He shook his head to clear the cobwebs. "Oh, yes, I'm sorry. You'll find this hard to believe. I'm Daniel."

"Daniel! Daniel who?"

"Daniel Santos."

"Humph," she said. "You lie. Daniel Santos is a nine year old boy. Not a grown man."

"No, I'm not lying; it's true. It's a long story. I will tell you, later. You don't know how much I've missed you and Ebony, how I've searched, how I've longed for this day. You have no idea what I've been through to find you again. I've been so worried for so long and now I'm back. It is such a relief, but please, have you seen Ebony? I must speak with him. He is the key to all this, I'm sure, and I must know why...."

"You are a strange one, whoever you are." Holly interrupted. She looked at Daniel with unbelieving eyes. "You can't expect me to believe you are Daniel."

"Please, you must answer me. Have you seen anything of Ebony?"

"No, I've not seen him since he jumped over the side of the canoe. I last saw him running for the trees. I assume he's okay. The Indians were more concerned about me and Daniel. They didn't bother with Ebony at all."

Daniel tried to move, but he was held fast by vines wrapped around his wrists and ankles. "Ow," he declared a frown on his brow. "It hurts this time. They obviously don't want us to escape again; they tied us really tight."

"Hey, whoever you are. You better stay still. They got really angry the last time. I thought they were going to kill me yesterday. Now, tell me that long story. This ought to be good."

Daniel told the story, but he left out all the anguish he had felt during his search, all the despair, and the times of near suicide.

Holly's face conveyed total disbelief throughout the telling. She laughed when he finished. "You can't expect me to believe that. It was only yesterday morning, Daniel escaped in the canoe. How could you be so much older in a little over a day?"

"What? What time is it then?"

"I don't know. I don't have a watch, and there is no clock hanging on the wall? But, seriously, it's gotta be late in the afternoon."

"Has it been that long since we first arrived here? How long was I asleep?" asked Daniel.

"You had to have slept three or four hours, at least. You were quite delirious at times. Why?"

"A day and a half, that means that the world out there, our world, has aged as much as fifteen years for you and another three or four years for me. And every minute we stay here it is multiplied by many hundreds of minutes in our world."

Again Holly laughed at the incredible possibility of what Daniel had said. "You can't expect me to believe that."

"As weird as it sounds, it's true, every word. If you go back, all your friends and family will be a lot older than the last time you saw them, as I said maybe fifteen years older. And they won't believe you. No one believed me, except my parents. And, even they had second thoughts lots of time."

"But, I want to go back. I don't want to stay here. Don't you want to go back?" Then Holly pulled back her statement. "Damn! Here I am already assuming you are Daniel. But, that's impossible."

Daniel sensed sudden despair in Holly. "I don't know," he said quickly to get her thinking about something else. "I've been very troubled the last few years. Most people thought I was crazy, and even I entertained the thought. I want to speak with Ebony. I can feel his presence very close right now. It's important I speak with him before I make any decision. I don't know how he fits into all this, but there is something about him that's stranger than the story I've just told you."

A drum began to beat and outside the wigwam there was much activity and yelling. A lone singer began a high pitched cry in time to the drum's beat.

A man entered the wigwam.

"Here comes that same guy, or sachem, medicine man or whatever he is. The same guy who was here before," commented Holly.

The Indian walked over to Daniel and Holly with an air of superiority. Everyone bowed to him as he passed. He was obviously a man of great power within his people. His long black hair fell across his shoulders, and interspersed within the hair were what looked like blue and yellow sea shells.

Daniel looked at the sea shells. *Must be some sort of status symbol*, he thought.

The warrior stood over Daniel and from a pocket in his white deer-skin shirt he pulled out a rattle and began to shake it over both of them while he chanted strange words. Much to Holly's surprise, Daniel spoke to this warrior in the Ojibwa language, and many of those words the warrior seemed to understand.

The warrior stopped what he was doing and stuck the rattle directly into Daniel's face. He spoke to Daniel; his voice echoed as if they were in a large cave. "You die, white skinned warrior," he shouted, shaking his rattle as he said it. He turned the rattle towards Holly, but his eyes did not leave Daniel. "You and your squaw woman, evil spirits that you are will die." The medicine man lifted the door flap, stepped outside and shouted orders.

"What did he say?" Holly asked, fear evident in her voice.

Before Daniel could answer, the medicine man re-entered the wigwam along with four Indians. The medicine man shouted commands and the warriors hurriedly untied Holly and Daniel, and dragged them outside.

They both resisted, but to no avail. They were re-tied, this time to a tall tree trunk buried in the ground. Once tied, women and children dragged bundles of branches and small logs over and spread them onto the ground around the base of the trunk and at Holly's and Daniel's feet. The drum suddenly stopped. The medicine man stood in front of the pile of sticks and pole to which Holly and Daniel were tied, his back to them. He raised his arms into the air and shouted more commands to the people of the village. Two Indians ran forward with burning torches and jammed them into the pile of dry branches. A great cry went up from the entire village. The drum began again but a faster beat. The flames took a moment to catch, but once burning, they spread quickly. The village people began to dance around the spreading fire shouting to the beat of the drum. Holly screamed as her inevitable fate became obvious.

Daniel raised his voice shouting at the warrior, but the noise of the drum, the shouting and the crackling of the flames drowned his words. Daniel could feel the heat now and he began to cough from the smoke. *At least Holly*

and I will be together, he thought as the flames drew closer.

The drum and the singing abruptly stopped, a startling hush prevailed, save the crackling of the fire. Everyone, including the head sachem, stared towards the lake.

Ebony had just entered the village. He stood up on his hind legs reaching his paws skyward. And as he did so, billowing dark clouds rolled into the sky that had no clouds a moment ago. A bolt of lightning flashed to the ground in front of the sachem and sent dirt up into his face and chest. All the villagers fell to their knees where they stood, heads bowed. Rain began to fall; within seconds a torrential downpour soaked the ground and all the people in the village. Thunder boomed across the land. The flames around Holly and Daniel smouldered and died, curling entrails of smoke all that remained. Ebony lowered himself back onto all fours; the lightning and thunder faded and the sky cleared.

An aura of light began slowly to surround the black wolf and when Daniel looked over to where the head warrior stood, a similar aura surrounded him too. Suddenly, they both vanished. This, indeed, was not the Ebony he knew. Certainly something had happened to him, but just what Daniel could not even guess.

Over to the right and to the left more billowing clouds, white clouds this time, rolled towards each other, rushing like giant waves cresting a celestial beach. Lights flashed within the clouds, but they were unlike any lightning Daniel had ever seen. A cold wind came up and blew into the faces of those watching. Great cries of anguish filled the air as if two mighty beasts were on the attack. The very air seemed charged and nothing moved, not even the village people who were where they had knelt at the first appearance of Ebony, their faces buried within their folded arms. Daniel feared for his friend's life, but Ebony had been acting so strange lately, Daniel wondered if it really was Ebony anymore.

It was many moments before any change occurred, but just as quickly as the strange clouds had rolled in, they withdrew, and a setting sun peaked out through wisps of early evening clouds and cast a yellow glow on the ancient village.

Silhouetted against the sun's back light, Ebony appeared at the edge of the water and slowly walked over to where Daniel and Holly were tied. He looked directly at Daniel. *It has been many summers for you, my brother.*

Daniel hadn't used his telepathic abilities for so long it took him a moment to realize Ebony had transmitted his message in plain words, and in the Anishinabe language.

"It is good to see you too," whispered Daniel. "I have been so worried about you."

Yes, I know. I have felt your concerns many times since you left. I am home now, Daniel, thanks to you.

"I don't understand, Ebony? Please clarify." Daniel was confused by Ebony's thoughts. He had never transmitted words before, or such complex images, and wondered about the change in him.

All in due time my brother. Ebony began to glow again until the light became so bright it outshone all images around it. Daniel watched in awe. The faint outline of Ebony's canine form stood up tall and lean; it lengthened, and then faded, replaced by a majestic warrior dressed in tan coloured leather. His long-sleeve jacket was adorned with porcupine quills and sea shells in a magnificent design depicting the sun, the earth and the moon and extended down below his waist. Traditional leggings and breechcloth covered his legs and groin. They were without decoration except the leggings had decorative fringes down the outside seam from waist to ankles. Ankle-high moccasins adorned his feet, again with a simple pattern of porcupine quills and sea shells. Two black feathers with white tips stuck out from the back of his head, held in place by a plain headband. His black hair, parted in the middle, was braided on both sides and hung down across his shoulders and chest. A small white feather, attached to the end of each braid, fluttered slightly in the light breeze. When he spoke, his voice resonated from deep within, and sounded all things holy. His first words commanded the villagers to rise and to honour the two visitors in traditional fashion. A young boy ran over, parted the smouldering brush and freed Daniel and Holly from their bindings. Holly collapsed into Daniel's arms and they embraced. She wept bitter-sweet tears. Daniel could feel the relief deep from within her body as well as his own.

The village was alive with activity; everyone seemed to have a pre-scribed task. Within minutes it became obvious a great feast was being prepared.

"Daniel, Holly, come with me," commanded the warrior. "We have much to discuss."

At first Holly shied away from the warrior's invitation and cowered closer to Daniel.

"It's okay Running Fawn. We are among friends now," soothed Daniel. With his arm around Holly's shoulders they entered the wigwam where they had been held prisoner and all three sat down around the fire.

"I feel a great confusion in you, my friend," said the warrior to Daniel. He spoke in English so Holly too could understand. "Let me explain. I am Tijus-Keha, one of the first-born sons of Kitchi-Manitou, the creator of all things. This is the East Colossus Village of my brother, Tawis-Karong. My village is on the other side of the Manitou Land, and it is known as the West Wolf Village."

"Is your village no longer there?" asked Daniel.

"My village remains, Daniel, but in my absence it has been ruled by a council of village elders. I have agreed to let the council continue to rule the Wolf Village. My father says it is best, but let me continue. Many years ago in your time, I came to visit my brother's village. I came as a wolf because I thought I would be able to watch my brother and his people without causing concern. I was wrong; my brother was waiting for me. We fought a great battle, a battle that I lost. I was unconscious lying on the ground. My brother picked up my body and threw me out into the mists where I was lost for a very long time. I emerged from the mists in a more modern time, not knowing who, or where I was. For many years, I occupied the minds and bodies of many wolves. Recently, in your time, I was Big Black, the black wolf your mother befriended. She saved me from a number of painful deaths. And when I was killed, my consciousness was transposed into your friend, Ebony and through your adventures, you stumbled upon the opening to my world and brought me home. I am eternally grateful to you, my brother. I have been away a very long time."

"What has just happened now?" asked Daniel. "Was the warrior who you just fought your evil brother?"

"Yes, Daniel. That was Tawis-Karong, my 'evil' brother, as you put it. He was not so evil, just a little misguided perhaps, but he had great power, power he abused and all his people feared him and suffered from his actions."

"All the stories I read when I was looking for you and Holly, they all said he was evil."

"Well, never mind. My brother will no longer trouble us. He has been banished into the depths of despair forever, never to be allowed to return, certainly not with the powers he had."

"Is that what happened in those clouds? You and your brother were fighting again?"

"Yes, my friend," replied Tijus-Keha. He paused for a moment, then stood. "I must go now to speak with my father."

"You mean all those stories about the great Manitous are true? There really is a Kitchi Manitou?"

"Yes, my young brother the stories are true. Although they are not exactly as told in the many songs sung by The Good People in your time. Sky Woman is my mother and Kitchi-Manitou is my father, but they exist only in spirit now. I must go and ask my father to free The Good People of my brother's village from the curse he put upon them and their village, so long ago."

"Oh yes, the curse, I read somewhere about a curse. What was it?" asked Daniel.

"When my father heard what my brother did to me, he came to the village and put a curse upon it and all the people within that changed time for them only. This is why you are now a young man and Holly has not changed. I must go now, but I will return, my brother."

"But what about Ebony, the Ebony I knew? Does he still exist? But", Daniel repeated as Tijus-Keha vanished.

Holly sat with a dazed look on her face, as if she was not seeing what was before her.

Daniel turned to Holly. "Running Fawn, are you there?" He knocked his knuckles lightly on top of her head, put his arm around her and pulled her to him, nestling her head on his shoulder.

Holly shook her head and replied. "Yes, I think I am okay. This is just too cool for words."

"All those weird clouds a few minutes ago," commented Daniel. "It's hard to imagine on what plain the two brothers fought. It was far beyond anything we can comprehend."

At that moment, four of the village women entered the wigwam bringing trays of freshly cooked meats and vegetables and a large pot of steaming tea. They placed the food on the ground in front of Daniel and Holly and began to withdraw.

"No!" shouted Daniel in words they understood.

The villagers dropped to their knees in a respectful bow.

"Please, rise up and feast with us. It is our wish that we eat together." It took much coaxing to get the villagers to obey Daniel's commands.

Still unsure of themselves in the presence of what they perceived to be Manitous in their own right, it wasn't until Daniel took the food out into the open air with the rest of The Good People that they understood. They smiled awkwardly, but soon began to relax and sing and dance.

For so long, they had been under the control of an unjust leader. There was much to celebrate and much to praise. The drum now beat a happier note and the song sung was sung by many more of the people.

After much eating and dancing by all the village people, Tijus-Keha returned and stood before Daniel for many moments before he spoke. "The curse is no more. All is as it was. I am pleased." Tijus-Keha stood looking at Daniel. "My father was pleased to see me."

Tijus-Keha reached out and touched Daniel's shoulder. Daniel could feel something probing his mind. It gently gathered his thoughts and feelings from the past 10 years, many events long since forgotten, sorted them and rearranged them in order.

"Are you still greatly troubled my brother?" Tijus-Keha asked.

"Yes, I am, or I was, I think." Daniel shook his head. "But I'm feeling much better now."

"Yes, I can feel your anxiety, my friend?"

"I've been so troubled for so many years. It is only the last few hours I've begun to feel at peace, being here with you and Running Fawn, I don't know what you did, but I feel at peace, more peace than I've felt for so long. Thank you."

"You have had many years to ponder your fate before returning to us here in this time and this place. It may be too soon, but I must know the future of your choosing. You must decide if you want to stay here or to return to the place from where you came. My father wants to close the passageway between your world and ours. But, before you choose, let me say, I ask that you choose to stay, and if that is your choice, I also ask that in your great wisdom, that you tend to my brother's people. They are in need of wise and just leadership. I see in you greatness yet fulfilled. However, if your choice is to return to your time and place, if that is your wish, it will be so."

"I would like to stay here, to do your bidding, but..."

"I do not understand my young brother, but what?" Now it was Tijus-Keha's turn to be confused.

"What about Ebony? Where is he? Will I see him again? And if so, will he be here?"

Tijus-Keha took in a deep breath. "Ebony will be with you, always, in body and mind regardless of your choice."

"Yeah, but, like, will he be real? Will he be the same; will he be more than just a spirit, a mere reflection of what he was?"

"Nothing stays the same, my friend. The Ebony you will experience will be mostly the Ebony you knew, and sometimes he will be me. He will also be different. But, he will be real. Have I answered your question, Daniel?"

"Yes, I think so. Thank you." Daniel paused for a moment, thinking then gave his answer. "I wish to stay. And I will be honoured to lead the people of the East Colossus Village, as long as you will be around to help me and to teach me the proper way."

"I am pleased. I know The Good People of my brother's village will flourish under your leadership. And I will offer what help I can."

The first-born son turned toward Holly. "Is it your wish to return to your people, Running Fawn?"

This was the moment Daniel feared, that Holly would choose to leave. After all he had been through to find her he feared he would lose her in but a few hours. "Please stay, Holly," he said. "I have looked for you for so long. I

don't want to lose you now."

Holly turned towards Daniel, took his hands in hers then turned to look at Tijus-Keha. Without hesitation she replied. "Yes, I want to go home, sir, Ebony, Mr. I'm sorry I don't know what to call you?"

"No matter, young friend of Daniel," replied the warrior. "Paddle out to the mist this evening and you will find the portal that will take you home."

"Thank you, replied Holly. She turned to look at Daniel. Never had she seen such a look of hurt on anyone's face. "Come back with me, Daniel."

"No, I cannot. It is my destiny to stay here. It is what I want."

Holly turned back to Tijus-Keha. "Will it be fifteen or twenty years later, like Daniel said?"

"Ah, you have so many questions, so many questions, but not to be concerned oh good friend of Daniel's. It is the inquiring mind that grows great wisdom." Tijus-Keha, paused for a moment then continued. "I have spoken with my father. The curse that was upon the village is no more. The days now pass in this world the same as the days in your world."

"But, how much older will all my friends be when I get home?" Holly asked again.

"Even I cannot control time, young friend of Daniel. My father has made some corrections, as much as he can. It will be when it is, but not so much will be lost." Tijus-Keha bowed his head. "I must go now and speak again with my father. He awaits me."

As the aura around Tijus-Keha dimmed, "Wait, wait, will we see you again?" asked Daniel.

"I will return," replied Tijus-Keha from amidst the fading light. Then he was gone and where the light had been, Ebony remained.

Daniel looked at Ebony, not quite sure what to expect from his old canine friend. Daniel could not feel any thoughts between himself and Ebony. *Is this how it's going to be now?* Daniel thought. *Maybe I'll only be able to read his thoughts when Tijus-Keha is present? Time will tell.*

While Daniel and Holly sat together, talking, touching and hugging, many of The Good People brought gifts of clothing, polished stone or jewellery. Each bowed in respect and presented their offering asking nothing in return. Daniel tried to refuse, but Holly advised him they would consider it an insult if he did not accept, so Daniel smiled and said thank you.

Daniel turned to Holly with one last attempt to convince her to stay.

"I want to go home, Daniel. I am not ready to give up all that I knew and wanted from my life as it was. Maybe you can, but not me, not right now. For me my life back home has only been a couple of days ago. It's different for

you. You've had so long to think about things."

Daniel sighed in resignation. "I understand," he said. "I will miss you. Please, tell my parents what happened; tell them I love them. I may never see any of you again."

"Yes, I will tell them, Daniel. Thank you. I will never forget you." They embraced one last time.

Holly bent down and petted the top of Ebony's head. "If only we had known about you before all this happened. Not that we could have done anything about it, but it would have been fun knowing." Holly turned to Daniel. "I wish we had more time to get to know each other better. You have known me as I am for many years. I have only known you for a few hours, but I feel we have been through so much together."

"We have," he replied. "You know. You could stay another day or two. There's no hurry now that time is the same speed on both sides of the portal."

Holly kissed him, first on his forehead, then worked down to his nose and each cheek, and finally pressed her lips gently to his. "It would be best if I go now. The longer I stay, the more difficult it will be to say good-bye."

"Yes, you are probably right. It may be better if you do. Take these as a remembrance of this place," he said, handing her some of the gifts The Good People had given them.

"Thank you." Holly took a few of the gifts, turned and placed them in Daniel's old canoe. She turned and smiled, slid the bow end of the canoe into the water and climbed into the middle of the craft.

Daniel handed her a paddle, then he pushed the canoe away from the shore. He and Ebony watched as Holly paddled out towards the mist.

Holly approached the white haze, turned and gave a last wave and then she was gone.

Chapter 8
Avalanche of Dirty Snow

Sharon and Ashley turned their canoe in the direction of the beaver lodge. As they approached the mound of twigs and mud, they could make out what appeared to be a stick growing out from the top of the lodge.

"That looks like a flag pole," laughed Ashley.

"It cannot be," giggled Sharon in return. "Beaver do not have flags." They floated closer. "It looks more like a paddle, or part of one," added Sharon. When within reach, she knocked the remnants of the pole towards her with her own paddle and retrieved it from the water. "This is Daniel's paddle," she said. "Or what is left of it. Look there." She pointed to another fresh piece of wood in the beaver's mound. "There is the other end. These teeth marks are fresh, maybe in the last few hours. It is not good to be in a canoe without a paddle. Can you see a canoe anywhere?"

Ashley looked around, but saw nothing.

"Even full of water, a canoe will not sink. Look closely near the shoreline. Maybe it has floated up one of the small beaver channels. Beaver dig small channels up to the trees so they can float the logs down to the lake. It also gives then an escape route in case a predator comes hunting."

"There aren't any channels big enough for a canoe," answered Ashley. "Oh, hang on. There's one over here," she said pointing beyond a large boulder to their right.

They turned the canoe around and let it drift up the channel. A short distance into the channel, it turned sharply left and virtually ended. Only a pair of Great Blue Herons were there perhaps tending to last minute preparations for their yearly migration. They both took flight at the sudden intrusion of the canoe into their space.

On the exit back into the lake, a cold breeze ruffled Sharon's hair and sent shivers up her back. It felt an ominous wind, unlike any she had ever experienced. Both women turned and looked in the direction of the wind.

"That mist wasn't there a moment ago," declared Ashley. "And does it ever look weird."

"Yes, it looks a bit frightening," declared Sharon.

Like a slow moving avalanche of dirty snow, the mist rolled towards them, overwhelming in size and volume. The air all around had turned decidedly cold as the cloud of mist approached.

Suddenly, a small arm of the mist shot out from the main mass and engulfed Sharon. "Aaaaaah," she shrieked.

The mist surrounding Sharon shot back to the main mass, just as the cloud crested and stopped.

Ashley sat staring at Sharon. "Are you okay?"

"I, I, I'm not sure. I think I am fine, but at the same time I am feeling strange," replied Sharon. "Look," she pointed. "What is that coming out of the mist?"

A vague object, darker than the surrounding multi-tone grey and dirty white, accompanied by a high shriek of rushing wind, appeared in the middle. A small canoe shot out onto the lake waters not twenty metres from Ashley and Sharon.

The mist slowly rolled back and within seconds had vanished and all was calm again.

"That is Daniel's canoe," stated Sharon. "But, it is not Daniel."

"Look, it's Holly." Ashley raised her paddle and shouted. "Holly. Over here."

"Ashley, Sharon. It is so good to see you. Huh," she gasped. "Is that really you? What's happened? You guys look so different."

"It's been many years, Holly."

"Oh, really, I know I only left two days ago. But, then Ebony did say it would be different." Holly smiled.

"Here we go again," replied Ashley. "Come on, follow us back to the dock. We can talk about it when we get home."

When they reached the end of the lake, Sharon excused herself saying she had some important things to do. "I will see you again, soon."

Ashley looked at Sharon. "Looks like you could use some rest, Sharon. You look so pale. Are you sure you're all right?" Ashley reached out to put her hand on Sharon's shoulder.

Sharon turned suddenly angry and slapped Ashley's hand away. "Do not touch me."

"Come on, Sharon," replied Ashley. "You're acting so strange. Are you sure you're all right?"

"I said I am fine. Now go."

"Okay, okay, we get the message. Stay cool, eh. I'll call you tomorrow."

"That wasn't the Sharon I remember," Holly said when Sharon had left.

"No, it wasn't the Sharon I know, either." Ashley explained what happened with the mist. "The mist must have freaked her out more than she admitted."

"Yeah, maybe," mumbled Holly.

"Come on. Let's go home."

"Hang on a minute. Let me get my stuff from the canoe."

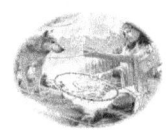

Chapter 9
Running Fawn

Holly's arrival home was greeted with a great deal of scepticism as to where she had been for the last nine years. Of course, the fact that she had not aged during that time lent some truth to her claims, but no one was eager to believe her. Even the Ojibwa elders from the reservation, considering that their entire religious beliefs are based on the Great Manitous, had trouble believing her story. To believe in a god is one thing, but to be confronted with a reality that Kitchi-Manitou, Sky Woman, Tijus-Keha and Tawis-Karong exist, and are presently occupying time and space in the mythical village of Daniel's long pursuit, was all but beyond reason. And what was even more difficult for the elders to accept: Daniel, a white man, and a human, now acting as a pseudo-Manitou, having taken the place of the banished Tawis-Karong, as the leader of an entire village. To have a non-Indian a leader went against all doctrine held sacred by the Ojibwa peoples.

If the village elders had opened their minds and considered all the evidence Holly brought back with her, they would have been more willing to accept her statements rather than considering them heresy. Both her people and the white authorities ostracized her, but the demands by her own people that she withdraw her stories and tell the truth about where she had been for the last nine years hurt her the most. Holly's subsequent refusal to change her stories virtually banished her from favour within the tribal hierarchy. And, as happened with Daniel, Holly lost all her friends and most people mimicked comments Daniel had heard when all his friends wanted little if anything to do with him.

The rejection was more difficult for Holly because she relied so much on friendships and human association for her well-being, whereas Daniel had been, for the most part, a loner. Now she had no friends, and not just because everyone she had ever known had aged so much since she last saw them, but mostly because they all thought perhaps she had lost it mentally.

Holly feared that first meeting with Daniel's parents when Ashley took her first to the Santos home. Knowing she had to tell them of Daniel's decision to stay behind was one of the most difficult responsibilities she'd had to date, but she had promised Daniel. However, the meeting had gone well. Both

of Daniel's parents were happy for him that finally he may have found some peace. They knew how troubled he'd been the last few years, troubles about which Holly new nothing. Of course, Holly never considered this aspect of Daniel. To her, it had all happened just a few days ago.

Daniel's parents were saddened by the knowledge they may never see their son again, even though their pain was consoled somewhat by the apparent peace he had finally found. It had already been some time since they had seen him, so, in fact, they had already partially accepted their loss.

Holly received a great deal of comfort at the home of Jennifer and Anthony Santos, a special connection she had no where else. They were the only people who really believed what had happened to her and Daniel. She had been the last person to see Daniel and consequently was able to describe to his parents how his life might develop. This was very comforting to both his parents.

"And, Ebony?" asked Jennifer.

"Oh, yeah, Ebony, you won't believe who Ebony is, or, was. It's so confusing all that has happened. Holly explained about Ebony and his and Big Black's true identity.

"Amazing," replied Jennifer, when Holly finished her story. "He is one of the first-born sons, a god in his own right."

Holly Kanipiswet, or Running Fawn, was a small woman considering she had reached the last of her teen years. She looked much younger than her true years and where age was a prerequisite for admission to some establishments, she was often asked for identification to prove her age. Of course, her birth documents gave her age as nine years older than reality.

Her mother had always told her. "Wait until you're older. You will be flattered that people think you much younger."

Right now, though, it was a point of annoyance. Holly had a typical round, but small, obviously Indian face with a pleasant, but shy smile. And when she did smile, which wasn't much lately, her almond-shaped eyes almost disappeared in the folds of skin above her high cheek bones. Her white teeth were exquisite, except for the two large front upper teeth that were separated by an abnormal gap that caused her to lisp at times as air passed through the gap.

In her youth, her mother had always parted her long black hair in the middle and braided each side so typical of that generation, a trait she now hated. She kept her hair short, preferring a more modern, convenient style. Her attempts to curl her hair always failed, as is often the case for women with

thick, coarse hair. Puffed up in the centre with a side part was her preferred style now, the sides curled under slightly just below her ears. The effect tended to square off her round face. She had a persistent dozen strands of hair at the crown of her head that refused to obey any command from combs, brushes, hair spray or gel, and always followed their own path, no matter what Holly did to correct them. In the end she gave up trying. They had a mind of their own, like the person whose head they occupied.

At the age of nine, Holly had unwittingly earned her Indian name. It happened one day when she and a couple of her school friends had been walking home from school through the woods. The three young girls had been arguing about something or other and Holly had become annoyed and ran off into the trees. Running through the brush, she disturbed two white tail fawns who had been hiding under a patch of brambles waiting for their mother to return. Not sure who was more frightened, Holly or the fawn, but to her two friends it looked like Holly was running with the young deer. The tale of her incident with the deer was told that evening over campfire discussions with the elders. In honour of the incident, Holly's grandfather thereafter named her Running Fawn.

Holly disliked being Indian with all the ramifications of aboriginal status. She always thought of herself as a person. What difference did it make if her skin was slightly reddish in colour, or pinkish, or dark brown, or ochre. For some reason she had yet to understand why many doors that were open to her white classmates were closed to people like Holly for no other reason than a different skin tone and eye shape.

Her grandparents told her many stories about their own childhood experiences growing up in a much less lenient white culture that prohibited them from being Indian. "For a while we were even separated from our parents to attend a special school," her grandmother had said. "We were forbidden to speak our own language or practise our many traditions. We were made to feel inferior. It was a very lonely time for me, and it was many years before I was reunited with my family."

Holly could not imagine such restrictions being placed on her just because she had been born Indian.

When she had reached her teen years, she rebelled against all authority, especially household rules laid down by her parents. She was out of control, according to her mother, and both her parents seemed powerless to have any influence on her actions. No one could advise her, no one could tell her anything; she took the attitude she knew it all, so had no need of anyone's advice. Her arrogance introduced her to a crowd of young people who seemed to be on a direct track for legal confrontation. In the eyes of the white authori-

ties, native people often walked a thin line between what is legal and what is slightly not legal according to white laws. It always seemed that local law enforcement came down harder on native offenders than comparable violations by young whites. By being a follower rather than an instigator, Holly had managed to avoid any major confrontation with the police during her teen years, but her name had been recorded in various reports as being an innocent accomplice.

During her first year at high school, her first time away form the native public school system, Holly had found junk food. Under its fattening influence, Holly ballooned, adding nearly ten kilograms to her small frame. Her mother took quick action, rallying a number of other concerned mothers both red and white, and protested the easy access vending machines in the school cafeteria. The popular vending machines had been removed, but Holly still found limited access to her beloved potato chips and chocolate bars at a local variety store.

In her mid teens, she had tried some of the softer drugs like marijuana and hashish, or Indian hemp as the natives called it. She managed to avoid the harder drugs with which many of the young people were experimenting.

As is so often the case with teenagers, almost overnight, Holly seemed to come around, realizing perhaps that she did not know it all, that her parents really did have her best interests at heart and that she really did have a brain worth developing.

Perhaps due to her Aunt Sharon's new appointment as clan matron that Holly seemed possessed by a new direction. Sharon had been Holly's role model to emulate and admire.

Holly always liked Sharon and had marvelled at her seemingly effortless ability to learn. It was perhaps Sharon who had the biggest influence on her, and by the time Holly reached eighteen, she seemed to be heading in the right direction with motivation and determination to succeed.

Once she had been able to curb her junk food addiction, and return to her normal size, cute, rather than pretty, was the word used most by her admirers. She'd been popular with the boys before her episode with the portal, but now, her new situation placed her in the weird category. Holly was having difficulty adjusting to this new status forced upon her by her time-frame in just three days.

A lot had changed for Holly during her absence from modern times, especially at school. History had gone on without her. News of her alleged experiences spread quickly within the school, news that other students used to ridicule her. Only a few days ago, to her time-clock, she had been a happy young woman, with many friends, a life-style she enjoyed, a promising future,

and a determination to get where she wanted. The constant mockery to which she was now being subjected, depressed her, put her behind in her efforts to again fit in, to make new friends and establish a new life with direction.

As is so often the case with shunned students, they frequently gravitate towards each other for comfort and companionship. And so it was with Holly. A young man by the name of Robert Conn, considered by most to be weird by normal standards, spoke kindly to Holly one day, the first words of friendship she'd heard from anyone at school since her return.

Robert was soft spoken with a forced lopsided grin. His eyes were the predominant feature of a long face, eyes that penetrated anyone he looked at. The uncomfortable feeling conveyed by people developed in him a habit of never looking directly at a person. He had a small nose for the size of his face, which was turned up at the end like a woman's, giving a softness to his expression that otherwise would not be found, hidden behind a permanent scowl. To compensate for his lopsided smile, he often cocked his head to one side to help counterbalance his peculiar grin.

A friendship developed between Robert and Holly. They hung out together at lunch time, and began meeting at a local pizza parlour after school for an hour or so.

"Did all that stuff that everyone says happen to you, really happen?" asked Robert, one day over a slice and a Pepsi.

Because of all the ridicule, Holly had become guarded, not readily sharing her adventures in time. She was reluctant to talk about them to anyone but Daniel's parents, young Brittany, or her own parents. However, her relationship with Robert had developed to the point she thought he could be trusted. "Yyyesss, they really did," she hesitated. "Do you believe me?"

"Well, I'm not really sure. It all sounds so weird, but if you say so."

The look on Robert's face, suggested otherwise.

"How do you account for the fact I look the same as I did when everyone last saw me?"

"Hey! I didn't know you then, so how can I say? For all I know, you could have made it all up."

"I don't know what I can do to convince you?" replied Holly.

"Well, you could take me there, and let me see for myself."

"Take you where?"

"To the village, you know. The Indian village so I can see for myself."

"No, I can't do that. I don't even know if the portal is open anymore.

Tijus-Keha said his father was going to close it forever after I left."

"Who?" Robert asked.

"Tijus-Keha, he's one of the first born sons. His father is Kitchi-Man-itou and his mother Sky-Woman."

"Oh, really, sounds like a lot of Indian witch-craft to me."

Holly tried to ignore Robert's remark. She tried to answer his question without provoking more anger. "The only thing he said was that his father took away the curse that had been put on the village. That means that time now passes at the same speed in the village as it does here. I don't know if the portal is still there or not, but it's probably closed now."

Robert began to laugh. "You don't really believe all that crap do you?"

"Robert," she said angrily. "It's not a question of belief. I was there; I saw it. I know it's real. And I don't need you to make fun of me. I thought you understood. That's why I was being your friend. Damn you!" Holly got up from her chair, grabbed her coat and stomped out the door of the pizza parlour.

Outside the wind was blowing and it was cold. Holly pulled her collar up tight around her neck in a futile attempt to retain what little body heat remained. She was both angry and hurt. "I thought he understood," she whispered to herself. The wind quickly froze the tears on her face. It was snowing, tiny flakes, more like ice crystals than snow, and they cut into her face like dozens of tiny needles. She arrived home cold and tired.

The next day Robert called, and he was very apologetic. "Hey, did you get home all right last night?" he asked.

"Yes, of course. I was cold that's all," replied Holly, her voice showing her indignation. She still felt the hurt from his remarks.

"Look, I'm really sorry about what I said. I didn't mean to upset you."

"You really hurt me, Robert. I thought you understood. Everyone's made so much fun of me, but I didn't think you would too. I'm fed up with it, that's all. I guess I'm too sensitive right now."

"Yeah, like, you know. It is weird. Anyhow, it's a lovely day. Why don't we walk over to the old village site, and see what we find? Maybe it'll make you feel better just being there. It's been cold enough lately. The ice on the lake has to be thick enough by now, and you can show me where it all happened."

It was indeed a lovely day. The temperature had risen to just below the freezing point and the wind of the previous day had dropped dramatically. The brunt of the winter's snow had yet to fall so early in the season and only about

fifteen centimetres lay on the ground, much of it blown into drifts under rock formations and trees. The coldest days bring the highest pressure zones, and that usually means sunshine and clear skies.

"That's a great idea, Robert. It's such a lovely day. I love days like this, with the snow all around, not much wind and lots of sunshine. Makes one feel good to be alive; don't you think?"

Robert agreed, although his idea of a great day was to spend it playing his favourite video games inside a warm house, looking at winter through an insulated window.

Like most young people, Robert came for the walk ill-prepared for the conditions - no hat, no scarf, a pair of light gloves. He did have reasonable boots though, but he kept them unlaced, and they soon filled with snow as they trekked along towards the clearing at the far end of the lake.

Holly ran ahead and scooped up some snow. Rolling it into a small ball she threw it at Robert, but it had little weight being so dry and fell short of the mark.

"Oh, it's a fight you want, is it," shouted Robert. "I'll getcha." He made his own snowball and let it fly.

Holly turned at the last minute and it hit her on the back. She bent down and picked up more snow and again threw it at Robert. This time it hit him in the chest. Robert ran towards Holly and tackled her throwing both of them to the ground. For a moment they both play-fought on the snow covered ice.

It started as a single crunch and grew into a cracking sound. Initially unheard by either Holly or Robert, but when the surface beneath them started to give way, they both instantly stopped moving. Fear engulfed them.

"Run," shouted Robert. He struggled to get up, helping Holly as he did so. Their arms and legs could not move fast enough; the ice beneath them broke apart. They scrambled for a foothold, searching for a solid footing, but failed and sank into the freezing water.

Holly grabbed the icy edge of the hole they had created and tried to keep her head above the water. "Help Robert, help," she shouted. But Robert had disappeared.

Chapter 10
The Truth

It had been six weeks since the incident on the ice. The police investigation had been intense, but to date, Robert's body had not been found. Sergeant Tom Adams from the Ontario Provincial Police had been the appointed OPP investigator. "We'll have to wait until the ice breaks up," he had said. "It'll be spring before we find it. We can't waste any more man power on a useless search."

Holly had said very little to the police about the incident; only enough to absolve her of any blame.

During the interrogation, Tom had stood looking at Holly. He'd lifted his hat and ran his hand over the top of his bald head. "You know, you should never have been out on that ice so early in the season. It's lucky for you that the two of you weren't walking together. Otherwise, you would both have fallen through."

Holly could only agree and had nodded yes. Her eyes filled with tears at the thought of Robert dying in the freezing waters of the lake and all because he'd wanted her to feel better.

In the end, it had been deemed an unfortunate accident. In most places around the lake, the ice had been thick enough to walk on, but at the mouth of the river where the currents run stronger, the ice takes longer to form. It was there the "accident" had occurred.

Holly sank into an even deeper despair during the following weeks. She didn't say much about it, but those closest to her could sense that she blamed herself for what happened. Had she not been so angry the day he'd made fun of her at the pizza parlour, they would never have been out on the ice.

There had been a reprieve at school, though, with everyone sensing the edge on which Holly's emotions perched. No one ridiculed her anymore. At first, no one noticed her deepening despondency, mostly because few people knew her at all. Her school grades were perhaps the first indicator of a problem. Within a month, Holly left school for an extended rest, as per her doctor's orders. The curriculum, the students and the school had become too much for her developing condition. Again, the only place she seemed to feel any peace was with the Santos family.

"You know," commented Jennifer one day when Holly was visiting. "I've been thinking, with all the work there is to do around here, we could use some help with things. I was wondering if you'd like to come and help us, you know, as a paid employee? You seem to enjoy being here and we like you here too."

"Good idea," replied Anthony before Holly could answer. "I've been after Jennifer for some time now to hire some new people. She could sure use the help in the classroom. It would be beneficial for all of us."

"Yes, that's right," said Jennifer. "Since Daniel spent so much time looking for the portal, he had little to do with the Wolf Education and Research Centre. And with Ebony gone, it's become necessary to try other attractions to get people to come visit. Nothing was quite as appealing as watching Daniel running with the wolves and having Ebony who people could touch. He was a great drawing card to get visitors to the Centre. Those magazine articles about Daniel and Ebony brought people from all over Canada and the U.S. and even parts of Europe."

Jennifer stopped and gazed out the window, her mind some distance away. She took a deep breath and let out a long and lonely sigh. "Ebony was such a treasure. None of the other wolves are as cooperative. I used to be able to coax Boots out into the clearing by the den opening sometimes, but he doesn't like it much anymore. I guess he's too busy playing Alpha Leader."

"What would I be doing?" asked Holly.

"Well, you'd be responsible for a variety of things. Since winter's started, the tourist trade has all but stopped, but I have a total of five schools that have contracted classes at the Centre. So your main job to begin would be to help me conduct these classes. With the absence of Ebony, we've had to expand our study program to include a broader overview of wildlife. Paramount in our new education program, we are discussing the ever increasing human encroachment of wild lands everywhere in the world and the increased interaction between wildlife and humans. Global warming is also a concern because it affects us all. We've introduced this into our study program, but not much because so many people believe it is a natural occurrence and not caused by human made greenhouse gases. However, survival of all animal species, including man, depends on an ever increasing need for humans and animals to better understand each other's needs. And that is what we are trying to teach now. And, of course, in late spring, the tourist trade will start too, but then the school business dries up with summer vacations. At first your biggest job will be to read this pile of magazines and take out any articles related to our studies."

"Well, yeah, it all sounds exciting, and I am interested. I'll have to

talk to my parents though, and my doctor. Can I let you know tomorrow? My parents would really like me to go back to school, but I'm not sure I want to."

"Sure, no problem," replied Jennifer. "Mention to your parents and to your doctor that this would only be a temporary job until you decide if you'd like to stay on a more permanent basis."

Holly was indeed interested in helping out at the Wolf Education and Research Centre. Her doctor was hesitant, but after talking it over with Jennifer and getting her assurances that she would not give Holly too much responsibility until they all saw how she adjusted to the work, he agreed it would be good for her. Holly started work the following Monday.

Young Brittany liked having Holly around, and seemed more than curious about all that had happened to her. Brittany always asked about her adventures travelling back in time to a place of fairy tales and real Manitous. At the age of eleven, for Brittany magic was still a very real possibility, and nothing seemed too extraordinary. She had become a great fan of television programs that involved time travel.

"Does the portal still open sometimes, Holly?" she asked.

Holly was reluctant to say anything. With all that had happened she had decided it best not to say anything to anybody anymore, taking the attitude of least said, least mended. But Brittany was different from the rest of the people. She felt she could talk to Brittany without the conversation going beyond the confines of the room. Still she hesitated. "I, I, um, don't really know, Brittany. Ebony, or Tijus-Keha, I forget that they are no longer the same beings anymore, although sometimes they are, not that Ebony is a person, but..... You know what I mean. The only thing he said was that his father wanted to close it after I left. So I'm assuming it's no longer open. I didn't press the point; all I wanted to do was come home."

"Do you think we could find the portal again and maybe go back and visit with Daniel? That would be so cool." Brittany had that innocent child's visage, eyes-wide-open look eager for any kind of magical adventure.

"Now that would be something wouldn't it." Holly laughed then paused for a moment deep in thought. "Tijus-Keha did say though, that his father removed the curse on the village. So now time in the village passes at the same speed as it does here. If it was possible to find the portal and we went back, then Daniel would be just as much older as us."

"Holly," hesitated Brittany. "About when Robert fell through the ice, I know you don't talk about it much, but I was wondering about it."

"Yyyess?" asked Holly, guardedly.

"Well, how did you escape not falling into the water too? When you

and Robert were together, you always walked side by side holding hands."

Holly was quiet for a moment, gazing at the floor. "Brittany, I'm going to tell you something and I want you to promise me you will never tell anyone else. Your word of honour not to say anything to anyone, agreed?"

"I promise," replied Brittany, excited about being pulled into Holly's confidence.

"You better close the door first."

After Brittany closed the door, Holly began. "For the longest time I thought that maybe I just dreamed it, but I know what I saw really did happen. When Robert fell into the water, we were together and I fell in too. We were playing in the snow having a snowball fight. He tackled me and we fell to the ground, and that's when the ice broke. I guess the combined weight of the two of us falling onto the ice was too much for it. We fell into the water, not just Robert, I fell in too. I know that I told the police it was only Robert."

"Really," exclaimed Brittany. "How did you get out of the water? How did you get back home without freezing to death when you were soaking wet? It was so cold that day." Brittany was so excited she squirmed in her chair.

"Okay, okay, one question at a time. Remember, what I'm going to tell you must not be shared with anyone. When I first fell into the water it didn't seem so cold, but within seconds the water filled my boots, soaked through all my clothes to my skin. It felt like I was being dragged down by the weight of all the stuff I was wearing. I grabbed hold of a jagged piece of ice at the edge of the hole, and tried shouting for help. But, no one was around to hear me. I got so cold everything was going numb including my voice. I never even thought about Robert. I was so scared for myself. Then, there was this circle of light in front of me and it grew bigger and bigger. I just looked at the light and suddenly the piece of ice I was holding onto broke off and I sank under the water. Then something grabbed my coat collar and pulled me out of the water. I was so cold lying on the ice. I looked up and there was Ebony, or a wolf that looked just like him. I couldn't believe it. I reached up and touched him around his ear, and that's when I felt warm all over, and I was no longer wet. I looked into the wolf's eyes and I could see an Indian person looking back at me. I then looked around for Robert. I think I spoke his name and something probed my mind and I could hear someone speaking to me."

"What did the voice say?" asked Brittany.

"It said: 'Robert is gone. I can no longer save him.' I looked at the hole in the ice and then back at Ebony, but all I saw was his tail disappearing through the circle of light. Then the light disappeared and I was all alone on the ice."

Brittany stood staring at Holly, her mouth open. "Wow," was all she could say.

"For the longest time I thought I had dreamed the whole thing, but I know it really happened. I know I fell into the water. I can remember how cold I was and the piece of ice I held onto. The memory is so clear. If it wasn't for Ebony, I would have died too, just like Robert."

Brittany stood up and put her arms around Holly and they both hugged.

In a few minutes Holly pulled back, and said. "Now, you have to promise me you won't say anything to anyone."

"I promise," replied Brittany. A few moments later she asked. "Do you think we could go out onto the lake in the spring and look for it, you know, try to find the portal again?"

"Oh, Brittany, I don't know. The lake frightens me a little now. I'm not sure I want to go back over there, at least not until they find Robert."

"I understand," Brittany answered. Then she had another thought and spoke about it to Holly. "You know, if we can go back, I should learn a few words of Ojibwa so I can speak to some of the Indians. Wouldn't Daniel be surprised? How much Ojibwa do you know?"

"Not much, I'm afraid. I've been thinking I too should learn how to speak it. Sharon's grandfather has been trying to get me to learn it for a long time."

Brittany kept thinking how wonderful it would be to go and visit her brother and to be able to talk to him in Ojibwa. She even talked about it that evening with her parents over dinner. "Do you think it would be possible to find the portal again and go back and see Daniel?"

"I'm afraid I can't answer that question, Brittany. Perhaps Holly knows," replied her mother.

"I've already asked her and she doesn't know either." Brittany hesitated then asked. "I've been thinking I'd like to learn to speak Ojibwa."

"I see no reason why not," replied Jennifer. "You should ask at the school and see if they have classes that teach it. If they do, we'll enrol you, no problem."

It had been two months since Holly started working at the Centre. During that time, she had fitted in well and seemed to enjoy her work. Her doctor too was pleased with her progress. However, lately, Jennifer had noticed a change in Holly. She seemed more distant, didn't smile often and was always so tired. When Jennifer asked her about it, she got angry and brushed her off

as if it was nothing. Jennifer asked Brittany if she had any idea why Holly was acting differently.

"I don't know, Mom. I've noticed it too. I'm a bit worried."

"Yeah, me too, I like Holly. She's a good kid really, a little misunderstood, but so are a lot of kids her age. Her experiences through the portal must have been very confusing for her. I hope she's all right." Jennifer had real concern in her voice.

Brittany too was worried for her friend. And her mother's comments did nothing but heighten Brittany's own anxiety.

The next Saturday, Jennifer asked Brittany if she wanted to help her with the weekend grocery shopping in Little Current. "It's getting late and the super market will be closing soon."

"I'm coming," replied Brittany. "There's a magazine I want to pick up if that's okay."

"Sure, no problem."

While Jennifer shopped for groceries, Brittany walked down the street to the variety store for her magazine. Across the road in the little park overlooking the North Channel, Brittany saw Holly. She called out, but there was too much traffic noise and Holly was too busy talking to a couple of other teens and didn't hear Brittany. Brittany ran across the road to say hi. When she got near, she again called out to Holly. Holly turned.

"Hi Hol..." She stopped in mid sentence. "Huuuhhh," she gasped, putting her hand to her mouth. Brittany turned and ran back across the road. She arrived back at the super market parking lot just as Jennifer was loading the groceries into the truck.

"Brittany! What's wrong? Are you okay? You're so pale."

"Oh Mom, it's Holly. She was across the road over in the park. You'd never recognize her. She looked awful. We saw people like that in videos at school that were spaced out on something, something really potent. It's more than just pot; she's high on something pretty strong. She looked half asleep, almost in a daze, and her eyes looked like she'd O/D'd on mascara and she'd been crying. They were so dark almost like they were bruised. Oh, Mom, what's she doing? I'm so scared."

"It's all right Brittany. Get in the truck. We'll drive over to the park. If she's still there, maybe we can help her." But when they arrived in front of the park, the small group of young people, including Holly, had gone.

Chapter 11
Oatmeal Porridge

Holly did not show up for work on Monday, and her parents were very evasive when Jennifer called to enquire about her well-being.

"All Holly's mother said was that things were under control. Whatever that meant", remarked Jennifer when Brittany asked about Holly.

At school, Brittany heard what had really happened and called her mother at lunch time. "Yeah, it's all over the school. Holly had been picked up by the police. She was found almost frozen in a snow bank over by Saunders' farm. It was the same night when I saw her in the park. The police don't know how she got there. Apparently, farmer Saunders was out checking his cows and he'd noticed Holly's yellow and red jacket in the snow. He called the police, and they took her to the hospital."

Holly's mother again was very evasive when Jennifer called, but eventually confided in her. "Once her condition stabilized, she was admitted to the rehabilitation clinic for drug abuse at the hospital."

"But drug abuse is a mental disorder and can be treated like any other illness," remarked Jennifer. "It's nothing to be ashamed of."

Holly's mother agreed, but she said that not everyone accepts that drug abuse is an illness. "Please do not tell anyone about this?" Holly's mother asked.

"Of course not," replied Jennifer. "Can I go and visit with her? Is it allowed?"

"Not at this time, Mrs. Santos; maybe in another week or two depending on how she responds to treatment."

Jennifer called back in a week, but there was no change in Holly's condition. When Jennifer talked to the doctors, they would not release any information.

"Can't anyone do anything for her, Mom?" asked Brittany.

"It doesn't seem so. If only we could get in to see her, maybe we could help," said Jennifer. "If only Ebony was here. He'd definitely be able to reach her."

Ebony, now there's an idea, thought Brittany.

To an eleven year old, the truth about Santa Claus and the Tooth Fairy are only just known and they willingly perpetuate the myth with younger children who still believe, but witchcraft and magic of any kind remain real possibilities. Even if no one else believed in Holly and what she experienced, that didn't matter to Brittany because she believed. And, if Holly said it was Ebony who pulled her from the water, then that's what really happened.

The next morning, Brittany got up early, dressed in warm clothes, her heaviest winter boots and slipped out the back door of the house. She first went to the barn where she picked up a pair of snowshoes, then headed off in the direction of the lake. With winter truly entrenched, the ice formation on the lake could support far more weight than an eleven year old girl, even though she felt she was wearing twenty kilos of extra clothing. There was little worry of the ice breaking, although she did stay clear of the entrance to the river.

A cold wind blew, but she was snug in all her winter gear. She trudged on glad she had the foresight to bring the snowshoes. It would have taken her twice the time without them. As she walked she questioned her sanity to be embarking on such a quest.

The wind blew strong into her face. She pulled her scarf up tight around her mouth and nose. Frost bite is a real concern on mornings like this. *It'll be warmer on the way back,* she thought. *The wind will be behind me then.* Her mind turned to Ebony. *If I actually get to talk to him, what am I going to say that he can understand? I don't know if I can talk telepathically like Daniel and Mom.* The more she thought about it, the more her resolve weakened. "Maybe this is not such a good idea," she said pausing, then turned around and began walking back the way she had come. "No, darn it, I have to at least try, for Holly's sake." She turned around again, bent forward into the wind once more and trudged forward.

Rounding the point of land at the far end of the lake, Brittany could see the clearing where the old Indian village had been. A few moments later she stood on the shoreline and called out. "Ebony, are you here? I need your help. Please Ebony if you can hear me. It's me Brittany." She paused for a moment, thinking. *I've never actually met Ebony. With all the stories and photographs my parents and Holly have, I feel I really know him. But would he know me; would my name mean anything to him?* "Ebony, please answer me. It's me Brittany; I'm Daniel's sister. You gotta help. Holly's in trouble."

For many minutes she repeated her plea without success. She plopped down in the snow and wept a few salty tears into her mitts. "This whole idea is so stupid. There's nothing here but wind and snow. This is crazy." She continued to sit in the snow undecided what to do. Once more her resolve began to weaken. In a last plea for help she called out again, but again she received no response.

Totally dejected she stared down at the snow. "I gotta get moving before I freeze," she whispered, and shivered as a blast of cold air and snow crystals slammed into her. "This is a stupid idea." Standing up, she bent down to adjust the straps of her snowshoes and turned to begin the long walk home. All around her the snow began to glow a faint yellow. She looked back behind her and everything was bathed in yellow light. As she watched the light grew brighter and a swirling window of glowing mist began to form where she had been sitting. Frightened by the intensity of the glow, Brittany jumped back as a huge black wolf jumped through the window and landed on the snow in front of her. She staring at him, his immensity startled her and because he was slightly uphill from her, he looked even more imposing. For a moment she was filled with fear. "Eeebbbony?" she stuttered and stepped back a bit. "Isss that you?"

Something probed her mind, more a suggestion than words, and she knew it was Ebony without him saying so. There was confusion in his thoughts and it seemed to Brittany that he was asking her what was wrong. Not sure how to communicate with the black wolf, she began talking and told the story about Holly and how much trouble she was having since she'd come back. All the time she was trying to envision images about the things she was saying so that Ebony could understand better.

"No one believes her and everyone, except her mom and dad and my parents make fun of her all the time. She's been so depressed for a long time and is now taking drugs. She's in the hospital and the doctors are worried she might not make it. They say she has lost the will to live and wants to die. I was hoping you could help her. Maybe if you went to see her and talk to her then maybe she would want to live again."

Brittany sensed a great misunderstanding coming from Ebony, and wasn't sure if he knew what she had just said. Then she thought, *how are we going to get a live wolf into Holly's room? The hospital isn't going to allow it, even if they think he's a dog.*

A glow engulfed the black wolf, and it grew in intensity, blocking out all other light. The light faded and there still was Ebony, but standing beside him was an Indian.

"I am Tijus-Keha, young Brittany, sister of Daniel," he said. His voice boomed out from deep within and conveyed a greatness. "Maybe now I can enter this place you call a hospital without raising concern."

Brittany stood looking at the Indian warrior, totally aghast at what had just happened. Then she began to laugh. "I don't think so; not in that get-up. And, you'll have to do something about your voice," she remarked before she remembered who it was standing in front of her. "Oops!" she said, a little embarrassed. It was a trait inherited from her mother who was famous for speak-

ing her mind, even when her opinion had not been requested.

Tijus-Keha only smiled. "I am not sure what you mean by taking drugs? Please explain."

Brittany compared Holly's condition to some teas used by the Ojibwa, that sometimes made a person dizzy and they see things that weren't there.

The Indian warrior nodded a partial understanding then added. "What do you mean by my get-up, and what is wrong with my voice?"

Again Brittany explained the problem with his clothes. "Maybe my dad can lend you something to wear that wouldn't, how would I say, wouldn't stand out so much. Anyhow, we can worry about that later. And, your voice, well, it does sounds like an electric guitar on high, but I don't think you will understand what that is. Anyhow, we'll worry about that later, too. Come on, let's go home. You can meet my mom and dad, and we can make a plan. And they can better explain what it means to be taking drugs."

Tijus-Keha reminded Brittany that as Ebony and Big Black he had already met her mother and father. "But it will be a joy to be able to talk directly to them," he said.

The three set out on the walk back across the lake to the Santos home.

Brittany had so many questions she wanted to ask of the first-born. She had been doing some reading about the Ojibwa and the old Anishinabe customs and religious beliefs and the name Tijus-Keha had come up frequently. She also wondered how much he remembered of the modern world, from his experiences in the guise of numerous wolves. The cold and the noise of the wind prevented much conversation on the walk back across the lake. It seems it was winter in the village too, and like it had been in Brittany's world, a cold winter. Brittany had wanted to ask about her brother, but thought it better to wait until later when conversation would be easier.

At the house introductions came with difficulty. Jennifer was in the kitchen making breakfast and was not even aware Brittany had gone out on her own. She had assumed she was sleeping in. Still in her night-gown and house-coat, Jennifer felt uncomfortable in the presence of the Indian warrior. At first, she smiled when Brittany said his name thinking it was some kind of early morning joke. She even looked at the calendar to see if it was April 1st. But when Ebony walked into the kitchen and stood beside them, Jennifer knew it to be true. Tijus-Keha gently probed her mind and spoke to her telepathically, further confirming his identity.

Jennifer bent down and tried to put her arms around the black wolf, but he shied away. "Oh, Ebony, do not be afraid."

"He is just Ebony now, a normal wolf. He remembers many things, but it is I who have most of the memories. It is I who was both Big Black and

Ebony in your presence all those summers so long ago."

Jennifer smiled. "So much has happened since those days. I have forgotten many things. But my memories with you as Big Black will be with me forever."

"Yes," replied the Indian warrior. "My times with you were very happy. You were my saviour on many occasions. I am eternally grateful to you. If it had not been for you, my life as your Big Black would have been cut short, and it is possible that Ebony would never have existed."

Jennifer asked how he came to be here, now.

He explained to Jennifer how Brittany had come to the far end of the lake that morning to ask for his help. "And, here I am."

"Yeah, you should have seen it Mom. It was awesome. I still don't believe what happened," quipped Brittany.

"It is wonderful that you are here. Did Brittany tell you what help we need?"

"She said that Holly was in a hospital and that she needed help. You will have to explain to me what a hospital is and just what help she needs."

Jennifer tried to explain and the first-born seemed to understand. "Do you think you can do anything for Holly?" asked Jennifer.

"If I can get to her, I can help. Holly is unaware of her importance to The People. She is destined for greatness. I cannot say more other than to emphasize the importance of her well-being."

Jennifer went back to preparing breakfast. She asked Tijus-Keha if he wanted something to eat, to which the warrior answered, "I have no need for sustenance. However," he said. "Ebony needs food and when I am in his body, I must feed myself to keep him healthy. And, on special celebrations I do sit with The People for a feast of deer meat, berries and root tea." For a moment he hesitated, then said. "When I lay on the floor in your parents' home in front of the fire, the day I lost my paw, I recall an aroma of grain cooking. It had a sweet smell to it and ever since I have always wondered what it was and how it tasted. Do you remember?"

"Oh my, that was so long ago; it's hard to remember, but it could only have been oatmeal porridge. That's about all the grain we ever cook in the mornings. Is that what you have in mind?"

"I hesitate to say yes, but I think so. Do you have any?"

"Yes, I do," laughed Jennifer. "Have a seat and I will prepare some for you and Ebony. It will take a few minutes."

"Thank you." Tijus-Keha sat down at the kitchen table. "But," he added. "I do not understand why you are laughing."

Jennifer smiled. "How can I say this without embarrassing you? You are one of the first-born children of Kitchi-Manitou. You are a god to the religious beliefs of the Ojibwa Peoples. And, here you are sitting at my kitchen table asking for oatmeal porridge. Don't you not find that, um, humorous?"

"I suppose so, but I never stopped to think about it when I sit and dine with The People."

"I hear Anthony stirring. I should go and tell him you are here." Jennifer excused herself and went upstairs with a cup of coffee for him.

Anthony came down and introductions were made. Like Jennifer, he too was initially sceptical about the identity of the Indian warrior and again it was Ebony's presence that convinced him it was true.

Anthony called his Ministry of Natural Resources office to ask if he could take the day as a vacation day. "Something important has come up that needs my attention," he said. He wanted to be included in whatever plans Jennifer and Tijus-Keha had in regards to Holly.

Brittany too wanted to be included and asked if she could have the day off school. Her parents agreed; after all, it was Brittany who brought Tijus-Keha to them.

Jennifer placed the bowl of oatmeal porridge in front of the Indian warrior with some maple syrup, soya milk and some banana slices. She felt comforted by his conversation and was surprised at how easily the first-born talked and shared his experiences. It was like talking to any of the elders from the Ojibwa Nation. Jennifer felt at ease in his presence. Hesitantly, she asked about Daniel and how he was doing.

"Daniel is doing well. My father and I are pleased Daniel chose to stay. I know it is a great loss for you and your husband, but be comforted knowing that he has become a great and respected leader of his people. We will talk more, later. I have finished my, what did you call it?"

"Oatmeal porridge," replied Jennifer, smiling.

"Oatmeal porridge, yes, thank you. It was as tasty as the aroma had suggested. Please, I think we have much to discuss. My time here is limited."

They all moved into the front room and sat by the fire to discuss what course of action they would take. Various sneaky tactics were considered, although no one wanted to do anything illegal. Jennifer suggested they try a direct approach and just go to the hospital and ask to see Holly. If that failed, then they would resort to more clandestine actions. Everyone agreed to try Jennifer's approach first.

After outfitting Tijus-Keha with some of Anthony's clothes that were more suitable for the 21st century, they all climbed into Jennifer's truck and drove to the hospital rehabilitation clinic. The nursing station was the first

hurdle to cross and they received an emphatic no to their request to see Holly. Jennifer then asked to speak with the supervisor and he also refused permission, saying. "I do not have the authority to overrule management policy in these matters. I would like to help, but I cannot."

"Please. You have to try to help. We've gone to a lot of trouble to bring my friend to see Holly," said Brittany, pointing to Tijus-Keha. "He can help her, but we just have to get in to see her. Please can't you do something for us?"

"Well, maybe I am being a little insensitive about this. Let me call downstairs to see if there's someone from administration who can help you."

The vice-president of the facility happened to be in the hospital and agreed to see them.

"Good morning," he said. "My name's William Slater. Please. Come in and sit down." After everyone was seated, he asked, "Now, how can I help you?"

Jennifer explained that they had come over specifically to see Holly in an attempt to assist with the mental anguish she was experiencing and that they had brought one of the respected elders from the Ojibwa First Nations who was famous for helping his people to overcome great troubles. And, as the hospital had so far been unsuccessful in reaching Holly, it was Jennifer's belief that the elder could help. "I have grown to accept many strange things in connection with the Native Peoples, sir, and strongly believe that if this holy-man says he can help, rest assured he can."

The vice-president sat back in his chair and thought for many moments. He turned and looked at Tijus-Keha. "What is your name, sir?" he asked.

Jennifer interrupted and said. "His English is limited, Mr. Slater. His name is Tijus-Keha. Let me write it down for you." Jennifer leaned over and wrote the name on a writing pad on top of the desk.

The vice-president took the pad and tore off the top page. "One moment please," he said, and got up from his chair and left the office. A few moments later, he returned and sat down again facing Jennifer, Anthony, Brittany and Tijus-Keha. "Is this some sort of sick joke, Mrs. Santos?"

"Hang on a minute, Mr. Slater," declared Anthony, not happy with the vice-president's tone or choice of words.

"No, you wait a moment, Mr. Santos." The vice-president got up from his chair and looked down upon the foursome sitting across from him. "I have just spoken with the administration office of the local Ojibwa peoples and, and," he gestured towards Tijus-Keha, "this so called holy-man, as you call him, is totally unknown to them. In fact, when I told them his name, they asked

if I was trying to be funny. I don't know what it is you are playing at, but there is no way I will allow you, or this sick excuse for a respected Ojibwa holy-man, to visit with Holly Kanipiswet. She is still a very sick young woman, far too ill to have some voodoo witch doctor shake some rattles over her and chant some ancient Indian medicine song. I cannot risk further damage to her already fragile condition."

Jennifer was looking at Tijus-Keha, trying to judge if he understood what was being said. She could both see and feel that he was becoming upset and angered. She tried to telepathically reach his mind and tell him not to respond, but she was too late. He rose slowly from his chair. An aura of light surrounded him and he grew in stature until he towered half a metre over the vice-president, who was still standing on the other side of the desk. Everyone went silent. Tijus-Keha spoke out. His voice echoed throughout the large room. "I am Tejus-Keha, first-born son of the Great Mystery, Kitchi- Manitou, ruler and religious leader of all The Good People throughout the Land of the Great Turtle. You dare address me in this manner. You dishonour me and show great disrespect for all that,,,, that…….."

Jennifer finally reached Tijus-Keha with her thoughts and he paused in mid-sentence, aware of the precariousness of the situation. The glow and his stature diminished. The room went silent. In one motion, Anthony, Jennifer, Brittany and Tijus-Keha, got up from their chairs and left the office, leaving the vice-president still standing at his desk with his mouth open, his complexion noticeably two shades whiter.

Outside in the truck, the Indian warrior apologized for his actions. "I lost my temper; I am sorry. It is rare, but it does happen. Even I am not infallible. We must use, what did you call it?"

"More clandestine actions," interrupted Jennifer.

"But we must wait until night has fallen in order to use the shadows to our advantage. I must first look for Holly's sleeping place from the outside of the hospital." They drove around to the wing that housed the drug rehabilitation clinic.

"How will you know which is Holly's room?" Jennifer asked.

"I will know. Already I can feel her mind. She is very troubled. I sensed it in the hospital when we first entered." There was a slight pause. "Holly is there," he said, pointing to the second window from the end on the second floor.

"What do you plan to do?" asked Anthony.

"I will return this evening. It will be no problem."

"How will you get in?" asked Brittany.

The Indian warrior turned from the front seat and touched Brittany's

arm.

"Oh, yes, I understand," she said, "More magic."

Tijus-Keha touched Jennifer's shoulder and she too smiled.

"Now wait a moment, you guys," remarked Anthony. "This ain't fair. Don't shut me out of the link with your mental telepathy stuff."

They were all still laughing at Anthony when Tijus Keha reached around and touched him on his arm. The Indian warrior closed his eyes and transferred his thoughts to Anthony.

"Oh, wow. Thank you," he said, smiling. "Yes, Brittany is right, more magic. Now I know what all the hype has been about for so many years. What a wonderful experience. Hey, wouldn't this be great if we could do this all the time, you know just think what we want to say to people without the hassle of getting someone's attention and then having to speak words?"

"It is not so good all the time. You must learn to block your thoughts so sometimes others cannot understand your true feelings. And that is difficult to learn. Daniel has learned it well, but in my world we do not have so many things that enter our minds. Here in your world there are many voices in the air from, what do you call it, radio and the picture box, and the small machines you talk into that you keep in your pockets."

"Television and cell phones," commented Brittany.

"Yes, but in my land, the air is quiet of unnatural sounds and clean of poisons that fill your air. It gives us time to think and clear our minds. To receive so many people's thoughts and conversations is not always an advantage in your time. Do you understand?"

Everyone agreed.

Tijus-Keha smiled.

Hospital visiting hours ended at 9:00 PM. From past experiences, Jennifer knew that staff changed shifts between 10:30 and 11:00 PM. During this half hour window, little staff activity took place with the patients. At precisely 10:30 Ebony stepped outside the truck and ran under cover of shadows from trees that lined the roadway to the edge of the hospital wing. Anthony watched from the truck. There was a slight glow from the darkness of the building, and for a moment Ebony seemed surrounded by a halo of light. It faded quickly and was instantly followed by a similar glow through the window of Holly's room.

Anthony picked up his cell phone and dialled. "He's inside," he whispered into the mouth piece. "You should have seen it. I'd never have believed it if I hadn't seen it for myself. Like magic, as Brittany so aptly put it. Anyhow, I'll keep you posted."

In Holly's room, Ebony stood looking at the bed, but had trouble seeing Holly because the bed was so high. He came closer, jumped up onto the bed sheets and straddled Holly's sleeping body.

She stirred at the extra forty-five kilo of weight on her bed, opened her eyes and stared blankly into the black wolf's face.

Ebony sensed a jumbled burden of thoughts and emotions. Nothing in her mind conveyed any order. Ebony knew if she continued in this condition, with all the guilt she felt over the events of her recent past, she would be lost to the sane world forever and might die. He probed deep into Holly's memory searched for and found the last time he and she met when they parted company on the lake the day Robert had died. There he found the root of her most recent problems surrounded by an enormous amount of guilt. He probed deeper back even farther in her memories to the day they paddled the lake and first found the portal. From that memory, he sorted her thoughts in order and stacked them neatly in her mind so they all made sense. On the way back to her most recent memories, he rearranged the sequence of events and replaced them with logic and order, too. He removed the guilt of Robert's death and replaced it with happy memories of their friendship together. He also found blame she carried for the pain her parents were suffering over her drug abuse and these he replaced with understanding and love. Leaving her mind, he stood quietly staring deep into her eyes.

Holly took in a deep breath; her eyelids opened. "Ebony, Ebony, is that you?" She squirmed her arms out from under the blankets, reached up and stroked the rough tangle of fur behind his ears, and ran her hands down his back and chest. "You are so heavy," she said.

Ebony transmitted a feeling of relief and joy that Holly's mind now seemed relaxed and calm.

"What are you doing here? How did you????" but she stopped in mid sentence when the bedroom door opened. Light spilled from the corridor into the room and onto the bed on which Ebony stood.

Chapter 12
A Big Black Dog

A nurse entered Holly's room holding a flashlight. She was making the early night rounds checking on her patients. At the sight of the large black dog standing over Holly, she shrieked and ran from the room calling for help.

Heavy foot steps came running down the hall and Holly's door crashed open. Three security guards burst into the room. Had they known what to expect, they might have caught the last remnants of a peculiar yellow glow from the area over Holly's bed.

Holly sat up and stared at the guards who were shining their flashlights around her room.

One of the guards went and looked into her washroom and then into her clothes cupboard. "Nothin' in here," he said.

"What is it? Is there something wrong?" Holly asked, while she casually folding her top blanket down to cover-up Ebony's muddy paw prints on the top sheet.

They told her what the nurse claimed to have seen on top of her bed. "She said a large black dog?"

"Ha, Ha," Holly laughed. "That's ridiculous. The door's been closed, the windows don't open, and, as you can see, there's no black dog in here now."

"Yeah, right, but the nurse was so positive what she saw," replied one of the guards. They all had a good laugh. "Sorry to have bothered you," he said, and they left her room.

In the morning, the cleaning staff looked curiously at the dusty dog prints on the top blanket of Holly's bed. Holly feigned ignorance and shrugged her shoulders. Her doctor came in the room at that moment; the cleaning staff got on with their duties.

"You are feeling much better today, Holly?" her doctor asked.

"Yeah, I am. I haven't felt this good in a long time. Must be the good hospital food I had for breakfast."

The doctor chuckled, then checked her blood pressure and pulse and took her temperature.

"When can I go home?" she asked.

"Well, we can't be too hasty. Give it a few days and we'll see how you get along."

"I'd like a telephone, please. I have to call some people. It's important I talk to them as soon as possible."

"Yes, of course, no problem. I'll have the nursing staff bring one in for you," he said. "Glad to see you are doing so well. We were quite worried about you. I'll see you later. Enjoy your day." The doctor left her room to go about his rounds.

William Slater phoned up to the nursing station on Holly's floor that morning having heard rumours about a commotion on that floor of the rehabilitation wing. "I'd like to be kept informed if anything unusual happens in regard to Holly Kanipiswet," he said to the head nurse.

The day-nurse then told him about the night-nurse, who reported seeing a large black dog on Holly's bed shortly before 11:00 last night.

Another report by the security staff denied the presence of a black dog on the hospital floor. The report suggested a passing car's headlights had reflected a shadow of the stuffed dog Holly had at her bedside and the night-nurse had overreacted to it.

After his earlier experience with the Santos family and that strange Indian witch doctor, the vice-president was not so convinced with this explanation, but for fear of sounding stupid and in need of medical help himself, he said nothing. He was also told about the miraculous recovery of Holly, which puzzled him even more. It seemed coincidental she should recover the very next day after the strange visitors were in his office. He stopped by Holly's room later that morning and casually asked her about an Indian named Tijus-Keha. Holly only smiled suggesting that you can never underestimate the power of Ojibwa medicine.

The vice-president was in Holly's room when the telephone was brought to her. He respectfully excused himself to give her privacy.

Holly called her mother first to let her know that everything was okay now, and that she was looking forward to coming home. "We have a lot to talk about, Mom, but that can wait until later," she said. "I gotta talk to Jennifer before Ebony leaves."

"Ebony?" her mother asked.

"Yeah, Ebony. You won't believe what happened. I'll call you later and we can talk after I call Jennifer. Okay?"

"Yes, of course, Holly. But isn't Ebony with Daniel?"

Holly ignored her mother's question and just said good-bye then called Jennifer.

"I am so pleased, Holly," Jennifer replied to Holly's excitement at feeling so much better. "Ebony was able to work his magic?"

"Yeah, I feel great. How did Ebony know I was in trouble?"

"You can thank Brittany. She just went to the old Indian village and started calling his name. In a few minutes he appeared, the same way he did when you fell through the ice."

"Oh, she told you about that, did she?"

"No, it was Tijus-Keha who told me. But, we can talk more when we come to visit."

"Jennifer, please. Where is Ebony now?" Holly asked again.

"They've gone back, left last night after visiting you. Tijus-Keha said their time here was limited."

"They?" asked Holly.

"Yes, Ebony and Tijus-Keha."

"Oh, yeah, of course, I just wanted to thank Tijus-Keha for what he did," said Holly.

"He knows; he could feel your gratitude. He was just glad to be able to help." Jennifer paused then added. "He said it was necessary; that there is something that you will do, something crucial, but he did not elaborate other than that. He said that you would see him again soon. But we'll talk later in more detail. Bye."

Holly held the phone to her ear for a few seconds after Jennifer hung up thinking she would call her mother back and momentarily heard a man's voice in the background, a voice she recognized. The line clicked and cancelled out. Rushing out into the corridor, she caught a glimpse of the vice-president entering the elevator. *No,* she thought. *He wouldn't do that. It must have been interference on the line.*

Back in his office, William Slater called the Ojibwa Administration office and asked more detailed information about Tijus-Keha. The office representative gave the vice-president a couple of web site addresses to get information about Ojibwa religious beliefs and stories concerning Kitchi-Manitou, Sky Woman and the two first-born sons.

"You mean Tijus-Keha is the name of one of your Manitous?" he queried.

The office representative explained that he was more than just another Manitou, but suggested all the information he needed would be found on the web sites.

"I have another question if I may?" the vice-president asked.

"Yes, of course."

"Is there anything in Ojibwa religion about a large black dog named Ebony?"

"Ebony? No, nothing in our beliefs that I know of; Ebony is not a Na-

tive name," replied the representative. "Don't know if it's the same Ebony, but the Wolf Education and Research Centre had a large black wolf named Ebony, if that's who you mean?"

"Not sure," replied the vice-president. "You said, HAD. Where is he now?"

"You best talk to Jennifer Santos. She runs the Centre and would be able to give you more detailed information."

"Jennifer Santos, eh. Okay, thank you for all your help," he said, and hung up. The vice-president spent the next two hours reading the web sites suggested by the Ojibwa representative. If he was to believe all that he read, the vice-president wondered if he really did have a live deity sitting across his desk yesterday.

Four days later Holly was released from hospital and a week after that she returned to work at the Wolf Education Research Centre. Spring was not far away and much preparation was needed in time for the opening of the tourist season the middle of May. Three school groups were due to arrive that week. Jennifer was glad of Holly's offer of help. During gaps in work duties, Jennifer had a good chance to talk with Holly asking exactly what it was that Ebony did.

"I don't remember much because everything was kind o' in a fog most of the time, but I remember something groping around in my mind, something gentle that sorted my thoughts, you know, like a computer defragging its hard drive and putting things in order. And when I woke up and saw Ebony standing over me, I reached up and touched him. I could feel how strong he was, and, and, he felt special, you know, when you're near someone important like. Well that's how I felt. I don't know how to put it, but it was a feeling of peace that was all around me. It was like, sort of floating in air and then being laid back down on the bed real gentle like."

"He is special, isn't he," added Jennifer.

"Ebony? Yeah he sure is. You should have seen the look on the nurse's face when she came in the room and saw him on the bed. She freaked big time. I thought she was going to run right through the door without opening it. Ebony began to glow and slowly disappeared. Then the security guards came in and they had a good look around, but obviously didn't find anything. We all had a good laugh. Ebony's paw prints were all over the bed, but no one saw them. I covered them up with the top blanket. After the guards left, I lay back onto the bed and had a good laugh before falling asleep. It was the best sleep I'd had for a long time. When I woke up in the morning, everything was great. All I could do was smile. I was so happy. And, I just wanted to go home and start making things better for all the rotten things that have happened to me the past year. Do you understand?"

"Yes, I think so," said Jennifer. "Before Ebony left he gave me some thoughts similar to what he gave you. I too can feel a peace now that I haven't felt for a long time, not since Daniel left. I wish Tijus-Keha could have stayed longer. There were so many questions I wanted to ask him, you know, about Daniel and his choices." Jennifer sat staring out the window, her mind far away in another time.

"Are you okay, Jennifer?" asked Holly.

Jennifer smiled and nodded yes, tears had welled up in her eyes. She sniffled.

Holly reached over and put her arms around her and they hugged.

"What now?" Holly asked, wanting to get Jennifer's mind onto something else. "Did Ebony say what it was I was supposed to do?" They broke apart. Holly handed Jennifer a tissue to wipe her nose and eyes.

"No," Jennifer replied through a large sniffle. "All he said was that there was something you would do, but he could not elaborate more. He said even he did not know what it was, but he did say that he would see you again, soon."

By the end of April, the ice had gone from the lake, and a search party had been dispatched to look for Robert's body. It didn't take long to find it at the shallow end of the lake. A few days later a private funeral service at a local church closed the chapter with Robert. The service renewed her memories of the incident, but at the same time finalized it totally. Thanks to Ebony, she no longer blamed herself for Robert's death.

Sudbury television news carried a small report of the drowning, the recovery of the body and the funeral.

William Slater turned off the news broadcast, reached over for his telephone and dialled a number. He introduced himself to the woman who answered and asked to speak to the manager in charge of programming.

"Yes, Mr. Slater. News or regular programming?" she asked.

"News please."

"One moment, please."

A moment later, the telephone was picked up, the voice distant and with a faint echo; the recipient using the phone's speaker. The man spoke abruptly, with an air of annoyance.

"Jim Kirby here."

Chapter 13
Ahawi
Gaa wiin daa-aangosh kigaazo ahaw enaabiyaan gaa-inaabid.
(You cannot destroy one who has dreamed a dream like mine.)

Ahawi straddled the dying embers of the communal fire in one of the main meeting areas not far from her wigwam. She felt the warmth rise up inside the skirt of her deer-skin dress. Loosening the belt around her tiny waist, she allowed the heat to flow up around her upper torso. She shivered in the warmth.

Ahawi stretched her arms up as the heat permeated her entire body, then she ran her hands down her svelte hips and smiled. At eighteen summers, she was enjoying her womanhood. The hardships normally connected to village life she found challenging, but since becoming a mother, the challenges developed new meaning. She was tall by village standards, and enjoyed the dominance her height gave her; she conveyed far greater confidence than most other woman of the East Colossus Village.

Many of the village squaws resented Ahawi for her fine facial features, slender nose and slim body that attracted the attentions of all the young warriors in the village. If Ahawi noticed the added attention, she said little. She was devoted to Mikya, her husband, and Bizaaz, their son who was almost two summers old now.

Stepping off to the side of the fire, she knelt down and leaned back against her heels. Extending her hands above the red coals, she soaked in the dying warmth. Tilting her head back, she gazed up at the night sky. She often watched the star children playing in the sky and wondered what they were, how they got there, how they were able to stay up there without falling and why most of them did not move. "But, some of you do," she said to herself and wondered about that too. She watched a sliver of a new eye of Brother Moon slowly rise above the trees beyond the marsh. "Such a strange and beautiful land we live in," she mumbled, "So many mysteries to wonder about."

"Yes, there are," replied Mikya. He had walked up behind her, his moccasins stepping lightly on the soft earth. He knelt down, put his arms around her and nuzzled his chin into the top of her head.

Ahawi was always awed by her husband's gentleness considering his immense muscular body. She envied the power it commanded. "Bizaaz sleeps?" she asked.

"Yes, soundly as all little boys should."

"Good. We have a long journey to make tomorrow. He will need his strength."

"So will you," said Mikya.

"Yes, I know. You are sure it will be safe?"

"Yes, of course. You are not still worried about the stories of all the ugly beasts, are you?"

"Well, yes it was a thought."

"You know as well as I do that before he went away, our leader's brother, Tijus-Keha, changed all the ugly beasts back into normal sized animals a few summer's ago."

"Yes, I did know, but I thought maybe he might have missed a few and maybe some are still out there."

"If there are, you have me to guard you and Bizaaz."

Ahawi smiled and felt reassured by her husband's confidence. "And our leader has given us permission to go?" she added.

"Yes, that too has been granted."

"Good," she said, and sighed. Ahawi leaned back against her husband. Looking up at the star children again, she asked, "Why does that one move each night, and not the others?" She pointed to the brightest star child in the eastern sky that even outshone Brother Moon sometimes.

"I do not know," replied Mikya. "The wisest of our elders, say it is Animoz, who is a servant to the other star children. He moves each night to bring wood for the other star children's fires. But I think the star children in the sky are like Giiz, our Mother Sun, the giver of light and heat for our land, but are so far away they are just lights in the sky to us. And the lights that move maybe are lands like ours looking for their own Giiz."

"Yes, you may be right," answered Ahawi. She took a deep breath and snuggled in closer to Mikya.

Mikya ran his fingers through Ahawi's long black hair. "It shines so bright in Brother Moon's light," he said.

"What does?"

"Your hair, it is beautiful."

Ahawi smiled. She loved the attention given to her so freely by Mikya.

A light breeze blew off the lake and brought with it the dampness from the mists slowly forming a short distance away from shore.

"The wind is cool," commented Mikya. "Come, we should rest now. I will bring some embers to start a fire in our wigwam."

The next morning, Ahawi, her husband and young son, set out on their overland journey to the eastern end of Manitou Land to visit with family members living in a small village outpost of the East Colossus Village on the edge of the Gichi Gumee, the great fresh water sea. Walking overland was a shorter distance, but going by canoe would have been easier. However, this late in the warm season, sudden storms were not uncommon on the Gichi Gumee. They didn't want to risk being caught in a storm in open water with Bizaaz.

It was Bizaaz's first journey away from the village and like all young boys he was overwhelmingly curious about everything he saw and did. Had he not been with them, Mikya and Ahawi could have done the journey in half the time.

After arriving in the village to the east and saying hello to all their family and friends, they settled into the guest wigwam. "It is so lovely here," commented Ahawi.

"Yes, I agree," replied Mikya. " But their cold seasons are very harsh. When the cold winds blow off the sea, it is much colder than in our village. There is more ice, and finding food is more difficult. Most of the animals they hunt go inland and are hard to find for the people here. They must gather more corn and many squash during the summer so they do not starve when it is cold. As you saw they already have a good supply of fish smoking over the fires, and many squash, corn and beans are buried in each wigwam's storage holes. They should be well stocked for winter food, but if the winter is very harsh, they may go hungry before Sister Spring comes."

Ahawi, Mikya and Bizaaz were sleeping when the night guard in the lookout tower cried out. His alarm was suddenly stifled when an arrow pierced his upper chest and he fell to the ground.

"What was that?" asked Ahawi, sitting upright on their sleeping platform.

"I do not know. I will go find Kaaki. He is the war leader. He should know. Stay here until I return." Mikya slipped out the doorway and was gone.

Most of the village had been asleep. No East Colossus warriors were on guard except the one lookout. He'd had a commanding view of the surrounding lands, but the early morning mist hid the approaching Wendowa war party who had beached their canoes along the shoreline out of view of the lookout tower. The attack took the village completely by surprise.

Kaaki had risen at the first alarm and quickly gathered a few of his warriors. They took their appointed places at the arrow slots in the palisade

walls and began defending the village. But the Wendowa warriors were too many and quickly overran the sparse defences. Many Wendowa warriors began entering the village proper. The intense battle seemed a sure victory for the invading Wendowa, but as more and more East Colossus warriors joined in the fight, the battle began to swing the other way.

"Mommy, I am frightened," cried young Bizaaz, sitting up in his hide robe. "We must run to find safety."

"No, your father said we should stay here. He will return."

A Wendowa warrior appeared at the entrance flap and bent down to enter. He screamed his war cry and raised his club to strike, then fell face down in the dirt; a spear protruded from his back.

On the far side of the small clearing Mikya stood with his fists clutched in success.

Bizaaz saw his father and started to run across the clearing towards him.

"Bizaaz! Come back," screamed Ahawi, but her words were lost by the cries from outside.

"No," shouted Mikya and he raised his hand. "Stop, Bizaaz, stop. Go back." When Mikya saw that his son did not turn back, he ran towards him.

Ahawi watched as little Bizaaz ran, his arms outstretched for the security of his father's arms. "No," she whimpered.

A Wendowa warrior met Bizaaz first and brought his war club down on the boy's head. Ahawi watched her son crumple to the ground; the crack of splitting bone would forever remain a horrible memory etched in her mind.

Mikya was upon the Wendowa warrior instantly and buried his antler stiletto into the warrior's stomach then jerked the short knife upwards tearing open his enemy's abdomen. The Wendowa fell forward, his hands groping to hold his internal organs in place and met Mikya's knee as he brought it up and slammed it into his enemy's face, flattening his nose. The Wendowa's body twitched and jerked a few times then lay very still. Mikya turned towards his son and immediately caught a wayward arrow that pierced his chest.

The enemy was being driven back and began a hasty withdrawal as Ahawi ran to her husband's side.

"Mikya, Mikya," she cried as she knelt down and cradled her husband's head in her lap. He reached up, touched her soft cheek and tried to say something, but a pool of blood gurgled out of his mouth and trickled down his cheek. He coughed once, stiffened in Ahawi's arms and slumped over in death.

Kaaki gathered a force of warriors, launched their own canoes and followed the retreating Wendowa war-party. Half way across the Gichi Gumee they caught the Wendowa unaware and sank all their canoes. All the Wendowa warriors were lost with no injuries to the East Colossus warriors.

Ahawi felt avenged by the deaths of the enemy warriors who had killed her son and husband, but it did not replace her loss. The image and the sounds of her young son's death were almost too much for her to bear. How quickly her life had changed.

It was customary for village women, who suffered such a loss, to go off into the woods to lead a solitary existence in mourning and sometimes when the pain is too great, to find comfort only in death. Living alone, a young woman usually died anyway from starvation, from the elements, killed by a predatory animal, or by an unfriendly warrior.

It was Ahawi's intention to do just that following the funeral ceremony for Mikya and Bizaaz once their remains had been placed on their raised platform in the sacred resting place to begin their journey to the Land of the Dead. But, Mikya's mother and father, White Shawl and Coyote Song, offered to take her into their lodge as their daughter, if Ahawi agreed not to go off into the woods by herself. This was an unusual gesture by grieving parents of an ex-husband. Ahawi accepted her in-law's offer and in so doing moved into their wigwam and became part of their family.

In time, Ahawi's heart had begun to heal, although the memory of her son and husband and the method of their deaths, lingered to torment her more than she cared to admit.

"Someday, you will marry again, my daughter," Ahawi's father-in-law, Coyote Song, had said.

"Yes," she had replied, but she felt great despair and knew that day would be a long time coming.

Ahawi awakened early from a troubled sleep.

"What is it, my daughter?" asked Coyote Song when he saw that she was so troubled.

"Oh it is nothing, just a dream. I have had it before; it will pass."

"Please you must tell me. Dreams are very important. The Manitous speak to us through our dreams; we must listen and share our visions to understand them."

Hesitantly, Ahawi tried to explain. "It is a clear vision of a strange white-skinned Manitou who commands a black beast. In my vision, Mikya and Bizaaz are standing in front of this strange white-skinned Manitou inside a large wooden wigwam. I have never seen such a large wigwam. Many people are inside the wigwam and all are standing and still there is room above them. I am in the vision too, and I walk up to Mikya and Bizaaz. It was so real, Father, I reached out and touched Mikya and I could feel the strength in his arm, see his smile and smell his scent. And, then the white-skinned beings black beast

extended his arms out for many lengths and wrapped them around all of us and bathed us in a yellow light. And suddenly I awakened. I am confused Father; what does it mean?"

"I do not know my daughter. We should talk with White Shawl. She understands dreams better than me and can often interpret them. We will talk with her after we finish the morning food."

After the morning meal, White Shawl put everyone's food dishes outside for the dog to clean.

Coyote Song had brought another armful of wood in from their wood pile outside and had placed some in the fire. Sparks rose up with the smoke towards the exit hole in the top of their wigwam and added another layer of black soot around the opening. The burning aspen filled the wigwam with warmth and comfort and a sweet aroma, mixed with the scent of so many corn husks and squashes buried in the storage hole inside the structure.

"My love," Coyote Song said. "Please come and sit by the fire with us. Ahawi has a dream vision she wishes to discuss with you. White Shawl did as she was asked.

"Tell me about your dream, Daughter." White Shawl listened carefully. When Ahawi had finished, White Shawl was silent for many moments, a look of deep concern on her face. Finally she spoke, hesitantly. "I,,, I am not sure what the dream means, my daughter. It is a very powerful message the Manitous are sending you. You say you have had this same dream more than once?"

"Yes, Mother, I can recall the same dream this many times in the last so many sun turns." She held up four fingers for the number of times she'd had the dream, and ten fingers for the number of sun turns. "And it is always the same dream."

"Having the same dream four times is very important. The number four has special meaning. That number represents the number of directions of creation, north is foreboding and brings an ill wind, east is the beginning of new life and new expectations, west is the ending of something like death or a change and south represents warmth, new growth and prosperity. These are all good signs. The other parts of your vision are unclear to me, but that number of times has other crucial meanings, too, that I do not understand. We must go to Otter and tell him the dream. He will know what it all means."

"But will he speak with a squaw?" asked Coyote Song. "He does not normally listen to what he says are the silly dreams of women."

"This is not a silly dream, my love. It is a strong vision that must be shared and understood. I will speak with Otter myself this morning. If I tell him it is an important dream; he will understand and will listen to the vision."

Later that afternoon, White Shawl approached Otter and as expected he initially refused. But then she told him some of the vision, which convinced

him to at least listen to Ahawi.

Ahawi entered the elder's wigwam for the first time. She knew he normally prohibited women from entering his living space, but she also knew how much he respected White Shawl's opinions. She had seen him talking with White Shawl many times and she had been privy to some of their conversations in her wigwam when they thought she was sleeping.

Ahawi retold her dream vision. Otter seemed greatly disturbed by what she said about the white-skinned being and the black beast.

"I cannot tell you the true meaning of your dream, but I can tell you that it has far reaching events that will happen to you. Seeing your husband, your son and yourself represents three events, and not all of them will be pleasant. It is the black beast that I cannot give meaning to, but it represents either a great evil, or a great blessing," and then he paused. "It is also your destiny, a destiny you must fulfill. I cannot tell you more."

"But," Ahawi hesitated not wanting to show disrespect to Otter. "I still do not know what the visions mean. You are the wisest of our elders. I believe what you say, but you have not told me much more than what White Shawl has told me. Please tell me the true meaning. If it is something bad and you are only trying to protect me from it, I will understand. But, I must know the truth."

"Do not dishonour me Ahawi by your persistence. I tell you what I believe is all you need to hear. I must think on it for a few sun turns then I might be able to give you a more detailed explanation. I must also go to our leader and warn him."

"Warn him; about what?" asked Coyote Song.

"I must warn him about the white-skinned being and the black beast, of course."

On Ahawi's and White Shawl's walk back to their wigwam, Ahawi said, "I hope I did not anger Otter, but I wish he would have told me more about my dream. I had a feeling he was not telling me all that he knew."

"He does not know," commented White Shawl.

"The Otter does not know?" asked Coyote Song.

"That is correct. He is as confused as me, and just as concerned."

It was two sun-turns later before Otter gave Ahawi any further explanations. During that time Daniel and Holly had arrived in the village. Ahawi stood and stared at Daniel when he was carried into the wigwam. Is this the white-skinned being of my dream, she wondered. But, when she'd heard rumours of a black wolf that had swum from the stranger's canoe before they were captured, she knew for sure that this was the white-skinned being of her dream, and the wolf was the black beast.

Rumours ran strong throughout the village about how their leader was going to deal with the strangers. Ahawi searched out whoever she knew to get first hand information, especially information about the white-skinned one. It was White Shawl who told her their leader was going to put them to death because he feared them after Otter's warnings.

Ahawi had to see the white-skinned being first before she could make any plans, to be sure she would do the right thing. She put on her best dress and waited just outside the wigwam until all the others had left. She then quietly entered and approached the two captives.

After being so close to the white-skinned being and praying for him, she was still uncertain how she should proceed. All she knew was that she had to save him from the death the village leader had planned.

"I must seek greater guidance," she whispered to herself. From her own wigwam she gathering a few things in a hide bag and sneaked off for a short canoe ride to a place just beyond the marsh behind a great willow tree. She often went to this place to find comfort away from children and the demands placed on all women by the men of the village.

A series of large boulders formed an odd shaped semicircle around a small clearing. Hidden by dense under growth, a slight crack between two of the boulders opened into a small cave. Ahawi parted the branches and squeezed into the cave. Inside, she made a small fire.

As far as she knew no one from the village knew about this little cave, but people once did, people from a forgotten past perhaps. And it must have been a holy place for these people. In the growing light of the fire, she could

see drawings and paintings on the high walls of the cave of overly large beasts being attacked by warriors throwing spears. Warriors attacking animals was nothing new, but these animals were very big compared to animals she has seen near her village. One beast in particular fascinated her, its bulbous body covered in long fur. Two large horns stuck out from the front of its head either side of its mouth and between these horns where the beast's nose should have been, a thing stuck out that looked like a thick serpent or snake. She had never seen such a beast and wondered if this was one of the giant beasts destroyed by Tijus-Keha two summers ago? Other drawings showed Mother Sun high in the sky and mountains with fire and smoke curling out from the tops. Many of the drawings had faded and she could not clearly see them in the flickering fire-light.

Around the fire Ahawi placed a few flat rocks. While the fire burned she went outside and cut a few small branches from the papakorsigun tree. Back inside the cave she carefully peeled the bark off the small branches. These peelings she laid on the flat rocks by the fire to dry. Within a few minutes the bark had dried enough she could pound it into a moist pulp. One of the flat rocks had a small natural bowl in its surface into which Ahawi placed the bark pulp. Pouring a bit of water into the natural bowl, it wasn't long before she had effectively boiled a small amount of water and made a tea from the papakorsigun bark pulp. She tipped the tea into a hollowed out animal horn-cup to cool. From her small hide bag she'd brought with her, she pulled a braid of dried sweet-grass, the end of which she held in the flames of the fire for a few seconds until the end began to burn. She pulled the sweet-grass from the fire, blew on the end to blow out the flame and let the sweet-grass smoulder. With her other hand she cupped the smoke from the sweet-grass and curled it around her head and shoulders inhaling the smoke and the sweet fragrance into her lungs. Sipping the tea, it wasn't long before Ahawi felt dizzy. She knew she was entering the dream world, but also knew it was dangerous to sip too much tea with the sweet-grass smoke. She also knew she had to have enough of the two to induce the vision quest she desired to take.

"Please, Great Spirit, come to me and speak to me. Guide me in making the right decision about the white-skinned being. Bring me the wisdom to choose wisely, I beg of you. I am but a weak squaw, but I am your obedient servant. Command me oh Great Mystery and I will obey. Otter says my future is important to The People. I ask for your guidance."

Ahawi's conscious mind went blank and she fell backwards; the horn cup in her right hand fell to the ground.

When she awoke, the fire was all but gone. It was still light outside, but Mother Sun was far down the western sky. Ahawi gathered up her things, returned to her canoe and paddled back to the village with a clear image of what she had to do.

Ahawi immediately put her plan into action. She sneaked around to

the back of the captive's wigwam, dug a small hole under the wall and crawled inside where the two prisoners were being held. She cut their bindings and motioned for them to follow her. Outside, she tried to guide them safely to a canoe. When they came to the clearing she told them to run then she hid and watched as Holly was recaptured, but was greatly relieved to see the white-skinned being escape in a canoe and re-enter the mist.

Upon returning to her parent's wigwam, Ahawi confided with Coyote Song and told him what she had done.

Coyote Song was astounded by her actions. "Why would you do such a foolish thing my daughter? "

"If the white-skinned being is so important to my future, he must live. If he dies, my destiny will never be fulfilled. This afternoon, I had another vision, a message from the Great Mystery himself, Kitchi-Manitou, and he told me what I must do."

"I understand your motives my daughter, but the village leader will be very angry. I fear what he will do to you. It is with a sad heart I say to you, for your own safety, you must flee this village. You must go as quickly as possible. My canoe is at the water's edge."

As Coyote Song had suggested, Ahawi gathered up what few personal belongings she had, placed then in the canoe and left the village.

Her departure from everything she knew, everything she held sacred, was so sudden, she was confused and scared. In the darkness, the world ahead seemed so empty.

Old fears die hard. Without the security and strength of Mikya, her husband, she kept an eye open for ugly beasts just beyond the confines of the village, especially for one like she saw in the drawings on the cave walls. "No," she reassured herself. "During our trip to the outpost village, we saw no such beasts. I will be fine."

She paddled north following the island to the beginning of the Gichi Gumee then headed out into the choppy waves farther north to landfall where she camped for the night. The following morning she headed east arriving at the mouth of the Great River, the Michi-ZeeBee early afternoon. Exhausted, cold and confused, she found a small clearing not far inland where winds were calm, game plentiful and the river close by. She built herself a temporary shelter. "Tomorrow I will search for a better campsite," she said to herself. Curled up in a hide robe she fell into a restless sleep wondering about the visions and the events that had changed her life forever. It had all happened so quickly, she'd had no time to consider what she'd done. She wondered too about Otter's predictions and how they might unfold.

Chapter 14
Big Brother

Jim Kirby and the William Slater met for lunch a few days following their initial telephone conversation and the hospital vice president told his story as best he could from the pieces he knew.

Kirby laughed between mouthfuls of French-fries and steak. "Sons of Indian gods growing in stature before your very eyes, changing into a black wolf, unscrambling a patient's mind using mental telepathy and disappearing into thin air like Tuvok being beamed back to Voyager, you must understand how ridiculous it all sounds. I don't know. If anyone else had told me this same tale, I'd have laughed in his face," replied Kirby. "But, I cannot ignore your credentials. And apart from your little involvement with the Davis and Santos families, I have had some first hand experiences with them too. Nothing as bizarre as what you're telling me, mind you, but there's definitely something very strange going on with these people. As difficult as it is to believe you, I cannot dismiss the possibility what you are telling me may be true."

"I am relieved," replied the vice president. "I'd have thought the story was crazy had I not experienced it myself. So what do you propose we do now?"

"Well, before we can do anything, we need irrefutable evidence. I think we should pay a visit to that old Indian village site and do some Ebony calling ourselves and see what happens. You have a boat?"

The vice-president confirmed that he did. Friday morning, Jim Kirby, a camera operator, and William Slater headed out from the Little Current marina for the little lake and the site of the Indian village.

"I brought some local charts in case you didn't have any," commented Kirby.

"That's okay. I think I know these waters well enough not to need them, but can't be too careful," replied the vice president.

Holly had just finished talking to her last group of school children at the Wolf Education and Research Centre when Brittany entered the class-room.

"I'm on duty until noon, Brittany. Then we can go," she said.

"Sorry, I'm just excited about going to the old village site. It'll be so much fun exploring around especially for you. And you can tell me where everything was when you were there. Mom said it would be okay to spend the whole afternoon. She packed some sandwiches and fruit for us and a couple of drinks. I'll meet you down at the lake. I can at least get the canoe loaded and in the water."

"No, just wait. We'll go together; be patient, I won't be long."

On the walk down to the canoe, Brittany asked Holly if she was still afraid of the lake.

"No, not really, well maybe a little. Since they found Robert's body and he's had his funeral I feel a lot better about it all. I'll be okay now, but thanks for asking."

Shortly after 12:00 the two adventurers pushed off from the dock. It was an overcast day, but rain had not been forecast. A slight wind had come up. If Holly had been on her own the canoe would have been difficult to steer. But having Brittany up front adding ballast and another hand to paddle, it was easy going. Both Holly and Brittany were expert canoeists and good swimmers and neither had any fear of the water, even considering Holly's fall through the ice the previous winter.

Brittany saw it first. They'd just paddled around the point of land that marked the middle of the figure eight shaped lake. "Look, beside the beaver lodge, there's a boat with three guys in it,"

People often sailed small boats into the bay to fish, so the presence of the boat did not alarm Holly, but this boat was a bit bigger than the usual boats seen in the area considering the underwater grasses that grew in this end of the lake.

"Oh, darn," said Brittany. "I wanted the village to our selves."

As they drew near, the two girls could see the occupants of the boat were not interested in fishing. And, then they both heard one of the men shouting.

"Ebony, where are you? We need your help. Please come and show yourself."

The men in the boat were too intent on what they were doing to notice Holly and Brittany until their canoe bumped into the side of their large craft.

"Hey!" Holly demanded. "What are you guys doing?"

The three men turned together to look at the girls.

"I know you," shouted Brittany pointing at one of the men. "You're the

vice president from the hospital."

"How did you..............." Holly let her comment trail off. She was thinking back to the vice president's visit in her room at the hospital and the unusual click on the telephone when she'd finished her conversation with Jennifer. She desperately tried to remember what she and Jennifer had been saying to each other to have some idea of how much he might have heard. "It was you listening on the other end of the telephone." Then she noticed the third man with the camera with Sudbury Television printed on the side. Her thoughts ran rampant. "Just what are you trying to do?"

"I would suggest you two leave," interrupted Jim Kirby. "You're way over your heads, girls."

Before Kirby could say anything more, Holly began poking her paddle at the man with the camera to stop him from filming what was going on.

Kirby grabbed the paddle and pushed it back. The canoe rocked to the far side. Holly grabbed the near gunnel to support herself which pushed the edge of the canoe under the water. Water rushed into the canoe and it tipped over dumping the two girls into the lake.

At that moment, from underneath the overturned canoe, a faint yellow glow appeared, then it was gone.

Kirby reached down, grabbed the canoe and turned it upright, but there was no sign of either girl. For many frantic moments the three men searched for the two occupants of the canoe.

"Damn, the water's not deep. They have to be here, somewhere."

William Slater was looking very distraught. "We have to find them. They can't have drowned. Come on Kirby. Find them. They were wearing life jackets."

All three men searched desperately for many moments. Finally Jim Kirby announced defeat. "We've got to get out of here before someone sees us," he yelled.

They all began paddling away to clear the underwater grasses before starting the engine. No one said a word, each fearing the repercussions if directly involved with the girls' deaths, if in fact they did drown.

Brittany and Holly lay on warm sand inside a strange hut, coughing up dirty lake water. They both turned over at the same time.

"Ebony," said Brittany.

She was about to say thank you when Holly shouted. "Daniel."

Both girls looked up at the young Indian standing off to the side of Ebony. It took Brittany a moment to recognize her brother. Those blue eyes and the braided blond hair hanging down both sides of his shoulders did look out of place with the leather headband and single feather casually fluttering in the slight breeze. His bare chest, breechcloth, fringed leggings and moccasins also seemed contrary to his white skin. But, the person standing above them could not be mistaken for anyone but Daniel.

"Are you two all right?" he asked speaking English.

They both confirmed they were.

Daniel turned and spoke to two Indians standing just outside the wigwam, who then turned and ran off. "I've asked them to get you some dry clothes and to prepare some food and tea."

"Didn't Kitchi-Manitou close the portal?" asked Holly. "How were we able to come through?"

"The Great Mystery, Kitchi-Manitou has temporarily given Tijus-Keha the right to open it once in a while as he sees fit," replied Daniel.

The dry clothes came and the two girls quickly changed. Holly looked right at home, except for her short modern hair-style, but Brittany's white features and brown hair were as out of place as Daniel's had been when he first adopted his roll as leader of the village.

"Please come and join me." Daniel extended both hands and led the two girls outside.

Brittany could hardly believe what she saw - the Indian village in its prime. "Look at this, Holly," she remarked, pointing to the early construction of a larger building surrounded by other smaller wigwams. In the centre of

the clearing a number of deerskin clad women tended a rack laid heavy with fish and a slow burning fire underneath.

"This way, ladies," remarked Daniel. Beside the wigwam they had been in was a roughly built picnic table made of tree branches laced together with vines. Four rocks placed around the table made sort-of comfortable sitting places. On top of the table a spread of food and tea steamed.

"I designed this table especially for guests. It's a bit crude, but it does the job. I have trouble sitting cross-legged for a long time in front of a fire," remarked Daniel. "And this is where I live, here," he said pointing to the small wigwam they had just been in. "Everyone in the village thinks I'm a bit weird, but that's okay. They have a tremendous respect for Tijus-Keha and, it seems, for me too."

The two girls explained what had just happened to them. "I guess those guys in the motorboat must think we've drowned," commented Holly.

"Yeah, serves them right," added Brittany.

"That may be so, little sister, but if they report this, which I doubt, then it would bring a lot of police and special investigators to the old Indian site. Much could be destroyed. But I expect they will just leave and say nothing, hoping no one will have seen them. If and when you two don't return home, Mom and Dad would call the authorities. They'd find your canoe and know where to search. Not finding your bodies, they'll think maybe you were kidnapped, eaten by a bear, or that your bodies were swept away down the river or something. You'll have to go back to let Mom and Dad know you're okay."

"Yes, you're right," said Holly. "But I would like to stay for a while. I have lots I want to talk to you about, if that's okay?"

"At least one of you will have to go back to let people know you're safe," replied Daniel.

"Brittany? Do you think you could find your way back okay without me?" asked Holly. "The wind will be in your back, so you should be able to paddle without a problem."

Brittany wasn't happy about it, but eventually agreed when Daniel said that Ebony would be with her when she appeared on the other side and would help her with the canoe. "As long as I can stay here for a while too, Mom's not expecting us back until later this afternoon, so I have at least a couple of hours."

Daniel agreed. They had lots to talk about, especially for Daniel to learn about the changes with his parents and how they were adapting to not having him around.

When Brittany was preparing to leave, Daniel handed her a piece of soft birch-bark with writing on it. "I've made a list. The next time you come, bring these things for me, please."

"Oh, I'm coming back am I?" asked Brittany.

"Yes, you are, and soon, when the sun is at its peak after seven sun turns and with those things on the list."

"What do you mean after seven sun turns? Have you forgotten what

noon is a week from today?" asked Brittany.

Daniel smiled as he handed Brittany back her wet clothes. "Sorry, I don't have a plastic bag to put them in."

"That's okay," said Brittany, smiling.

"Now go so Mom won't worry."

"Hey, hey, slow down Big Brother. You're letting all this chief stuff swell your head too much. But, that's okay. You can boss me around all you like. Stay cool, eh. Now how do I get outta here?"

"Ebony will take you back," replied Daniel. He turned and looked over towards Ebony who had been lying on the ground by Daniel's hut.

The black wolf got up and came over to Brittany and looked up into her eyes.

Brittany stared back into his and everything around them began to glow. Brittany could hear a rushing wind sound and then everything around her began to spin. She kept her eyes on Ebony and as the yellow glow around them began to fade, they were back on the ancient Indian village site in modern times.

Ebony jumped into the water and swam out to the canoe a few metres off-shore, grabbed the rope dangling from the end of it and pulled the craft to shore. Brittany dragged it up onto the beach, tipped it over to drain the water and pushed the bow back into the water. Both paddles had remained inside, trapped under the seats.

After she had loaded all her things into the canoe she turned to Ebony to say, see yuh in a week, but Ebony had already gone.

Brittany stepped into the canoe and pushed off from the shoreline. She had just paddled around the point of land and out of sight of the Indian village clearing when a boat floated out from the narrow beaver channel beside the beaver lodge.

"Wow! Did you see that? Did you see that? Did you get it?"

The camera operator put down the camera and replied. "Yup, I got it all, Mr. Kirby."

Chapter 15
The List

" A CD player, a 12 volt motorcycle battery, a solar battery charger and all these albums," laughed Anthony, looking down at Daniel's list. "He's really missing his music. His guitar's probably on here too," he commented looking down the list. "Oh, I'm surprised he didn't ask for it." He turned to Brittany and asked if she read the list

"No, not really, Daddy."

"Do we have any Beatles or Supertramp CDs? He's also got Kenny Loggins, John Denver and Liona Boyd on the list. Brittany, can you go up to his room and see what's there?"

"Yeah, sure, but most of his albums, I have in my room, now. I'll have a look and see what's there." Brittany headed for her room.

"Well, I guess we'll take what we've got. We can always take more later." Anthony turned to Jennifer. "You know he's asking for a couple of hundred packages of vegetable seeds, an old plough like the ones horses pulled and a book on elk farming. He wants some steel nails and a couple of good hammers, axes, four chisels, a large two handle push/pull saw and a few hunting knives. Back in their time, they only had stone and bone tools. Quality steel didn't appear for another six or seven thousand years in his time. He's also asking for construction books with building design codes. What the hell's he got in mind? I see what he's thinking for some of this stuff, but we have to be careful here. The time he's in is a volatile period in native history. Having certain knowledge could really sway power in the area, not to mention what it could do to history. Think about the wars between the various Indian bands. If Daniel imparts his 21st Century knowledge onto the Indians in his village, that village could overthrow any power for centuries. I wonder if there is any way of accurately determining just what year he's in. It's at least seven or eight thousand years ago, maybe more."

Anthony put the list down on the table and took in a deep breath. "It's a known fact that one of the Indian's biggest problems was their inability to get along with each other. Within a village it was okay, but bloody squabbles between neighbouring nations was the norm. In later native history, it's a known fact that if the Indians had banded together as one fighting force against the Europeans when they first set foot on this side of the Atlantic Ocean, par-

ticularly in the United States, the whites might never have conquered North America. You know, when the Europeans first arrived here there were close to thirteen million indigenous people from southern Mexico to Northern Canada. If Daniel gets all the local nations together under one central command, with his 21st Century knowledge, history could be completely re-written and life as we know it could be irreparably changed." Picking up the list again, he added, "I have some serious talking to do with Daniel before I'll bring some of this stuff."

At the same moment as Anthony was arguing over the birch-bark list, at the far end of a marsh-ringed lake on a small bit of solid ground in an age a long, long time ago, Holly and Daniel walked the full length of the Indian village. Many of The Good People remembered Holly from her previous visit when she and Daniel were held captive by Tawis-Karong, and acknowledged her presence. Most willingly accepted her, not only because of her Indian heritage, but because it was Daniel's wish that it be so. As they walked, he introduced her to many of The People. Her knowledge of their language was sparse, but she learned quickly. Many of the Ojibwa words taught to her at her school over the last winter were not recognized by the village people, but likewise many were understood. It was the same problem for Daniel when he first came to live in the village. His dialect at the time was strange to these people, but both he and they adjusted.

At the back end of the village site, Daniel pointed out some of the changes he'd been able to initiate since he took over as leader of the village. "One of the first things I had them do was to strengthen the palisade surrounding the village. The initial problem was that the villagers were afraid to venture too far from the confines of the existing village to gather enough trees to build a proper protective wall. I had to reassure them that all the wild beasts created by Tawis-Karong had been tamed and reduced to normal size by Tijus-Keha. Many still believed that some had been missed and were still running around. I had to personally go out and cut down a number of trees to show them it was safe. My plan nearly backfired though. A black bear came lumbering along and I only just made it back inside the palisade. Everyone watching laughed. I felt like a real jerk, but it helped the village people to accept me as one of them."

Holly snickered. "Did the bear screw up your plan?"

"No, not really, they knew it was just a regular bear, not a beast, so it was all right. Actually, it helped. After that all the warriors came down and we had a pile of trees cut in no time at all. As you can see, there's now a much stronger wall around the village with a platform near the top for lookouts to walk along the entire perimeter of the palisade."

"That's great Daniel," commented Holly as she surveyed the extent of the palisade wall. "It feels very secure inside. But isn't it a bit of an overkill?"

"I don't think so. One of the biggest concerns for these people is pro-

tecting themselves against warring nations and small war parties out for blood. Killing for sport seems to be a way of life for many of these warriors. Not so much with my people, but more so with some of the warriors from villages off the island. I still have a lot to learn about their culture. I called a council meeting with some of the elders and from the conversation I gathered that was one of their biggest concerns. So the stronger palisade was the first thing I had them do and everyone is really happy with the results."

I don't have the same fears here as the locals, thought Holly. *Cause I don't know what to be afraid of. At home I'd be worried about walking down a lonely road at night, being abducted, or raped by some sex crazed freak, muggings, petty robberies and home invasions. It's just different here, that's all.*

"And this construction here," Daniel said, pointing to a large framed building under construction. A dozen young warrior were climbing all over the frame lashing rawhide and vines around tree branches to secure the framework together. I'm acting as construction boss for this thing. I've tried using charcoal drawings on birch-bark to show them what I have in mind. They find this an odd way of building things. If we ever get it finished, it's going to be our council chambers and general meeting hall for various celebrations. It'll be big enough we can all get together in one spot without worrying about outside weather. I'm also trying to introduce the idea of more communal living and building larger wigwams. These people haven't reached the point of thinking big. They still think small and portable."

"Yeah?" asked Holly. Why's that?"

"They're so stubborn sometimes; too set in their ways. They don't like the idea of changing anything. Small bands of warriors go off on hunting trips and make hunt camps for a few weeks of the year. The elders argue that they need animals not only for food, but for tools and clothing. And once they kill all the animals in a given area they have to move to find more. They say it's also harder for their enemies to find them if they are not in the same place all the time. My argument is that warrior's should stay close to the main village to defend it. By getting them to do more farming, they'd be forced to stay at home and create a good living without having to move all the time, but traditions are hard to change. It's easier to keep vegetables fresh over the winter than meat. And if I can get them to reduce their dependence on animals, there'd be lots of wildlife left in the same area all the time to fulfil their needs. Then they'd not have to go on these hunt parties for so long. Sometimes they're gone for a few months."

"It's a problem, isn't it," replied Holly.

"I thought the elders at the Gore Bay reservation were adverse to change, but these people are so entrenched in their way of life, it's like hitting your head against a stone wall to get them to make changes."

"Well, they've been around for a long time already, Daniel. Their way of life may not be all that wrong. Maybe you think too much in the 21st century?"

"Yeah, maybe so, but I will say, I'm getting through to some of them, slowly."

"Well, that's progress, I guess," replied Holly. "How are you going to get them to all live more communilly?"

"I haven't figured that out yet. We'll build a larger wigwam first then it might be easier to show them than tell them."

"In our time," commented Holly. "We've become accustomed to having our own personal space. I'd find living in such close quarters with others difficult, especially if I didn't like someone. These people might feel the same way."

"The key word here is survival, Running Fawn," remarked Daniel. "Winters are really cold here and many die of starvation. You know, it's happened that some die without others knowing, even though their wigwams are only a few metres apart. The larger wigwam idea would allow everyone within a family group to keep watch on other family members and to share needs. With a couple of good fires going, it'll be really warm and comfortable inside. The only construction problem is to think of a good way of getting rid of the smoke so people can still breathe. Smoke holes in the roof are okay, but gusting winds often blow the smoke right back inside. I'll have to think of some way of preventing that. What we need are some lengths of steel chimney pieces. I was thinking of tree bark but I don't know if it would take the heat without itself burning. Maybe a big upside down funnel would work. I'll think of something."

"Winters are difficult enough in our time," remarked Holly, "I can't imagine what it's like here without really solid houses, good insulation and central heating systems, not to mention running water, toilets and warm footwear. I visited a museum in Midland once and they had a recreation of a Huron longhouse. It was so cool; I loved the idea of sleeping on animal skins laid out on sleeping platforms." Holly could feel the warmth and comfort they provided just thinking about it. "Daniel?" she asked. "I've been wondering about the young girl who untied us that day when we first came through the portal? I've not seen her anywhere. Where is she?"

"That was Ahawi. She's not here. The day she set us free, she took a canoe and left. She knew Tawis-Karong would be furious with her and she was so afraid of his rage and what he would do to her for what she did. So she left without confronting him. She was sure he'd kill her. He probably would have; she was smart to leave before he found out what she'd done."

"Yeah, but where did she go; to another village?"

"No! She knew no other village on the island would take her, even a village of her own family clan members, for fear of what Tawis-Karong might do to them too. He was a very powerful and evil leader. Apparently he got mad very easily and his people always paid the price."

"How can she survive by herself?"

"She probably can't for long. A predatory animal or maybe an unfriendly war party might find her. If not, she'll probably eventually die of starvation or cold, or take her own life because of loneliness."

"You say that in such a matter-of-fact way. Don't you care what happens to her?"

"Yes, I do, but........."

"But what, Daniel?" Holly was getting quite angry at Daniel's apparent lack of concern.

Daniel tried to ignore Holly's question. "It is believed she has a small camp not far from the mouth of the Michi-ZeeBee to the east."

"Hey, come on Daniel. Don't give me that crap. This is Holly you're talking to. You know, Running Fawn? Don't you talk down to me like one of your subjects; get off that high horse of yours."

Daniel was shocked by Holly's reprimand. He took a deep breath then looked away. "Yes, you're right. I'm sorry. Please forgive me, The People look to me for guidance. No one talks to me the way you just did. You must appreciate; I have to maintain a certain respect with The People. If I should appear weak at any time, I will lose credibility. You understand, don't you?"

"Yeah, I think so. I'll try to hold my tongue in the future. But that doesn't change anything. What about Ahawi? We have to do something."

"She seems to be doing okay."

"Okay! Is that all you can say? Don't you have any more concern than that? She risked her life for us, We owe her." She took a deep breath realizing there were things here she did not understand. "All right then, she's doing okay you say, but for how long? She can't live there indefinitely."

"No, she probably can't."

"Are you just going to leave her there? Can't someone go and get her?"

"This is difficult to explain so that you'll understand. As far as I'm concerned, she is welcome to come back. In her mind, she betrayed her People by going against Tawis-Karong's wishes and before she will come back, she must feel she has earned the right to do so. Then, none of The People will question her right to be a member of this village. We must bend with the wind when it blows, or be blown over and have our roots torn apart."

"That's a lot of crap. You're sounding just like my Aunt Sharon. Maybe the problem is yours, not hers. Maybe you've been here too long. We owe her. Ebony owes her. She didn't do anything wrong."

"But, Running Fawn, in the eyes of The People, she did. I don't fully understand all the whys of it, but nothing I say will make her come back."

Holly argued for many minutes, but Daniel was adamant that Ahawi would not return without earning the right to do so and that, she had to do on her own.

"Damn, this is impossible to understand," Holly remarked. "And just where is this Mish Zee thing you mentioned?"

"The Michi-ZeeBee is the French River, you know, north of Parry Sound."

"Yes, I know where the French River is."

During Holly's brief time in the village, The People had been friendly, but it was an arm's length friendship. Everyone tolerated her and her many questions because of her relationship with their white-skinned leader, but few went out of their way to be friendly. One in particular did, however, Makadewaa, an aging elder, no longer able to walk without the aid of a cane, had shown her unusual kindness. In return, Holly had helped him with his daily chores. Under his tutoring, her knowledge of village customs and language had improved measurably. He asked Holly if she would call him Grandfather, and asked if he could call her Granddaughter. She later learned that he was in fact Ahawi's grandfather. She assumed his friendship was because he really missed his real granddaughter.

It was Makadewaa that Holly went to whenever she had difficulties understanding village culture, or language, or for that matter, opinions on just about anything. Holly thought that he would have made a great modern day Guru sitting at the top of some mythical mountain offering advice to whoever chanced along.

"Daniel is correct," he said when Holly asked him about Ahawi. "She cannot return until she feels she has the right to do so. It is not The People who make this law, but Ahawi herself."

"And just what is it she is she suppose to do, Grandfather? She probably doesn't even know that Tawis-Karong is no longer here."

"It is difficult to explain, Granddaughter."

"Yeah, that's what they all say," replied Holly in English.

"I do not understand your strange tongue, Granddaughter."

"It is okay, Grandfather," she replied in words he understood.

All day Holly thought about Ahawi, perhaps more than she should. Holly felt a strong bond with this woman, an unpaid debt owed to her, a debt she felt compelled to repay. *Without her help, both Daniel and I would probably be dead now,* thought Holly.

As summer had progressed, the days were growing noticeably shorter. Holly was worried Ahawi would not be able to survive the next winter, assuming she had survived the last one. Holly devised a plan to rescue her and went to Grandfather to ask his advice.

"Do not do this without considering all the difficulties carefully, Granddaughter. However, I agree with you. Ahawi should return. I miss her and would do almost anything to see her again before my eyes close for the last time. Go, my child, and may the Great Kitchi-Manitou guide you on your path. You will find a small canoe over near the entrance to the village. It is mine. It is a fine canoe and it will take you across the waters to the Michi-ZeeBee. It is a long journey. Are you sure you know the way?"

"Yes, Grandfather. I have been there many times. I know the way."

Holly had done the trip four times in the 21st Century, once as a little girl with her parents and three times on school trips with professional guides. She'd never done it alone and certainly never in this time and not in a birchbark canoe with the many inherent dangers of a wild and untamed land.

"What you do is a great sacrifice, Granddaughter. Return safely to us," were Makadewaa's parting words.

Holly had already gathered together some things to take with her. She packed them into the canoe and early the next morning quietly pushed the small craft into the water.

No one who saw her leave thought anything of it. Young people often went for short paddles on the lake. And, Holly's presence in the village was strange enough that no one thought her actions odd.

By late morning, she had just cleared the last of the small islands on the north of Manitou Land. Across the open sea, she could see the mainland where she planned to make the first night's camp. The last time she had done this trip there were always numerous sail boats, motor boats and people enjoying the deep blue waters surrounding the islands. Cottages and docks had dotted the landscape everywhere, but in this time, with the total absence of such things, the risks of what she had undertaken seemed overwhelming. But, having embarked on the journey, she was committed to it. She had to continue, but fear of the unknown lay heavily on her mind.

The winds were calm, which made crossing the sea comfortable and the extra weight of her pack in the front of the canoe reduced wind effect. As remarkable as was this canoe, it was not like other canoes she'd paddled. Modern designs had many advantages, not to mention strength. She was afraid the

crude stick ribbing and the birch-bark main hull would not hold her weight and the weight of her gear with the constant splashing of small waves against the hull. Undaunted, she carried on, and late afternoon she made the beach that is today the town of Killarney.

"Damn, wouldn't I give for a camera about now," she whispered to herself. "This is real history, nothing like dull school stuff."

She dragged the canoe up onto the beach, hid it under some bushes, and raked a large tree branch across the sand to hide her tracks. At the far end of the beach was a slight hill with trees all around and a small clearing in their midst. *This is a great place to make camp,* she thought. *Good thing I still have my lighter. Doubt I could get a fire going the way they do in the village. Oh what I'd give for a few drags on a cigarette about now.*

By late afternoon Daniel had begun asking questions about Running Fawn's whereabouts. He had not seen her since late the previous evening. Seeking out Makadewaa, he asked if he knew where she had gone.

Makadewaa was reluctant to say. Memories of Tawis-Karong and his violent nature, hung long and deep on all The People's minds.

Daniel was aware of the long ingrained fear and assured Makadewaa there would be no repercussions. Finally, Makadewaa told Daniel what he knew, that Running Fawn had gone looking for Ahawi with the intention of bringing her home.

Daniel was very angry at what Holly had done, but there was little he could do about it. "Thank you, Makadewaa. If she does not return by next sunrise, I will send a search party looking for her."

Holly had slept poorly. She had not gathered enough wood to keep the fire going all night, which was probably a blessing not of her doing. A night fire can be seen and smelled for some distance. She had to constantly remind herself to be extra vigilant against unknown dangers. Her problem was that she really had no idea what dangers might occur.

She was frequently awakened during the night by animals crashing through the bush. The stone club Grandfather had given her gave some security and she kept it close by at all times. Something big once had crashed through nearby undergrowth and she'd sat upright in fright. She stared into the black, but had seen nothing. It seemed where she had chosen to camp was near a normal pathway that many nocturnal animals used to reach drinking water. She turned and saw three deer at the water's edge silhouetted against the dark star-speckled sky and a short distance away, a bear had just arrived for a drink of fresh water from the lake. Neither predator nor prey seemed to take much notice of each other.

The early morning sun brought relief and she lay resting for some min-

utes in its welcome warmth, drifting off into a heavy sleep for another hour, an hour of quality sleep.

A quick breakfast of dried venison, berries and corn kernels washed down with cold water and she was on her way again. A slight mist covered much of the water near land which shrouded her view, but at the same time hid her from any spying eyes. She paddled on into a heavy head wind until mid-day and making little progress made for shore where she ate another quick meal and had a short nap to recharge her batteries hoping the winds would lessen by afternoon. Fortunately, she had taken the precaution of pulling her canoe up onto the beach and hiding it behind a bush. She had just re-packed her things away and was about to drag the canoe back to the water when she heard what sounded like paddles in the water and mumbled voices. The wind had died considerably but mist remained along the shoreline off to her left. She ducked down behind her canoe and waited. A few minutes later a canoe emerged from the mists travelling at great speed pulled forward by two Indians. Their sweat-covered bodies glistened in the sunlight. They both had shaved heads except for a strip of hair running across the tops of their heads and down to the nape of their necks.

"They're not from our village," she whispered to herself. She cowered down behind her canoe and waited, fearful of being seen. She'd talked at length to Grandfather who'd told her to be wary of people she didn't know. Many of their enemies took few hostages and those they took were usually for sport and a slow torture.

It seemed the beach that invited her to stop, beckoned to the warriors too. She heard their canoe hit the soft sand at the water's edge and heard their words, but nothing they said made any sense to her. *What to do, what to do,* she thought, her mind working overtime. *Should I run; maybe they won't find me? Fat chance of that; wish I had a gun.*

From behind her came a gruff huffing of air and a mumbled roar. A large bear had come out of the bush to her right and reared up on its hind legs at the sight of the two warriors. They too saw the bear and must have thought better of dealing with such a large animal, because they made a hasty retreat back to their canoe and were away. Holly breathed a sign of relief. *Thanks, Mr. Bear,* she thought. *But what now, what's worse, the Indians or the bear?* She clung to her hiding place behind her canoe and watched the bear. He stomped over to the water for a drink then turned and began eating berries growing wild not far from where Holly hid. He looked over in her direction, but showed no hostile intentions. With few other options, assuming he was not interested in her, she quietly dragged her canoe over to the water, grabbing the remains of her stuff and pushed off. When she was in deep water, she turned and gave a wave of thanks to the bear who was still busy eating berries.

By mid-afternoon, Holly beached her canoe on a spit of land at the

mouth of what she thought was the French River. "I think it is," she said to herself. "It looks so different than I remember. I guess things change a lot in a few thousand years." She let her mind return to her last visit here trying desperately to remember some detail that might not have changed much. Then she spied it. A small island in the mouth of the river just where the rapids end and the calmer waters of Georgian Bay begin, although much larger now it was basically the same shape. The rapids too were similar enough to confirm in Holly's mind that this was the mouth of the French River. A lot more water tumbled over the rocks now, and the water flowing into the Bay ran faster.

"Well, I'm here," she said aloud, "Now what? Make camp I guess." Climbing the bank, she walked a short distance inland and found a quiet clearing. *This will be perfect*, she thought. She went back to her canoe and dragged it up onto the sand, and hid it behind some trees and shrubbery. And, again, she wiped her tracks in the sand with a tree branch.

Feeling a little more secure in the clearing, she had a more restful night. The next morning was cool and a strong wind lashed light drizzle into her face. Veils of mist raced through the trees at the edge of the clearing and obliterated anything beyond, but the trees afforded her some protection from the wind and rain. A fire was out of the question. Nothing in this dampness would burn, anyway, so she kept warm by keeping busy. Walking into the bush, she found some raspberries and blue berries and began filling her mouth with the succulent fruit. It was a pleasant change from the dried venison and cold tea. Hearing voices, she stopped what she was doing and listened. A woman was shouting words she partially understood and a man was yelling at her, but she could not understand what he said. She heard a slap and then a woman's scream of pain.

Holly crept to the edge of the clearing. Two warriors were inspecting her camp, perhaps the same two she saw in the canoe the previous day, for they both had the same shaved heads except for a strip of bristly hair down the middle. One of the warriors held a woman. Was this Ahawi? She assumed it must be. She couldn't remember what she looked like from their brief meeting in the past.

Holly retreated back into the woods, turned to her left and climbed a large rock which placed her about three metres above the ground. Cupping her hands and projecting her voice towards the trees, she let out a slight whistle trying to impersonate the squawk of a Blue Jay. The two men turned in her direction. The warrior not holding the woman walked quietly to the edge of the clearing and peered into the bushes. He had his war club raised in anticipation of trouble. He walked a few metres into the trees.

Holly quickly reviewed her options wishing she was somewhere else than in her present predicament. She remembered what Grandfather had warned her not to afford any hesitation and to strike first and hard if she should

encounter an enemy. Hesitantly and without making a sound she picked up a small rock at her feet. When the warrior walked underneath her, she dropped it onto the warrior's head. The crack of crushing bone was clearly heard as the rock caved in his skull. He fell lifeless to the ground. At that same moment, the woman pulled herself free of the other warrior and ran towards the trees in Holly's direction, perhaps assuming there were friendly Indians in the trees. The warrior ran after her. With no more rocks to drop, as they past Holly's vantage point she jumped down on top of the warrior, and they both fell heavily to the ground. The warrior jumped up quickly and raised his club to strike Holly lying winded on the ground.

The other woman rushed up behind the warrior and smashed the side of his head with a long stick. He fell to the ground clutching his head, but was not seriously injured. Holly lashed out with her feet and smashed them into his stomach just as the other woman brought the stick down hard, point first, into his face. Blood oozed from several severe wounds on his head and he went all limp.

Holly lay in partial shock, not totally comprehending what had just taken place. The other woman eyed her suspiciously. Holly reached over to check the man's pulse. It was weak, but he still lived.

"Is he dead?" the woman asked in words Holly understood.

"No," replied Holly.

"Good, we must make him talk. Help me drag him over to that tree."

The two women did so, tied his hands and feet with some nearby vines and wrapped more vines around his body to secure him to the tree trunk and then they waited.

"Who are these people?" asked Holly.

"Scouts from Wakemsiu war party camped not far," the woman said, pointing up river.

"Are you Ahawi?"

"Yes. Ahawi," she replied pointing to herself and then pointed at Holly with a questioning expression.

"Holly," replied Holly, pointing to herself.

"Oh!" and a look of recognition crossed her face. "Holly," she said.

Holly smiled. "Yes," she said in English.

Ahawi looked puzzled at the sounds of the strange language. "Why are you here?" she asked.

Holly tried to explain to Ahawi that she had come to bring her home. She told her that Tawis-Karong was no longer and that Daniel was now the

119

leader of her people.

"Dan'l? Who Dan'l?" She had trouble pronouncing his name.

"Daniel is the boy I was with that day you set us free. He is a man now. Tijus-Keha has made him the leader of your village."

Ahawi looked confused. "Tiju-Keha has returned?"

"Yes," said Holly emphatically.

"How?" asked Ahawi.

Holly explained a little, but for obvious reasons could not give all the details.

"I am pleased that Tawis-Karong is no longer the leader of The People. But, even if Tijus-Keha himself bids me to return, I cannot." Ahawi shook her head to confirm.

"But, Daniel says it is okay to come back to your people. Do not worry. You do not have to be here alone anymore."

"No! I must earn my right to return home and I will do that soon."

"You don't have to do anything. Just come home. Everything will be all right. You'll see for yourself."

The two young women continued to debate the situation.

It was almost an hour before the warrior began stirring. He'd lost a lot of blood and seemed to be partially blinded by the blow Ahawi had inflicted on him.

"What are you going to do with him?" asked Holly.

"I must force him to tell me what I need to know. You may leave if you do not wish to watch."

Holly nodded her understanding and returned to the centre of the clearing.

Within a half an hour, Ahawi too returned to the clearing.

"Did he tell you what you needed to know?" Holly asked.

"Yes, he told me the war party's plan. I was surprised that he talked so easily. He was weak, but at least he showed courage by not calling out when in pain." Ahawi laughed. "He say that two squaws would not be able to stop his people. That is why he talked so easily."

"What are we going to do with him?" Holly asked.

"I have killed him."

"You killed him?" Holly was surprised. Ahawi said it as if it was a normal thing to do - to kill someone., but then she remembered how easily it was for her to drop the rock on the first warrior.

"Yes," said Ahawi. "It was necessary so he could not tell the war party

what he knows about the river."

Now it was Holly's turn to be confused. "What does the river have to do with all this?"

"The war party is many warriors. They are from the Wakemsiu village many sun turn's journey away and are going to attack the village of the Great White Leader. At first, I did not understand, but he means your Dan'l. Their war leader says they must kill the white leader to save their own people. This, I do not understand, but whatever it means, I must stop them. Tomorrow I will earn the right to return to my people."

"Tomorrow, what happens tomorrow?" asked Holly.

"Tomorrow I go to the Wakemsui encampment." Ahawi explained to Holly her plan to destroy the enemy.

"Come on," Holly said in English. "They'll kill you."

"I do not understand the words you speak?" remarked Ahawi.

"It is okay," replied Holly in Ahawi's language.

"Come, we go to my camp now and rest."

Ahawi's camp was not far away. The two women walked in silence both deep in thought.

Nice to be sleeping inside, thought Holly when she saw Ahawi's bark wigwam.

"I will try to make a fire for warmth and tea."

"Good," replied Holly. "It's so cold and damp with all the fog. Wait a moment," she said when she saw Ahawi rubbing two sticks together to create friction. Holly picked up some of the soft wood and with her flint knife, cut up a few small slivers. These she piled in the shape of a miniature teepee in the fire pit. Next she took out her lighter and set the tiny teepee on fire.

"Ah," shouted Ahawi and jumped back. "You have strong medicine. How did you do that?"

Holly tried to explain, but her limited knowledge of the language prevented a detailed explanation. In any event, Ahawi was very impressed.

The tea and a few strips of smoked venison hit the spot. The two women bedded down for the night beside a warm fire.

The next morning, when Holly awoke, her hands and feet were tied with rawhide and Ahawi was no where to be seen.

Chapter 16
The Gauntlet

Kwa-Erha had been appointed war leader of the Wakemsui village only the summer before and he had yet to prove himself a worthy leader in matters of war since his appointment. However, he had earned a great deal of respect from other warriors in battles already fought. The previous war leader of the Wakemsui had been killed shortly before this appointment in a minor skirmish with the neighbouring Daga village. That winter had been particularly severe and many people of the Wakemsui village suffered greatly, but the neighbouring Daga village, during the same winter, were almost completely wiped out by famine and disease. The previous summer's war against the Wakemsui had left the Daga ill prepared for the hardships of the cold and they paid a heavy price. Kwa-Erha had considered raiding the other three local Nations, but felt a victory with them would carry insufficient war honours to justify the obvious losses so close to the cold season. He thought long and hard on who would make an adequate adversary to prove his fighting prowess.

Forced to spend long hours in his wigwam during the early spring black fly season, Kwa-Erha needed a strong vision to convince the Wakemsui elders to wage war somewhere on some Nation. He began a fast to induce this needed vision. On the third day of his forced starvation, a vision of a huge enemy encampment seen from above came to Kwa-Erha. All around the outside of the encampment lay bodies of warriors, and looking closer he saw that the warriors were Wakemsui warriors, all of them. Standing on the wall of the edge of the camp near a wooden gate a mighty enemy warrior shouted at him, an enemy warrior like he had never seen before with white skin and yellow hair. Great anger raced through Kwa-Erha, but when he tried to avenge and kill this warrior, a black beast ran from the open gates and charged Kwa-Erha. He fell to his knees to protect himself from the charging beast and that's when the vision ended.

In Kwa-Erha's mind this was a clear vision, but a vision he did not understand. He consulted with the village elders in a special council meeting and asked for an explanation of his dream. Dreams were never taken lightly, especially those dreams experienced by important members of the village, like a war leader.

During the council meeting, Kwa-Erha told his dream vision. Some interpretation was given, but none that was of any major concern or importance until Gonkam, one of the elders remembered a trading party that had visited

them late the previous summer who told stories about a white skinned leader of a peaceful nation on an island many sun-turns away towards the one star child that is always in the same place in the sky.

"Peaceful, you say," shouted Kwa-Erha.

"I am only saying what the trader told me," replied Gonkam.

"Gonkam is a wise and respected elder of our people, but clearly I have had a vision that must be acted upon." Kwa-Erha clearly wanted to get the attention of the elders and for their ultimate approval to attack the village of the white-skinned leader. If he did not speak carefully, the elders would not approve the attack. "This white skinned leader," he continued, "he must be eliminated. He is a threat to our entire Nation. We must destroy him before he destroys us. I have seen it in my vision. If we do nothing in response to this vision, we will all perish."

"Kwa-Erha has had a strange vision," replied Gonkam. "Do we listen to the spirits who sent the message and follow their guidance? It is a long journey from here and we do not know the way. If he takes all our greatest warriors with him, our village will be defenceless against our enemies while they are away."

Discussion went long into the night, and it was finally decided that Kwa-Erha's vision had to be acted upon. To do nothing would surely invite major displeasure from the spirits who gave him the vision. It was agreed that Kwa-Erha would take eight of their largest canoes with half of their best warriors and kill the great white leader. The other half of the warriors would stay to guard the home village.

Ahawi walked into the temporary Wakemsui camp and asked to speak with the war leader. She had learned a bit of the Wakemsui language from a Wakemsui squaw who had spent a number of moons in the East Colossus Village. It was from this squaw she also learned of the Wakemsui reputation for being a very violent people. She was now going to find out if there was any truth to that reputation. Five warriors ran over to her and pushed and shoved her. One of them prodded her with the point of a knife, and drew blood. They made her undress, and forced her to stand naked in the middle of the clearing while several men poked at her with the points of spears and shouted obscene remarks at her. One of the warriors grabbed her by the hair and dragged her around the camp. She shouted back her own barrage of obscenities some in their language, but most in her own language. Such words coming from a squaw infuriated her captors even more.

One of the warriors shoved and pushed her to the far side of the clearing. There was a lot of noise from behind one of the make-shift bark wigwams. Around the other side a double row of shouting warriors, all armed with sticks and clubs, greeted her. "Ahh, the gauntlet," she gasped. Fear gripped her very

being.

Someone from behind poked her in the buttock with the point of a spear. She felt a warm trickle of blood run down her leg. "Gor!" shouted the warrior with the spear, and he pushed her forward into the chaos.

And, run Ahawi did. She stumbled forward on the uneven surface of the ground underfoot. Sharp stones and tree roots cut into her bare feet. She managed to duck the first club that glanced off her right shoulder, the pain deadened by the panic within. She lurched to the left, but someone's hand pushed her off balance to the right. Clubs and sticks were swung in her direction. There were too many to avoid. Sticks lashed at her legs and back. Long scratches covered most of her body, and most of them oozed blood, but she just kept running. Close to the end, a club was swung straight and took her hard across the chest just below her breasts. She doubled over as another club swatted a glancing blow just behind her left ear. She rolled into the dirt, and lay very still. A thorny tree branch stung her legs then another lashed hard across her buttocks. Her knees jerked up in a reflexive action and she found herself on her hands and knees. Blood ran down her face and into her eyes. She crawled blind, reacting instinctively. Reaching the end, she collapsed into the dirt. Shouts and cheers from the Wakemsui warriors were the last words she heard before everything went black.

The bindings were tight, and struggle as she might, Holly could not undue the rawhide. She struggled all day without success. In the drying warmth of the sun the rawhide shrunk and tightened even more making it all but impossible to free herself. She kept the deer hide moist during the day with her own saliva and some tea left over from the previous night. When evening came and the dew lay heavy on the ground, Holly wormed her way over to the edge of the camp and soaked the rawhide in the condensed water droplets clinging to the tall grasses. It took over an hour before the leather strips softened and loosened and Holly was able to slip her hands free. Untying her feet, she stood and rubbed her hands and feet to aid blood circulation. They tingled for many minutes before they again felt anything like normal. Gathering up her few belongings, she stumbled up the path beside the river in the direction Ahawi had said was the enemy encampment.

No moon shone to help light her way, but she followed the river as best she could. It took her three hours before voices in the distance and the smell of burning fires guided her to the Wakemsui camp. She worked her way up a steep hill and there below was the war camp. Three fires burned, the flickering light casting strange shadows on the faces of the many warriors sitting around the fire closest to her. Holly was undecided what to do, not knowing for sure if Ahawi was here. She had no idea of the reception she would receive if she just walked down into their camp. She remembered a book she read a few years before about the Lakota Sioux people of the American plains and their strong

beliefs in evil spirits, especially at night. It was one of the reasons the Sioux almost never fought at night. "Did the Indians of this time believe in similar night spirits?" she asked herself. "If so, maybe I can use that to my advantage."

Such a large encampment has little concern for security. From her vantage point she let out an eerie scream, trying to sound like a wild animal in pain. Three warriors sitting by the fire leapt to their feet and stared into the darkness. Holly worked her way down the hill between the trees and continued to scream. When the trees thinned she lit her lighter, held it up high and bravely stepped out into the open. Slowly she walked into the camp. Not one warrior approached her.

At Holly's first scream Kwa-Erha had stood and looked in her direction from one of the far fires. He was the only warrior to approach Holly as she stood in the middle of the camp screaming. He walked towards her, his eyes fixed on the flame coming from what looked like Holly's pointed finger. The war leader held his position and Holly came up to within arm's reach of this ferocious looking warrior. She released her finger from the lighter and the flame went out.

"I come in peace," she said in English, and held out her hand with its palm facing the war leader's direction. She then pointed her finger at the war leader and re-lit the lighter.

It startled him, and he jumped back in reaction. Holly admired his courage under what must seem extreme magic to him. Hesitantly, the war leader returned the peace greeting.

The three warriors who had been sitting around the fire had circled around behind Holly and jumped her wrestling her to the ground. The lighter fell from her hand and the war leader picked it up.

Kwa-Erha raised his hands and shouted. Holly did not understand his words, but the three warriors immediately let her go. The war leader shouted more words and Holly's hands were tied and then she was dragged into a wigwam and dumped unceremoniously in the dirt. Beside her in the dark enclosure was another body. Whoever it was groaned and rolled over.

"Ahawi, is that you?" asked Holly. It took a few minutes for her eyes to adjust to the low light flickering in from the fires outside, but when they did, she could see some of Ahawi's injuries. "Oh my god, Ahawi," Holly said in English.

Holly stood and began shouting for the war leader. He came, but he was not pleased at being disturbed. He was also visibly cautious. Holly did not understand his words, but she assumed correctly they were not pleasant.

Holly responded in all the four-letter English words within her vo-

cabulary and then spat in his face.

Kwa-Erha raised his hand to strike then decided not too. "You speak a strange tongue, squaw," he said, wiping the spittle from his face.

Holly understood nothing of what he said, but she also realized at that moment that he was afraid of her. "You are wise to fear me," she said in Ojibwa and smiled an overconfident smile.

They stood looking at each other for many moments, both extremely angry. Holly thrust her hands forward and motioned for her hands to be untied.

The war leader took out his flint knife and cut the rawhide.

Holly took a deep breath and asked for food and water to tend to Ahawi's wounds.

"You are very brave, squaw." said Kwa-Erha, but otherwise ignored her request. "We will test your courage in the morning when you run the gauntlet. This squaw braved many clubs before she fell," he said pointing at Ahawi.

Ahawi had struggled to sit up by this time. "This woman can tell you nothing," gasped Ahawi to the war leader. "She does not speak your tongue. She is the Great White Leader's Wakonk. Do not harm her. If you do, you will have every Manitou fighting against you. You cannot defeat the Manitous. All your people will die. If you spare the Wakonk of the Great White Leader, I will lead you to the Great White Leader's camp on Manitou Land."

Holly asked Ahawi what she had just said to the Wakemsui war chief.

When Ahawi had translated her statement, Holly shouted, "Ahawi, no. You cannot betray your people."

Ahawi looked at Holly while the war leader considered what she had just said. Her eyes searched Holly's.

Holly understood and remained silent.

"I know of your dream," Ahawi said turning back to Kwa-Erha. "I, I can help you," she added then slumped over.

"Why would you do that? Why would you betray your own people?" demanded the war leader, and he kicked her when he got no response.

Holly realized the war chief understood a few words of Ahawi's language. "She cannot hear you," Holly said in Ojibwa. "She is badly hurt. Bring me food and water and I will help her. Then she can answer." In conjunction with her words, Holly made enough hand gestures for the war chief to understand. Holly waited a moment when he did nothing. "Now," she shouted in English.

The war leader ordered food and tea and arranged for his medicine man to attend to Ahawi's needs.

Ahawi slowly responded with the food and hot tea and the medicine

man's rattles and chants. Holly thanked the medicine man and quickly dismissed him.

He left willingly, having kept one eye on Holly the whole time.

Kwa-Erha returned. "Now tell me why you want to betray your people he demanded of Ahawi."

Ahawi again struggled to sit up. Holly tried helping her but Ahawi shrugged her off. "My people banished me from my home, from my family. I am alone living here in the wilderness. Life is not good for me. I will die soon if I must stay here. I hoped to win your favour by doing this for you. Maybe then you will take me with you, and let me live in peace with the great Wakemsui Nation. I hate the Great White Leader. I want my revenge." Ahawi repeated in Ojibwa what she had said so Holly could understand.

"No, Ahawi. Daniel has forgiven you. Do not do this to your own people."

"Be quiet, squaw," shouted the war leader and ordered one of his warriors to hold a knife to her throat to keep her quiet.

The warrior did so, but he was shaking when he did as the war leader commanded.

The war leader of the Wakemsui listened with interest to Ahawi and agreed to spare Holly from the gauntlet. "I warn you. If there are any tricks, you both die and your deaths will be long and painful."

Ahawi told the war leader about the fork in the river not far from where the big river empties into the big sea and about the fast moving water down the rapids. "There are many forks and little islands in the river. You must have a guide to show you the way. If you do not, you will take the wrong fork and die in the rapids."

The war leader agreed to use Ahawi as a guide down the river. In a meeting with all the warriors, the war leader told them what Ahawi had said. They all understood and were in agreement, except Haku, who questioned Ahawi's honesty.

"How can we be sure she speaks the truth?" he argued. "Maybe she will take us down the wrong fork and then we will all die in the rapids."

"Haku speaks wisely," replied the war leader. "Go, and take Ondawa with you down the river to see if she speaks the truth."

It was a gamble for Ahawi. If the warriors found the falls on the right, her plan would fail and both she and Holly would be put to death. Her only hope was that the warriors would not cross the river to the island in the middle to see what was on the other side.

It was three hours before the two scouts returned to the camp. "Ahawi speaks the truth," Haku told the war leader. "Ondawa and I ran along the river on this side and came to the rapids. There are many islands and little rivers and

we got lost many times. The rapids are very high. The water runs fast and dangerous. We came upon the rapids quickly. It would be easy to get lost and crash down the rapids. The journey to the big sea will be very dangerous without a guide. We must go very carefully."

That night Ahawi slipping in and out of consciousness, but during one stage of consciousness, Ahawi said that Holly would have to lead them down the river. "I cannot."

"But, I don't know the way. How can I do that?"

"You must. Tonight I may die. You must do it. I will,,,, I will," she took a deep breath, "tell you," she stuttered, closed her eyes and blacked out again.

It was two hours before Ahawi awoke. She began telling Holly the way down the river and just where she was to trick the Wakemsui to take them over the falls. "It will not be difficult. Always keep to this side of the river," and she indicated the direction with her left arm. "When you come near the rapids there is a large tree that grows out over the water. Here the river starts to run quickly and the rapids begin, so it will be easy to convince the Wakemsui to take the river this way just past the tree to side with the falls," indicating her right arm. Ahawi, took a deep breath. "Do you understand?"

Holly indicated she did.

"When your canoe starts to go over the falls you must leap forward as far as you can. There are no rocks at the bottom a short distance beyond the falls, and the water is deep." Ahawi slumped into unconsciousness again and slept.

In the morning, mist lay heavy on the land all around, and clung in thick patches along the river's surface. The war leader came to the prisoners' wigwam.

"We go now," he demanded.

Ahawi was awake, but when she tried to stand she collapsed back onto the ground.

Holly signed to the war leader that she would lead the Wakemsui. Turning to help Ahawi, she led her outside.

Ahawi stopped her when she saw the mist. "The mist is a good sign," she said with a smile. "Bring the war leader to me. I will tell them they must tie all the canoes together so that none will be lost in the mist."

Holly brought the war leader to Ahawi and she explained her plan.

The war leader agreed.

Holly sat in the front canoe, immediately in front of Kwa-Erha.

Ahawi was placed in the second canoe, wrapped in a fur robe. She lay back, closed her eyes and slipped into unconsciousness.

Holly looked down the river and struggled to remember what Ahawi

had told her. Doubts began to fill her mind, and fear of the unknown. *Am I prepared to die to protect the village?* thought Holly. *Ahawi was.* But Holly wasn't sure her resolve was so strong. *What other option do I have? I'm in too deep to get out of this now. What else can I do? I have no other choice. Daniel and all his people will be destroyed if I don't do this. I must remember to jump far forward when we go over the falls like Ahawi said.*

The Wakemsui were a mighty force especially if they had surprise on their side. The war party navigated the many small rapids with ease and under Holly's direction she guided them down the left side of the river as Ahawi had instructed. Within a few minutes guiding the war party along the river, she had successfully planted a false trust with the war leader. And Holly too was gaining her own confidence and remembered the details of Ahawi's directions.

They approached a large fork in the river. *Is this where I am supposed to go to the right?* thought Holly. *No, we've not see the tree yet.* Holly turned to Kwa-Erha and pointed down the left side of the river. "We go this way."

He shouted the instructions to the other canoes and for them to be careful, and they all followed line astern down the left fork.

Thick fog still restricted visibility and confused Holly. Her confidence began to wane. *The tree Ahawi mentioned, I've not seen it yet, or have I missed*

it? she thought. Holly had expected to see it before this, but suddenly there it was, looming out of the mist, hanging over the water just as Ahawi had said. Holly smiled. "Good," she whispered to herself. A huge boulder appeared in front. Holly pointed to it and the Wakemsui war leader was quick to take action

to avoid the hindrance. He shouted a warning to those that followed. The river began to run quicker now. *We must be coming to the rapids,* thought Holly.

Various obstacles kept the war party busy. One of the trailing canoes struck the rock and nearly capsized, but the warriors were able to regain control. They were all still strung out, tied together by long rawhide ropes.

What looked like an island loomed in front, "There's the island," Holly said to herself. "We must go this way past the island," shouted Holly, pointing with her right hand and hoping this was the way to the falls that Ahawi had told her. "There are rapids down this side," shouted Holly pointing to the left and she shook her head so the war chief understood not to go down the left side.

Kwa-Erha guided his craft to the right not questioning Holly's directions.

Watch for the smooth waters, had said Ahawi. That will tell you the falls comes next. Ahawi's words echoed clearly in Holly's mind. She strained, searching for the smooth waters to be sure she had led them in the correct direction.

The war leader pulled hard on his paddle, as did the other Wakemsui warriors in their canoes. A sudden still fell upon the small crafts as the waters turned strangely calm. The canoes glided swiftly into the smooth waters. The war leader stopped paddling and took a deep breath, relaxing his strained muscles.

Just beyond the pool of calm water, the river appeared to vanish. The war leader stared at the edge of the river and suddenly realized what lay ahead. "No, he shouted to the other canoes. "Turn back. Turn back, now."

Her resolve strong, her course of action determined, Holly stood, raised her arms and shouted Daniel's name, ready to leap forward as Ahawi had told her when the canoe crested the falls.

Accepting the inevitable and in a last futile attempt to avenge Holly's deception, Kwa-Erha swung his paddle around and slammed the tip into Holly's back.

Holly crumpled forward over the bow of the canoe. Water engulfed her and she fell aimlessly down followed by the first canoe.

Chapter 17
Honour a Fallen Warrior

Kizhok pulled his deerskin shirt up around his neck and shook his shoulders to ward off the chill wind blowing through the trees. "Cold," he shouted to Zoong in the bow of their canoe.

"Ugh," grunted Zoong.

Kizhok guided their canoe close to the shoreline to afford some shelter from the wind and rain. They neared the last point of land before the open waters of Gichi Gumee.

Clear of the land, both squinted into the weather and pulled hard on their paddles. Heavy waves crashed against the right side and freely splashed over the gunnel.

"We must go with the waves," shouted Kizhok.

Zoong, grunted agreement. They both swung their paddles out farther into the rough waters on their right to swing the bow of their craft hard to the left. The canoe instantly swung left moving with the wind and waves.

Zoong's hair, hanging loosely across his shoulders, whipped around and lashed against his round face. He grunted again, lifted his paddle into the canoe, and reaching around, pulled his hair together and quickly tied it into a knot.

"Ha, ha," laughed Kizhok, who had taken the time to braid his long black hair into a single strand. But even it lay heavy on his back soaked with water.

Their deerskin jackets offered little protection against the rain and they too were soaked through and clung heavily to their muscular bodies.

Kizhok shouted to Zoong to turn into the wind. They both switched sides and paddled hard on the left. The craft slowly turned into the wind.

Every fifteen or twenty minutes they repeated the process and zig-zagged back and forth in a rudimentary tack, thereby gaining distance straight ahead, albeit slowly. To do otherwise would have filled their frail craft with water in the heavy swell.

What should have taken a couple of hours to cross, took Kizhok and Zoong almost the entire day of hard paddling to achieve. Exhausted, wet and

hungry, Kizhok shouted to stop over there pointing to the same beach area where Holly had spent her first night.

They dragged their canoe up onto the sand. Kizhok gathered tree branches and erected a small lean-to against the canoe. Zoong struggled with a pair of fire-sticks to build a fire and eventually managed a smouldering semblance of one that offered only slight warmth, but insufficient heat to consider making tea. They settled in to a cold meal of dried venison, and berries picked along the shoreline.

The night passed cold and restless for the two warriors. Morning dawned reluctantly with an overcast sky, but the rain and the wind had gone. Glad to be on their way again to generate some body heat, it didn't take them long to journey the remainder of the distance to the mouth of the Michi-Zee-Bee. They beached their canoe on the same spit of land as had Holly and found her canoe hidden in the bushes.

"Ugh," grunted Zoong.

"Yes," remarked Kizhok. "I agree. Running Fawn is not stupid."

They dragged their own craft over and hid it beside Holly's. Running inland, they found Holly's camp almost immediately. Investigating farther, they found the two bodies of the Wakemsui warriors.

"Running Fawn a great warrior," said Kizhok.

Zoong, responded with his usual grunt, but this one with an unaccustomed air of respect.

The damp grass of Holly's camp revealed few secrets, but the two warriors found two faint sets of tracks leading off into the woods. A half hour trot following the tracks brought them to Ahawi's camp. If they thought Holly's camp was confusing, Ahawi's camp was all but impossible to read.

"Ground is too busy to know what happened." commented Kizhok. What puzzled them both were the bits of rawhide that had been used to bind Holly's hands and feet. "Someone was held captive, but only the tracks of Running Fawn and Ahawi here."

"Ugh, strange," replied Zoong.

The two East Colossus Village warriors found the two sets of faint tracks leading away from Ahawi's camp site, but the warriors wondered why one set of tracks was made at a much earlier time. Following them, they soon arrived at the hill overlooking the abandoned Wakemsui encampment. Cautiously, they waited out the night for any signs of returning Wakemsui warriors. In any event, the darkness would reveal few secrets. In the morning, they ventured down to the encampment and spent an hour investigating the events of the immediate past.

"Gauntlet," said Zoong, pointing to the two rows of logs laid on the ground, about a metre apart.

"And recent," remarked Kizhok.

A couple of dozen long sticks were scattered on the ground nearby, some with dried blood on the pointed ends and many heavy footprints on either side of the logs clearly indicated the gauntlet's recent use. Not far from the far end of the gauntlet, a dark stain had soaked into the ground. "A warrior had fallen here. This is her blood. She was dragged to that wigwam." Kizhok pointed to the wigwam frame where Holly and Ahawi had been held captive.

The animal hides and bark coverings had been removed, which was normal practice for Indians vacating a temporary camp. Standing in the middle of the wood frame, Kizhok closely examined the ground and suggested two people had been held captive in here.

"Both alive," confirmed Zoong.

Marks in the sand at the shoreline showed where a number of canoes had been beached. "Big and heavy," commented Zoong. "And many moccasin prints."

"Yes, many warriors," replied Kizhok.

Zoong grunted.

"If a large war party is heading for our village, we should have seen them on the Gichi Gumee. But, we saw no one," replied Kizhok. "Where have they gone?"

"Maybe over the falls?" said Zoong, and he laughed at the end of this unusual long statement for him.

"I think the Wakemsui are not so stupid," laughed Kizhok. "Come, we should go down the river."

The two warriors ran along the left bank of the fast flowing river. A couple of kilometres down river, Kizhok pointed at marks on a rock.

"Wakensui passed this way. Those marks left by a canoe."

To the left of the point of land where Holly had taken the war party to the right, the rapids began. The noise of cascading waters and heavy mist hung heavily on the air.

An infrequently used portage followed the river at the head of the rapids. A difficult portage with a heavy canoe considering the steepness, but without a canoe, the two East Colossus warriors quickly arrived at the bottom of the rapids a short distance upstream from where the two forks of the river re-joined. Here the waters tumbled noisily down the remainder of the gorge and out into the Gichi Gumee.

Bodies of Wakemsui warriors littered both banks of the right fork of the river.

Kizhok laughed and pointed. "Look, Wakemsui are so stupid."

The two warriors walked farther down to the mouth of the river and retrieved their canoe. Paddling out into the Bay, they circled around the turbulent currents and came back on the far side of the river.

Walking back along the far shore of the right fork to the base of the falls, they found the Wakemsui war leader. He was still alive, but his body lay twisted and contorted out of all proportions. Both his legs appeared broken, his right leg was bent back underneath his body and remained attached to his torso by fragments of skin and bits of tendon. His left arm dangled helplessly to his side and it too appeared broken.

"Ah," moaned Kwa-Erha, in obvious pain when Zoong rolled him over with no regard for the discomfort his actions added to his enemy.

Zoong raised his club to administer the war leader a fatal blow.

The Wakemsui war leader raised his remaining good arm and muttered, "Running Fa..," and then slumped back to the ground and appeared dead. Zoong brought his stone club down hard against the war leader's skull to ensure he was, indeed, dead.

A short distance away, a large rock lying on its side looked like a bench and an ideal viewing seat upon which to sit to observe the falls. Looking as if she was admiring the beauty of this place, sat Running Fawn. She was propped against the boulder, one of her outstretched arms resting on the natural seat. Her facial expression conveyed peace and joy. Kizhok touched her, half expecting her to turn and smile, but she fell gently into his arms.

He felt for a pulse, but found none. He gently laid her on the ground resting her head in his lap, reached around for his amulet bag and took some tobacco from within. He sprinkled a bit on Holly's resting body, uttered a few words of praise then threw some tobacco pinched between his fingers to the wind to honour the Great Kitchi-Manitou for granting a great warrior an honourable death.

"We must return Running Fawn to our village and honour her in traditional manner," commented Kizhok.

"Ugh," grunted Zoong.

Wedged between two dead Wakemsui warriors lay Haku. He had been the stern paddler in the third war canoe. As his canoe had crested the falls, he had pushed off forward into the air and projected himself clear of the rocks and boulders at the base of the falls. He landed in the pool of quiet waters beyond danger. Hitting his head on the stony bottom of the pool, he had been knocked

unconscious and was then washed ashore where he lay in a confused stupor for many hours. At the sound of voices, Haku opened his eyes and raised his head. He immediately recognized Kizhok and Zoong as enemy warriors. They had their backs to him, busy with the body of the white skinned leader's squaw who had guided the war party warriors over the falls to their deaths. On the ground in front of Haku was a Wakemsui stiletto bone-dagger. He carefully reached out and wrapped his fingers around the handle. Slowly and quietly, he got to his feet, lunged at Zoong and slashed out with the knife as he did.

The blade cut deep into Zoong's neck and severed his jugular vein. Blood gushed from the deep wound in a mighty flow of red. Gasping for breath, Zoong grabbed his throat, but within seconds he went all limp and his large body crumpled heavily into Kizhok's arms.

Haku attempted the same tactical manoeuvre on Kizhok, but Kizhok swing Zoong's body around to shield himself from the attack. Haku suddenly straightened up, his back arched, his forehead frowned in pain. He fell face first into the gravel. An arrow protruded from his back.

Kizhok turned to see what big medicine had cause an arrow to fly into the back of his enemy.

A short distance up river, leaning against a large boulder, stood Ahawi. At her side, hanging limp in her hand was the bow that had projected the arrow. Seeing Kizhok was no longer in danger, she too collapsed to the ground.

Kizhok laid Zoong's body on the ground, ran to Ahawi and quickly checked for a heart beat. "She lives," he whispered to himself then ran his fingers over her entire body checking for broken bones, but found none. He gently gathered her up and carried her away from the noise and dampness of the rushing water. He laid her down on soft pine needles beneath a tree some distance from the river and covered her in a warm robe from his canoe. He struggled with a fire, finally managed to get one going and prepared some warm food and tea. After feeding her a small portion, and confirming she slept, he returned to the river to bury his friend, Zoong, under a pile of rocks. What little tobacco remained in his amulet bag, he sprinkled on the rocks and threw the remainder to the wind saying a little prayer as he did so. The bodies of the Wakemsui he left to the crows and the ravens, the foxes and the coyotes, the wolverines and the bears and the many smaller carrion eaters that had begun to gather for the unexpected feast.

After taking care of Zoong's body, Kizhok paddled across the river to retrieve Holly's canoe hidden in the bushes. He carefully washed away the grime from Holly's face and hands then laid her on pine branches in the bottom of her canoe. He covered her body with more branches ready for the return journey to their village.

I wonder what part Ahawi and Running Fawn played in the slaughter of the Wakemsui war party. thought Kizhok. *When Ahawi awakens, maybe she can tell me what happened. But, how could two squaws defeat the powerful Wakemsui? If they did, they no doubt saved our village from a surprise attach that would have killed many of The Good People.*

Kizhok brought water to bath Ahawi. When he removed her robe, he was appalled at the numerous puncture wounds and deep gashes that covered much of her body.

"So it was Ahawi who ran the gauntlet," he whispered.

Many of her wounds had festered, and puss ran freely, much of it now encrusted on her legs and arms. *She is close to losing her inner self,* he thought. *It is amazing she survived the plunge over the falls.* Her body did not appear otherwise damaged. Kizhok bathed Ahawi's body in the cool river water to wash away the encrusted body fluids. From the river he had also brought some bull rush roots, crushed them into a pulp and laid the pulp into the open sores on Ahawi's body.

Each new day brought added strength to Ahawi. On the third day her fever had broken and her many wounds no longer oozed puss and appeared to be healing. She had awakened and for the first time she was able to speak coherently. She described in detail what had happened in the Wakemsui camp and how, thanks to Holly, or Running Fawn, as Kizhok knew her, they were able to carry out the plan to trick the Wakemsui. She confirmed that, yes, the war-party was planning an attack on their village with the intent of killing Daniel. She told Kizhok about the war leader's dream of a great impenetrable encampment ruled by Daniel and all around were the dead and dying bodies of the entire Wakemsui war party.

"I was unconscious most of the time after running the gauntlet," commented Ahawi. "I tried to tell Holly what she must do, to tell her the way down the river. Are the Wakemsui dead?" she asked. "And, how is Running Fawn?"

"Yes, all Wakemsui are dead," replied Kizhok. "No more talk; you should rest now."

"But, Running Fawn, does she live?"

Kizhok look at the ground and was quiet for a few moments. "I am sorry," he said.

"Oh, no," said Ahawi. "She was a great warrior. Without her we would not have defeated the Wakemsui. I wish I had had more time to get to know her better."

"Yes, me too." answered Kizhok.

"She seemed a strange squaw and often spoke a strange tongue," com-

mented Awawi. "But she was a person of deep convictions. I would like to have been her friend."

"You were," replied Kizhok.

Early morning on the fourth day since the Wakemsui defeat, Kizhok was becoming increasingly anxious to be gone from that place. He mumbled something about needing to be gone away from Wakemsui evil spirits seeking revenge and the overwhelming smell of decaying bodies even at the distance of their small camp from the falls. He could see that Ahawi was feeling much better and expressed his desire to begin their journey home.

"Yes, I will be fine," Ahawi confirmed.

"Good. Then we go." Kizhok packed all their things in the lead canoe and tied Holly's canoe to it.

Ahawi settled into the bow of the lead birch-bark craft and picked up the paddle as Kizhok pushed the canoe away from the shore and climbed aboard the stern end. The two crafts were picked up by the swift currents and pushed out into the deep blue waters of Gichi Gumee.

Kizhok smiled. *What a great reunion Ahawi will have with family and friends,* he thought. *No one can now question her right to return home.*

Chapter 18
The Home Coming

On the prescribed day, at the arranged time, Brittany and Anthony arrived at the old village site in a rowboat filled to overflowing.

"No one's here to meet us," said Anthony. "Now what do we do?"

Brittany laughed. "Just watch, Dad." Brittany looked around to be sure no one else was watching them then cupped her hands around her mouth and called out, "Ebony, Ebony, we're here." She called a second time and a circular light appeared almost immediately and grew in intensity, the same as the last time Brittany called for Ebony. Out from the middle of the light jumped Ebony. Brittany knew what to expect, but the magical appearance of the large black wolf startled Anthony.

"Hhhii, Ebony," he said, still unsure of himself in front of this creature, who in reality, was an Ojibwa god.

Something probed his mind, a greeting of sorts. Brittany received the same telepathic message. She leaned over and gave him a hug. "Nice to see you too," she said.

"We brought some of the stuff that Daniel wanted," said Anthony. "Where should we put it?"

A picture of all the goods piled on land was planted in both Brittany's and Anthony's minds. "Okay," said Anthony, and he began unloading the small craft.

Once everything was piled on the beach and the empty row boat pulled up on land, Ebony planted an image of all three of them crowded around the pile of goods. They stepped close to the pile, and Ebony looked up at the two visitors, who looked down deep into the black wolf's eyes. Everything around them began to glow and spin and became a blur. A few seconds later, the apparent whirlwind dissipated and everything surrounding them fell into focus again.

"Wow!" said Anthony. "What a rush, like being in the centre of a tornado. Too bad we couldn't bottle it. We'd make a fortune."

Anthony looked around the building they were it. It appeared newly constructed. "What a marvellous place. Look at the workmanship here and without modern tools and equipment, not yet anyway." He touched the animal

hides stretched across wood frames hanging from the main building supports. Moving past the smouldering fire in the centre of the building he walked down the far side of the structure and admired the wood carvings and paintings hanging along the wall. At a door, he lifted the hide covering and looked outside. "This is amazing. Now I see why Daniel wants the drawing pad and pencils. I'm surprised he didn't ask for a camera."

"Dad," Daniel spoke from the far end of the structure.

Anthony turned and there in the doorway stood Daniel in all his grand Native attire. They walked towards each other and embraced.

"It has been too long," said Daniel.

"Yes, it has, son. I've missed you. Wow, let me look at you. Don't you look impressive. How are you?"

"I'm fine, thanks Dad. Jennifer couldn't come?"

"She wanted to, but I suggested next time. She had a couple of school groups coming to the Centre this afternoon and couldn't really get out of the classes. Besides, with all the stuff we brought, we really didn't have room for another person in the boat. If it had been windy we might have had to leave some things behind. We were quite low in the water as it was. You and I have lots to talk about, especially about your list of equipment."

"Hey! What about me, Big Brother." Brittany stood beside the two tall men, and tugged at Daniel's leggings.

"Hi Brittany," said Daniel, and he bent over and gave her a long hug. "It's nice to see you again."

Brittany looked at her hands. "What's all this stuff on you?" Brittany asked.

"Oh, it's an ointment one of the women gave me to protect my skin from the sun."

"It makes you look like you've got red skin. If it wasn't for your blond hair, who'd know you weren't Indian?"

"Daniel, I'd like to see the village, if that's okay," asked Anthony.

"Yes, okay. But, it will be necessary for you to change clothes first. I have some things for you here." He pointed to some deerskin clothing lying across a rack in the corner.

"Me in a breechcloth, leggings and moccasins?"

"Yes, it is necessary," replied Daniel.

Brittany was dressed in the small deerskin dress, leggings and moccasins she wore the last time she visited the village. "These are so cool," she said running her hands down the sides of her dress and spinning around on her

toes. "Can I have an Indian name too?" asked Brittany.

"Yeah, probably, we can give you a play name to begin with, but a real name is one you have to earn by doing something brave or having something noteworthy happen to you. I have been considering a name. How about Waabooz? That means rabbit in Ojibwa."

"Oooh," squealed Brittany. "I like that." She raised her right hand, palm facing her brother and said, "How, me Waabooz," and giggled.

"Come on, let's go." Daniel and offered his hand to his sister.

They had a tour of the village.

"Where's Holly?" asked Brittany. "I thought she'd be here."

"Yes, well. Running Fawn was here, but she's not now. I'm not exactly sure when she'll be back. I think she's gone to find Ahawi and bring her back to the village."

"Ahhh, who?" asked Anthony struggling with the unfamiliar name.

"Ahawi is the young woman who untied us when we first came to the village. You remember, I told you what happened."

"Oh, yes. That was ten years ago you told me that story."

"It was not that long ago in village time," replied Daniel.

"Where did you say she went?" asked Brittany.

Daniel explained.

"With any luck then, Holly and Ahawi could be back before we leave," said Anthony.

"Yes, I hope so. I've sent Zoong and Kizhok to find them. The land is not as friendly in this time as it was the last time Running Fawn made the journey to the French River. There are many dangers she's not aware of; I am worried. She has been gone too long."

"Zoon,,, and who? Whatever their names are? Who are they?" asked Anthony struggling with the strange names.

"They are the two best trackers in the village." Daniel assured Anthony these two warriors would find them where others might fail.

"Do you have any idea where she's gone?"

Daniel told the story as best he knew. "Kizhok and Zoong paddled over to the Michi-ZeeBee, oh sorry, The French River. That's where we think Ahawi is camped, so we assume that's where Running Fawn has gone."

Anthony was somewhat relieved, and said so. "Good. Let's hope they find them and bring them both back. In the meantime, son, we have a lot to talk about."

"Yes, okay. We can do that in my wigwam." Daniel turned to look for

Brittany. "Any idea where Brittany's gone?" he asked.

"She's down by the shore playing with the other kids," commented Anthony.

"Brittany," shouted Daniel. "You'll be okay for a while? Dad and I'll be in my wigwam if you need us."

She shouted back that she'd be fine.

Inside Daniel's wigwam, Anthony handed Daniel his original list on birch-bark and a piece of paper. "Here's the list you gave Brittany. And here's a list of what we brought. I have no problem with the music stuff that you wanted. We couldn't find all the albums, but there's a good selection. We can always bring more, later. The CD player is an automotive player and works on 12 volts, so it'll be a direct connection to the motorcycle battery. We also brought a small 12 volt solar battery charger. There're a couple of good hammers and chisels, some nails and two good axes. The plough you wanted is here and a book on elk farming. What are you planning to do?"

Daniel explained his plan to clear a couple of acres of land to develop for farming. "We've started to cut down some trees to clear a large area of land. I'd like to grow enough food for winter consumption. Winter's a huge problem here. People often go without, and when starvation is imminent, many of the old just leave camp to die in the cold to reduce the burden on the young. It's a major problem I want to stop. I'd like to develop this village to be more of a permanent central farming community for all the local villages around the island. Over top of the hill behind us is a perfect spot for a farm. It's great soil over there and as I said before, we've already begun to clear the land to make a large field for crops. The People already grow a variety of veggies, but they do so only within the confines of the palisade, or in small fields around the palisade walls. They're afraid to venture too far, especially the women and children, without some sort of protection from marauding war parties. It's not a big problem, but it does happen."

"I brought some construction books you asked for, what I could find. Have a look at them to see if they're what you want. If you need others, I'll have to bring them at a later time, if that's okay?"

"Yeah, that's no problem. I'll let you know if I need more things before you leave."

"What are you planning to construct other than a few bark buildings? Oh, by the way. I really like what you've done with the longhouse, a great building."

"Yeah, The People really like it too. We'll use it as a central meeting hall or council chamber. The next step might be to suggest a similar large building for families to live in, but I'll have to swing the idea of communal living first; maybe next year for that idea. What I want to build sometime in the

future is a stone wall around the couple of acres of fields we're clearing, so the women and children will feel safe so far from the protection of the palisade. There's millions of field stones around that'll be perfect for the walls. We can create a crude mortar from a nearby clay bed and mix some sandstone, lime and water with it. After that, who knows?"

"Okay, but take it easy. Now what's this about elk farming?"

"Oh yeah, well, there are no horses here yet and there won't be for a long time. So, I thought we might be able to domesticate some wild elk, like the Lapps do with the reindeer in Finland. I was hoping to use elk as plough horses. Worth a try I think. If the elk don't work, maybe moose might."

"Don't know, Daniel. It could work. Elk maybe, but moose are not very clever and don't take direction easily. Good luck with that. What do the village elders think of these ideas?"

"I've already talk to some of the elders and some are in agreement with doing a little more farming, while others are sceptical, but everyone laughed when I suggested taming elk to use as farm animals. And there's a group who are a little concerned about their hunting traditions. They don't want to totally abandon them. It's been tradition for so long. It's long been their habit to set-up these hunting camps three or four times in different places each year. They usually deplete an area of most of its animal population and then move on to another area and do the same there. By the time they return to the first camp, the animals have re-populated and the process begins again. If I can swing them over to a more balanced diet with more fruits and vegetables there will be less need for meat. If that happens the animals within a given area could remain plentiful throughout the year. And that would eliminate the need for the constant moving to keep up with game."

"Sounds like a good plan, but don't force too much change too quickly. You have to prove yourself a worthy leader before they will follow you without question."

"Yeah, I know, Dad. I can lean on my friendship with Tijus-Keha only for so long, but most of The People seem to have accepted me."

"I've not brought many of the vegetable seeds you asked."

Daniel looked disappointed. "But, why not?" he asked. "They don't have much in the way of vegetables for making salad."

"Some of these vegetables you've asked for will not appear until the Europeans arrive however many thousands of years from now. By introducing these seeds now, you could dramatically change the course of history."

"Come on Dad. They're only a few vegetable seeds. What difference could it make having a bigger variety of them to eat? All I want is to have some stuff that will keep during the winter so we don't go hungry."

"I know, son. It seems trivial now, but think about the long term ramifications should these seeds get out into other villages and then spread across this province and then into what will become the northern United States? How are you going to prevent these seeds from spreading? What if you're attacked and the war party over-throws your leadership, and then takes control of what you have? How can you be assured these seeds will go no farther than this village?

"I don't know. I guess I can't. I never stopped to think of the long term effects. I miss my salad, that's all, and they don't have much like it here."

"Well, get used to it, son. And you really have to stop and think of the effects on history you will have on this time period with your knowledge of the 21st century. Who knows how the changes you make here will effect us in our time."

"Yeah, but who says it hasn't already happened, that all I am doing is reliving what is already history in your time?"

"I know it seems of little importance, but just think about things before you do anything crazy."

"Yeah, okay," agreed Daniel. "Couldn't you just bring a few packets of potato, carrot and tomato seeds? I guess I can make salad out of some of the marsh plants, like water cress. It won't be the same as lettuce."

"Daniel! Are you not listening to me?"

"Yes, I am, and I have thought a bit about it. But, I believe that history will be a lot harder to change than you suggest with a few packets of seeds."

"Okay, okay. I'll bring a few the next time."

Daniel smiled. "Oh, there's something else I want from you, Dad."

"What now, an electric generator or something? No gasoline here, remember."

"No nothing like that," snickered Daniel. "I have arranged a special meeting with all the elders of the village, including the clan matrons. I would like you to join us. I have some ideas to run by the elders and your input would be welcomed, if that's okay? You'd be there as an observer and advisor. You won't have to say anything to anyone expect me maybe. You won't understand the language anyway and they won't understand you."

"Yes, I guess so, son, but what's it all about?"

Daniel explained a little about the present leadership role that he plays, that he is the sole leader in charge of every decision and every policy within the village. "And some of my decisions are not good because I do not yet fully understand the culture. I want to try to build proper leadership governed by all the people, not just me. In the past with Tawis-Karong, he ruled absolutely and everyone was deathly afraid of him. Much of that fear still exists, but it's get-

ting better. I'm just trying to remember how Sharon's grandfather explained to me the way it was back before there was total dominance by the white authorities. That's how I want it now."

"Shouldn't you talk to Ebony, I mean, Tijus-Keha first?"

"I already have and he likes a lot of the ideas. But, like you, he wants to make changes slowly. I also had to ask him to allow you and Brittany to come through the portal this time."

"You know, Daniel, you really need Sharon here. She'd be able to help you."

"Yeah, you're right, but not sure if that's possible. Tijus-Keha is very guarded who comes through the portal. And his father has concerns too."

"Have you met his father, Daniel?"

"Kitchi-Manitou?"

"Yes."

No, Tijus-Keha says he exists only spiritually now, no longer taking human form."

"Now that would be something; to meet the Great Kitchi-Manitou himself," commented Anthony.

"Yes, but what would I ever say to him? All I hope is that he is pleased with the way I'm running the show here."

"I'm sure if he was not, you'd know about it." There was a pause in the conversation.

"You're right, you know. Sharon would be the perfect person to have here to help me, but there's no time. And, I'd have to ask Tijus-Keha. For this meeting, I just want to talk with the elders, plant the ideas so to speak. I have some basic thoughts. I'd like them to think about these ideas for a while and afterwards, in a few days we can decide how best to handle things depending on the initial response from this meeting. I can then ask Tijus-Keha if we could bring Sharon. You could bring Jennifer too, maybe."

Anthony smiled then cocked his head to one side. "What's that?"

"Oh, sounds like someone's arrived at the water's edge."

Chapter 19
Unwelcome Guests

For days following the incident in the old village site, Jim Kirby had mulled over the events that had taken place there, watched the film footage of the sudden appearance of the black wolf and the young girl and continually shook his head in disbelief.

He kept asking himself, "If I have trouble believing it, how am I going to convince others that this really happened?"

He did have proof, though, the video tape and two reputable witnesses besides himself that it really did happen. The problem with such things as video tapes, they could easily be doctored to look real with modern digital imaging and computer technology.

"And that's exactly what most people are going to believe," he said aloud and slammed his fist down on his desk. "I've got a million dollar story here and no one's going to believe it. This thing could put me back on the map."

He re-read his proposal to Sudbury television and the rejection letter in response to that proposal given to him by the CEO of the station. He'd even been called into the big office where the conversation had ended with the CEO recommended Kirby take some time off to relax, rethink what's important in life and to get his act together. It was even suggested that his job could be in jeopardy should he continue in his present direction and not get back on track with the network's normal mandate.

He wanted to comply with his bosses' wishes, but every newsman instinct he possessed tingled knowing there was a revolutionary story going on around him with the whole Wolf Education and Research Centre, Jennifer Santos and Jason Davis. *Damn it,* he thought. *I saw that wolf and the young girl just appear out of nowhere. There has to be a way to prove it to the world. And I'll do anything to get even with that Jason Davis bastard. He really screwed up my status here.*

Kirby had previously searched through a list of television networks and newspaper groups for a reputable network that could air his film, but he had eliminated most media. Consequently, he'd started looking to smaller networks that perhaps would not be so afraid to air something controversial.

Sample query communications had already gone out to a select few of these smaller networks and to other forms of mass media. A para-normal newsletter had responded with a polite email saying they were tentatively interested and would consider it for a publication later in the year, but requested more information. *Obviously, they too are sceptical,* he thought. SETI the Search for Extra-Terrestrial Intelligence declined any interest saying the subject matter was an earthbound phenomenon, not extra-terrestrial, and the National Enquirer and The Star had yet to get back to him. ABN the American Broadcasting Network and its television show, Stranger than Fiction, was the only semi-reputable network that showed any interest. A more detailed package of the events had been sent to them. However, Kirby had little faith that anything would come of it.

The whole thing is just too impossible.

He was about to shelve the entire project and get on with his normal duties when his program assistant brought him a large manila envelope. It was from ABN.

Fat chance, he thought as he struggled with the perforated strip on the envelope. But, contrary to expectations, ABN was interested, and claimed to have had the film he sent down analyzed by their experts. ABN said they could find nothing untoward about it. "It appears to be authentic," the letter said. They wanted to discuss copyright on the film, future filming rights, required permits and other necessary details regarding costs, accommodations, etc. Kirby was ecstatic. *At last.*

Permits to do just about anything were relatively easy to come by on Manitoulin Island compared to many other communities across the province. Anything that would bring a few needed dollars into local government hands was always welcomed. Kirby had been told there would be no difficulty obtaining the necessary permits for filming in the area of the old Indian village site.

"Just let us know the dates," the clerk at the local township offices had said. "We would issue the permits almost without question, but we'd also have to notify the Ministry of Natural Resources, as well as the local office of the Ontario Provincial Police. Standard procedures," she had said. "Oh, yes, almost forgot. Because this is a National Heritage Site maintained by the local Ojibwa Nation, they too would have to be informed."

This is becoming too complicated, thought Kirby. *All these bloody permits and permission from who knows who else, and the Indians will probably raise a stink, that's for sure.*

The crew arrived about a week later.

"One camera; that's all?" queried Kirby when he met the crew.

Kevin Russell, the crew chief, conveyed his and the networks concern over the validity of Kirby's story. "We are willing to give you the benefit of the doubt, only because our analysis of the tape could not detect any trick overlay, or alteration of any kind. In truth, the film looks genuine. It is difficult to believe, but it may be true. Now the permits, you have them?"

"They're being issued as we speak." In truth he had not applied for them when he made his enquiry. He'd assumed that permission from the various groups needed would not be forthcoming, or if they did approve, it would take forever to get and would require mounds of paperwork to satisfy some back-bencher who wanted forms filled in for this and for that for no other reason than to justify his or her position as a government clerk. "I'll deal with it at the last moment," he'd said to himself. "That way we'd get the permits before responses from everyone could come back to stop the whole thing."

The next day, the crew visited the village site and were not impressed. "I had expected to see something," commented Kevin Russell, "Some walls or remains of buildings, not just nothin'."

"Excuse me, but you have to remember; this site's thousands of years old," retorted Kirby, sarcastically. "And their villages were all made of wood. As you know wood's life expectancy ranks in the tens of years, not hundreds, and certainly not thousands.

"Yeah, I guess so," was all the crew chief could say. "There's just nothin' to film here. We could maybe dub in some stuff to make it look more authentic."

To stir-up interest and a future viewing audience, Kirby had called the local newspaper in Little Current and leaked the story of ABN's involvement in the filming of a Stranger than Fiction episode; he did not leave his name.

After inspecting the village site, the ABN crew chief had told his crew that he didn't think there would be enough material for a full twenty minute segment let alone the forty-five minutes that Kirby had requested, unless they could somehow activate the illusive portal and get the black wolf to suddenly appear like he did in the tape. "If that happened," he commented, "we'd have the story of the century."

Canadian national television networks picked up the article that appeared in two Manitoulin Island newspapers and a dozen major newspaper chains across the country ran stories. City TV in Toronto heard about the

planned filming and contacted Jennifer asking if this story had any relationship to Big Black. Jennifer didn't know what to say other than denying any connection. She had read the local newspaper article only that morning, but she denied any knowledge of the events and suggested it was just some publicity-hungry newspaper journalist out to make a quick name for himself.

"We made some enquiries with ABN in the States. Apparently it's a Jim Kirby whose behind the original story," said the City TV representative.

Jennifer raised her hands in exclamation. "Oh, well. That's it then," she said to City TV. She explained her previous encounter with Jim Kirby and the misinformation story that was aired on Sudbury television over the disappearance of Daniel when he was very young. She reminded the City TV rep, with whom she was talking, that it was this encounter with Jim Kirby that precipitated her first involvement with City TV and its subsequent filming of Big Black and the reattachment of his paw, the paw that had been severed in a leg hold trap.

"See you in the morning for breakfast in the hotel restaurant," Kevin Russell said to Kirby as they left the bar. "And don't forget those permits."

At 7:30 the following morning Jim Kirby called Kevin Russell to say he was going to be a little late and for them to start breakfast without him. At 8:00 AM he waited on the steps to the local municipality offices desperate to get something at least that looked like a permit. At 8:10 the clerk arrived to open the offices.

While the clerk drank her Tim Hortons' coffee and ate her cheddar bagel, Kirby pleaded his case saying the crew arrived unexpectedly late last night and wanted to film for an hour or two before noon today. "Can you help me please? I'd be willing to pay a little extra to get something that would allow the crew to get started, at least. They're on a really tight time frame. Surely they can do no harm in that time. Please, can you help?" He smiled that confident smile and twitched his moustache that always seemed to get middle-aged women's attention.

The clerk looked at him and smiled back. "I always watch you on Sudbury News. I love the way you tilt your head and look so forlorn when you describe the gory details of a car crash or the victims in an overseas disaster. You should leave that day's growth of beard. It looks good on you."

"Yeah, I'd like to some mornings; it's against network policy. But, I'll tell you what I can do though, I'll do a special wink just for you the next news broadcast I do, if you can help me?"

"Well, I suppose," she said. "A couple of hours can't hurt, I guess, as long as you assure me you will not disturb anything, not that there's much to disturb?"

"No problem," said Kirby. "You have my word. You're right though, there's not much there to disturb."

She looked at Kirby and smiled, pulled open a drawer and began filling out a special temporary one day permit.

Kirby paid the fee, handed her a $20.00 tip and an autographed photograph. "Thanks, darling," he said with a wink and a smile and left the government office to meet the film crew.

The crew finished their filming before noon. There wasn't really much to film, other than the open space where the village had been and the lake itself, but nothing looked any different from a dozen other lakes and clearings in other places nearby. Ebony never did make an appearance. They'd given up after constantly calling his name for over an hour and feeling silly doing it.

"We'll get back to you, Jim," said Russell. "I'm not sure we can do much with what we've got. Too bad the black wolf didn't just appear out of nowhere, like in your tape. Now that would have been a story, but we can still dub in your original tape and make it look like something really did happen. I'll go over to the Indian administration office and see if we can get a taped interview. That might add some credibility to your claims and fill the time to complete a twenty minute episode. And we will want to tape a brief interview with you tomorrow, if that's all right. I'll call you later tonight to arrange a time and location."

They shook hands and parted. Kirby didn't think too much would come of it, but was pleased he would be interviewed.

The following morning one of Manitoulin's newspapers carried an in depth story about the upcoming ABN Stranger than Fiction episode with details about a black wolf named Ebony who would appear out of nowhere upon demand just by calling his name. By noon there were maybe twenty-five boats docked at the end of the lake by the old village site and perhaps sixty people. They poked and probed every metre of the old site. And every once in a while one of them could be heard shouting.

"Ebony, Ebony. Where are you?"

Chapter 20
Daniel's Grief

A gusting wind curled off the lake and blew dust and falling leaves into Daniel's face. His long blond hair hung down around his shoulders and flew back into his face. He reached up and gathered the loose strands and curled them around his ear. The single eagle feather tied to a bone pin stuck in the back of his hair fluttered in the breeze. He stood back from the beach behind the crowd of villagers who had gathered to welcome the occupants of the canoes. He surveyed the scene with an air of concern and fear.

"Who is it?" asked Anthony.

"Kizhok and Ahawi," answered Daniel. "No Holly and no Zoong."

Her muscles not yet seasoned for many hours in a cramped position in the bow of a canoe, Ahawi had difficulty standing. Coyote Song stepped forward and took her hand and helped her onto the shore.

"Welcome home, my daughter. Are you well?" he asked.

"I am better now Father. Happy to be home, but I am saddened by the events of the last few days."

Coyote Song looked puzzled, but said nothing. He bent down and pulled the lead canoe up onto the sand to allow Kizhok to get out. Then Coyote Song grabbed the second canoe, its weight told him what it was he lifted and he understood Ahawi's sadness.

Daniel walked down through The People who had crowded around Ahawi, his soft moccasins treading lightly on the sand. He touched Ahawi on her shoulder.

Ahawi turned and when she saw him, she fell to her knees in front of him. "I beg your permission to take my place among my People, oh great leader. I have earned the right."

Daniel took her hands and pulled her to her feet. "You do not kneel to me, Ahawi. I am but a mere mortal and do not deserve, nor do I demand such status. Welcome home." He smiled a welcome smile that Ahawi returned. He turned to greet Kizhok who had stepped onto the shore. "Your search was successful Kizhok. Glad to see you home again. Ah," hesitated Daniel. "Running Fawn and Zoong?" he asked.

"I am sorry, Daniel," interrupted Kizhok and he bowed his head.

"Running Fawn?" asked Daniel again.

"She is here, Daniel," said Ahawi pointing to the canoe. It was her turn to reach out and touch Daniel's arm. "She saved us Daniel. She destroyed the Wakemsui war-party that was coming to attack our village. Their war leader was obsessed with killing you and destroying our village. Had it not been for Running Fawn we might all be dead now. She sacrificed her life for us."

"Then she died honourably?" he asked, his voice choking.

"Yes," replied Kizhok. "And so did Zoong. We did not have room in the canoe to bring his body back as well."

Anthony, not having understood the conversation, asked what was being said.

Without turning to look at his father, Daniel replied in English. "It's Holly. She's dead."

"No," Brittany screamed. She had been standing behind her father and heard Daniel's words. Tears streamed down her face as she ran to the canoe. She pulled back the tree branches covering Holly's body.

The village people all gasped at Brittany's actions.

Holly's body had begun to decay. To Brittany, her friend looked like some aberration from a horror movie. Brittany screamed and dropped the branches back onto Holly's body then ran to her father and buried her face in his arms.

"This child has dishonoured the remains of Running Fawn," shouted Bear Tooth who had been standing in the midst of the villagers and now walked to the front. "This young squaw has looked upon her body before it has been cleansed. Running Fawn's spirit will now never find its way to the Land of the Dead and will be cursed to live in dishonour amongst the trees in the Black Woods."

"I gave Running Fawn her cleansing after we found her at the base of the falls on the Big River", interrupted Kizhok. "Her spirit is ready to begin its journey to the Land of the Dead."

"No," shouted Bear Tooth. "The cleansing must be done by her clan Matron or by a blood relative. You, Kizhok are neither. Running Fawn's body is not properly prepared to go beyond."

Few villagers disagreed with Bear Tooth. For the last few years he had been claiming to possess special powers that made him understand dreams, one who could tell the future and who could bring fortune to some and curses to others. Some believed he had the gift, but most thought he did not. He had never proven he had special powers, but everyone agreed he had shown some potential. At this point, no one was willing to dispute his claims for fear of raising his potential wrath and being cursed by him. His assumed role as a Dreamer had given him more confidence than the other members of the village to speak out against Daniel.

"Waabooz is only a child," shouted Daniel. "She does not know the ways of The People."

"That is no excuse," accused Bear Tooth. "She has lived with us long enough to know right from wrong. She must be punished." Bear Tooth rallied support and more and more of The People began to agree.

"We will discuss this at the next council meeting," argued Daniel.

"And in the meantime, what happens to Waabooz?" asked Bear Tooth.

"She will stay with me. I will see she does not dishonour anyone again."

"Not good enough," demanded Bear Tooth. "She must be held in the Black Hut to keep her from bringing more shame to The People."

Shouts of agreement came from most people.

"She is only a child," argued Daniel. "It is not fair."

"It is the law of The People, Daniel," stated Bear Tooth quite adamantly. "You cannot have one law for some and another for others. The law has to be obeyed by all."

"It will be done," agreed Daniel. "But, Waabooz does not know what she has done and does not know why she is to be held captive. First let me explain to her before she is taken to the Black Hut."

"Ugh," grunted Bear Tooth, and The People agreed.

Daniel turned to his sister and father and explained what had just happened.

"But Daniel," replied Anthony. "This is not fair. Brittany has done nothing wrong."

"I know she hasn't, but to The People she has and she must be brought to the council to answer for her actions. It has been agreed by The People that she must be kept in the Black Hut until the next council meeting."

"And how long will that be?"

"Three days."

"Three days! Daniel, you can't expect her to be locked in the dark for that long." Anthony paused then added. "And if she is to be punished, what form of punishment will that be?"

"She will not be punished. Trust me. It will never happen."

"Come, Brittany," said Daniel extending his hand. "I will take you to the Black Hut and will see you have a small fire, some food and a proper sleeping place."

Anthony took Brittany's other hand and all three walked to the back of the village where the Black Hut sat.

"Can't you do something, Daniel?" asked Anthony. "This is crazy."

"But, I have not done anything wrong Daniel. Holly was my friend and now she's, she's...." At the thought of Holly's smiling face and knowing she will never see her again, Brittany began to cry. "Can't you just tell them to get lost? You're their leader," she mumbled.

Daniel tried to explain that the village had certain laws that not even he could disobey. "The People believe that the dead body of a noble warrior had to be honoured in a certain way, otherwise his or her spirit would never reach the Land of the Dead where it would exist forever and ever in peace. I know it sounds silly, but that is what they believe, so I have to accept it too."

Tears rolled freely down Brittany's face as she looked into her brother's eyes. "If you won't help me Ebony will." She began calling his name and looking around for him.

Ebony was lying in Daniel's wigwam and came when Brittany called his name.

"You see, Ebony is here, but Tijus-Keha is not, Brittany. He has gone to speak with his father. I don't know when he'll be back. I too wish he was here to guide me in this situation."

Resolved to her predicament, Brittany looked down at her feet. "How long will I have to stay in the Black Hut?" she asked.

"No longer than is necessary," replied Daniel. "The council meeting is not for another three days. I will speak to the elders today and see if they will allow you to be in my custody until then."

"Three days? I have to stay in that horrible thing for three days?"

"Yes, Brittany, I'll stop by after I speak with the elders. Just stay cool."

After seeing that Brittany's needs were taken care of, Daniel went immediately to speak with the village elders.

"Just because she is your sister we cannot make an exception in her case," said the elders. "What kind of example would that make for The People? Waabooz must remain in the Black Hut until the council meeting, but....."

It had taken Brittany's eyes a few moments to adjust to the darkness inside the Black Hut. Some light came through cracks in the walls and through the smoke hole in top. In addition, the small fire in the middle of the hut gave a yellowish glow to the interior. Along one side was a low platform on which lay an animal skin robe for sleeping, and virtually nothing else adorned the interior. "Just what am I suppose to do for three days?" she asked herself sniffling. She wiped her nose along her sleeve. Tears came freely and an uncertainty concerning her immediate future. She wondered just how much influence her brother had over the village people. "I thought he was their leader, their chief, and that they had to do what he said. It's not fair. I didn't do anything wrong." Tears began anew and fear crept in where before had been nothing but joy. She

kept thinking about Holly. "I'll never see you again." She began to cry again.

Lying down on the musty robe she remembered back to the good times she and Holly had at the Wolf Education and Research Centre. The more she thought about home and the Centre, the more she began to miss her mother and her life back there.

Following his meeting with the elders, Daniel returned to the Black Hut. "Brittany. May I enter?"

"Yes!" came a weak reply.

Daniel opened the flap, went inside, and sat down by the fire with Brittany. "The elders refused to allow you to return to my wigwam. But they did say they would bring the council meeting forward to the day after tomorrow. So you only have to be in here for two day, not three. The time will go quickly, and I will return as often as I can to check on you."

Brittany didn't like it, but she had no other choice.

Daniel left Brittany and returned to his own wigwam.

Later that evening, food was brought to Brittany. She ate sparingly. "If they think I'm going to stay in here for two days, they've got another think coming. Now just what can I do? How am I goin' to get out o' here? What would Holly have done?" *Humm,* she thought. *If Holly can do it; so can I.*

In protest to the ruling, Daniel showed his disagreement by refusing to come out of his wigwam and declined any visits.

"Daniel?" asked Coyote Song the next morning. "May I enter?"

"No," Daniel replied. "I wish to be alone."

About noon the same day Anthony came to Daniel's wigwam with food. "Daniel?" Anthony asked. "I have some food for you."

"I am not hungry. Please leave."

"But, Daniel," argued Anthony.

"No, just go," shouted Daniel in the village language.

The guard on duty in front of Daniel's wigwam moved in front of Anthony and held his hand out, palm facing Anthony; his actions gave Anthony no recourse but to leave.

Later that afternoon, Ahawi came to Daniel's wigwam. "Daniel, may I enter?" she asked.

"No," replied Daniel. "I wish to be alone."

"It is important. It concerns Running Fawn."

"What about Running Fawn?"

Her body has been taken to the burial hut. She is not a member of any clan here in the village other than you. And you are the closest she has to a

blood relative. It is your duty to perform the cleansing of her body so we can proceed with the honour ceremony. We must talk about it. I also want to tell you how she died. It is important you know the complete story."

"You may enter," replied Daniel.

Ahawi lifted the door flap and stepped inside, sat down around the fire and looked at Daniel. The redness around his eyes, and the sadness in his face, shocked her, but she said nothing. A few moments later she began relating all she knew about what had happened.

During the telling, Daniel sat quietly, an expression of total despair his only visible emotion, and when Ahawi had finished his eyes were filled with tears.

Ahawi sat looking at Daniel, saying nothing. When she saw the tears overflow his eyes and trickle down his cheeks, she reach out with both her hands and her heart and took Daniel's hands in hers.

Daniel looked down at their entwined fingers. His eyes opened and tears flowed freely. "Running Fawn," he whispered in English. "I miss you so much. Why did you have to die?"

"I know Running Fawn was special to you, Daniel," said Ahawi, her voice tender and soothing. "Please be assured, what she did was not only for The People, but because of her love for you. It was a great sacrifice. I had told her to jump forward when the canoe crested the falls. If she had, she should have landed in the deeper water away from the rocks. Something must have happened that prevented her from doing so." Ahawi paused for a few moments to let Daniel get control of his emotions. Cautiously, she extended her hand to touch Daniel's shoulder, not sure if her actions were permitted to such an important person as the leader of the village. Daniel responded by burying his face in her shoulder and openly weeping. Ahawi put both her arms around Daniel and rested her cheek on top of his head.

"I know no one can replace Running Fawn in your life," she whispered. "But if you would accept me as your slave, I would be honoured to live in your wigwam, to make fresh clothing for you, to prepare your food and to keep your wigwam clean and your sleeping robes warm."

Daniel lifted his head and looked into Ahawi's eyes and realized she was serious. He appreciated that her offer of friendship was not given lightly in view of her own recent problems and losses.

"Thank you, Ahawi," replied Daniel. "Not sure I would be a worthy mate to you. My heart is not capable of loving anyone right now."

"Maybe in time you will come to accept me as your squaw? I would

make you proud if you would give me the chance?"

Daniel smiled. "Yes, maybe," he replied, and squeezed her hands.

At that moment, Kizhok knocked on Daniel's door flap. "Daniel," he interrupted. "May I speak with you? It is urgent."

Daniel wiped the back of his hand across his eyes and looked towards the entrance of his wigwam. "What is it Kizhok?"

"It is Waabooz. I was bringing food and tea to her and I called out to the wigwam if I could enter. She did not answer, so I called again. And again she did not answer. So I opened the flap and looked inside. I could not see her, so I entered, but there was no one there. In the back under the wall, there was a hole. She is gone."

"Gone?" asked Daniel. Gone where?"

"I do not know."

Daniel got to his feet and stepped out into the sunlight. "Coyote Song," he shouted. "I need you."

Coyote Song came running. "Yes, Daniel, what is it?"

"Have you seen Waabooz in the last little while?"

"No I have not seen her since she was put in the Black Hut."

Daniel explained what had happened then told Kizhok and Coyote Song to look everywhere in the village for her. They returned a few minutes later.

"She is not in the village, but one of the smaller canoes is missing," commented Coyote Song. "It looks as if she has gone from the village."

"What's happened?" asked Anthony who had heard Daniel calling out for Coyote Song.

"Brittany's gone. She dug a hole out the back of the Black Hut. It looks like she's taken a small canoe and run away."

"Oh no," said Anthony. "Not in this wilderness. What are we going to do?"

"We'll go after her."

"We've got to find her, Daniel. She has no idea what's out there."

"I know," replied Daniel, "And it'll be dark soon."

Brittany had been paddling for a couple of hours when she rounded a point of land and was met by loud honking and trumpeting.

Surprised by the sudden intrusion of the canoe, a family of two adult trumpeter swans, and seven grown young cygnets scattered, flapped their wings to gain airspeed, their heavy bodies struggling for lift. After a run up of about 30 metres, all nine took flight and disappeared beyond the trees.

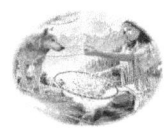

Brittany smiled at the wondrous sight of these nine huge birds flying together. She stopped paddling and just watched the birds disappear behind the trees. It was then she heard voices, muffled voices of many people some distance away.

Fear struck her suddenly and an awareness of just how precarious she was in this unknown world. "I better get out of here," she whispered to herself, turned the canoe toward the land and beached it. Quickly climbing out, she pulled the small craft out of the water and dragged it behind a fallen tree. She huddled down behind the canoe and waited.

The sun had just gone down behind the far trees across the other side of the river. A chill wind had come up and blew across the water into her face. It was noticeably cooler than a few minutes ago.

A canoe came around the point of land to her right moving very quickly with two Indians in it.

"Who are they?" whispered Brittany. "They don't look familiar. If they were from Daniel's village they would have come from the other direction." *Hum,* she thought. *They must have wondered what disturbed the swans.*

Fifteen minutes later the same canoe with the two Indian warriors returned, passed by her hiding place and disappeared back beyond the point of land again. She stayed crouched down for another thirty minutes until she was sure they would not return.

It was getting quite dark now and she could see a yellow glow reflecting off the low clouds. She quietly crept along the beach sand, and over a few rocks and logs. Just at the point of land before the open waters of the Gichi Gumee began, a large tree had fallen and its roots afforded a great hiding place. Brittany peered out from between the sweet smelling roots. In a small clearing a hundred metres away, at least a dozen campfires blazed, and what seemed like hundreds of warriors sat around the fires laughing and talking.

Who are these people? wondered Brittany. *They're certainly not from our village. I have to get back and warn Daniel.*

As quickly and as quietly as she could, she returned to her canoe, dragged it back into the water and began paddling back the way she had come.

Once clear of the reflected light from the fires, the darkness seemed to crowd around her. The near full moon had fallen behind a cloud and visibility was down to a few metres. "I'm going to get lost if I'm not careful. Must remember, must remember," Brittany said to herself. She guided her canoe closer to the shoreline to prevent taking a wrong turn. *If I stick to the left shore I should be all right,* she thought.

Suddenly another canoe loomed out of the black and nearly ran into her. She steered her canoe quickly towards shore, jumped out into the shallow water and ran inland. She was running blind, unable to see more than a metre or two in front. A hand grabbed her and dragged her to the ground. She kicked

and tried to bite and scratch her assailant.

"Waabooz! Stop it. I am your friend."

Brittany did not understand all his words, but she recognized Kizhok's voice and stopped resisting.

"Come," he said, and took her hand.

"Brittany," said Anthony when they had reached the canoes. He held out his hand, drew her to him and engulfed her in his arms.

"Oh Daddy, I was so scared." She then told him what she had seen. The next problem was telling Kizhok and Coyote Song so they too would know what she had seen. Eventually she managed to get the idea across.

Through a series of hand signs and what few words Anthony and Brittany understood of the Indians' language, Kizhok managed to convey to Anthony and Brittany that they were to return to the village in the smaller canoe, and he and Coyote Song would go ahead and check out the large encampment of which Brittany spoke.

The moon peaked out from behind scattered clouds and helped to light the way back to the village for Anthony and Brittany. Rounding the last bend and finally seeing the village fires burning, both were relieved that they did not get lost. Immediately upon beaching their canoe, Brittany ran to find Daniel to tell him what she had seen.

She ran into Ahawi who was tending the fire in front of Daniel's wigwam. "Ahawi, where is Daniel?" she asked in the Ojibwa language.

Ahawi pointed to the council chambers and tried to tell Waabooz that she was not allowed in the council meeting, but Brittany ran off too quickly. She burst into the meeting in the middle of a heated debate. The room went suddenly silent and everyone stared at her.

Bear Tooth stood and pointed a finger at Brittany. "You see, this is the insolence I am talking about. She has no respect for our ways and does exactly as she pleases whether it dishonours The People or not. For many sun turns she has disrupted the entire village. Something must be done about this young squaw before she influences all our young people."

Daniel grabbed Brittany and was about to escort her out when she hurriedly told him what she had seen. Daniel listened. "Are you sure of what you saw, Waabooz?"

"Yes, I am sure. Kizhok and Coyote Song went to have a look."

The village elders began shouting for Brittany to leave. Daniel raised his hand to silence the council members. "My sister brings important news of a large war party camped where the river joins the Gichi Gumee. We must prepare for battle."

"You would prepare for battle on the word of this impudent child squaw?" demanded Bear Tooth.

Many of the elders agreed with Bear Tooth, saying that this could easily be a ploy devised by Waabooz to avoid punishment for escaping from the Black Hut and running away.

At that moment, Kizhok entered the council chambers. "Waabooz speaks the truth," he shouted. "There is a large war party of Wendowa and Wakemsui warriors camped at the mouth of the river."

A sudden silence fell upon the elders. "How many warriors were there?" Daniel asked.

"Many. I counted this many hands of large war canoes on the beach. If each canoe holds this many warriors, (he held up eight fingers) then there are enough warriors in the war-party to defeat our forces in a surprise attack."

Daniel turned to the elders. "They will not attack at night. We have time to prepare. Gather the war leaders and bring them here," Daniel ordered.

As the war leaders were being gathered, Daniel turned to Brittany. "Thank you Brittany. You did the right thing. If our village is attacked, we will be ready. Go now and find Dad. Stay with him."

The war leaders gathered to discuss a plan of defence against their mighty enemies, the Wendowa and the Wakemsui. "It is revenge they want for the deaths of their warriors at the hands of two squaws on the Michi-ZeeBee," suggested Coyote Song who was the appointed war-leader for his clan."

"We can talk later about why the war party has gathered to attack our village," shouted Daniel to quiet the war-leaders. "We must plan carefully to minimize our losses."

Coyote Song stood and spoke. "There will be mist in the morning in front of our village. It will be easy for our enemy to come very close to the village without us knowing. The Wendowa are skilled canoeists."

"But there is rarely heavy mist on the river," remarked Daniel. "We should send a warrior over to the river who can use the mist to quickly return and warn us when the war party comes."

"Ugh, ugh," grunted the war leaders in approval.

"We must also send a runner to the West Wolf Village to inform them of the pending attack and for them to send their warriors to help us."

"But they maybe not get here in time," shouted Bear Tooth.

"That is true," replied Daniel. "But maybe they will and maybe we will need them." Daniel continued, "If the sky is clear in the morning, the sun will be in our enemy's eyes. It will make it difficult for them to see us clearly. We must divide our forces. Half will hide in canoes in behind the point of land over there." Daniel pointed off to his left opposite to where the river begins.

Coyote Song stood. "Sounds like a good plan." He raised his hands and began singing his war song and was soon joined by other war leaders. Someone started beating a drum.

Daniel had to shout for the leaders to be silent. "We must be quiet. It is possible enemy scouts have been sent to spy on our village. If that happens, the scouts must not see us preparing for battle. Our village must look peaceful. And, I have another suggestion if you will listen."

"Yes, speak," shouted one of the clan war leaders.

"We can use the mist to our advantage. I agree that we will not be able to see the Wendowa and Wakemsui until they are close to our village, but they will not see us very well either. I would like five hands of our best archers with many arrows, to crouch down along the palisade wall just outside the entrance. The enemy will not be able to see them, but when the enemy comes into view, our warriors will shoot their arrows as fast as they can into the air so there will be a rain of arrows falling onto the Wendowa and Wakemsui. The arrows will kill many enemy warriors and will put holes in their canoes too. This first attack of the rain of arrows will be the signal for our warriors waiting in their canoes behind the point of land to attack from behind. Once our warriors outside the palisade wall shoot all their arrows, they will run inside the entrance, which we will then close, and they will begin shooting more arrows through the arrow slots in the walls and from the top of the palisade."

"Daniel," said Coyote Song. "Are you sure you are telling us the truth when you say you have had no experience making war? These are different ways to make war, but they are clever ways."

The war leaders laughed.

"Yes, they are good ideas," added Bear Tooth, reluctantly.

The sun had just risen above the horizon behind the village when the sentry from the river emerged from the mist to warn the village that the enemy canoes were coming.

Daniel signalled the warriors outside the palisade wall to get ready. It was many agonizing minutes before the first enemy war canoe came into view through the mist. Daniel shouted. "Fire."

The first volley of arrows took flight in a whoosh of displaced air and arced upward, quickly followed by another volley and then another. Cries of pain came from the Wendowa and Wakemsui in their canoes just off shore. By now ten or twelve canoes were visible six of them were floundering in the water. Many warriors had already fallen from their small crafts and lay floating in death. As the mists slowly lifted an orange sunlight reflected off the lake waters that had turned a bright blood red.

Shouts from behind the Wendowa and Wakemsui canoes could be heard as the other half of the East Colossus warriors launched their attack from behind effectively blocking any retreat by the main enemy war party.

The war party was caught completely off guard by the different war tactics. Their entire plan of attack was based on surprise. Immediately, they

realized the East Colossus warriors were waiting for them their forces scattered, thrown into total chaos. The battle was over in minutes and most of the Wendowa and Wakemsui warriors lay dying or dead on the water's surface killed before any could gain a foothold on land. Some enemy warriors had been captured and would be kept as slaves to serve the East Colossus Village, or would be traded back to their Nation for future favours. Those who could not or would not adjust to the ways of The People would be put to death. A few enemy warriors had used the mist to make a dishonourable retreat away from the slaughter, and no doubt would return to their villages to tell the story of their defeat and disgrace.

"So many Wakemsui and Wendowa lives have been taken, Daniel," commented Coyote Song.

"Yes," replied Daniel. "It will be many summers before either of these two Nations will be strong enough to be a threat to the East Colossus Village again, if ever."

"Oh, look," said Coyote Song pointing out into the lake when a dozen war canoes appeared through the remaining mists. "Now that the fighting is over, our brothers from the West Wolf Village arrive."

"Good, they too can help celebrate our victory," replied Daniel.

A feast of food and dancing took place to celebrate the great victory and to honour Waabooz for her heroic actions of alerting The People to the war-party's imminent attack.

Brittany was brought forward to the middle of the ceremonial circle surrounded by The People. Daniel took her hand. "Thanks to you, Waabooz," he said. "We are here today to celebrate an overwhelming victory against the mighty Wendowa and Wakemsui Nations. Had you not brought us news of the impending attack on our village, many of us here today might now by lying dead or dying on the ground. Not one of our warriors was seriously injured during the fight. To honour you for your heroic act in the face of great danger, from this day forth, you will no longer be known as Waabooz. I bestow upon you your earned name, White Swan." He then repeated the announcement in English so both Brittany and Anthony understood the great honour being shown her by The People. A great cheer went up.

Brittany stood in awe of the glory and support shown to her by The People. She smiled. *Running Fawn and White Swan,* she thought, *Sisters forever.*

Chapter 21
Feast of the Dead

"**B**ut Father, you cannot close the portal for all time. It must stay open."

"I am sorry, my son. It is already closed."

"Can it not stay open, at least some of the time?"

"Have you not heard the voices on the other side gathered at the old village site, my son? So many voices were calling for you. It is crucial that no one comes through the portal uninvited into this time and this place. There is a great unseen danger. I am very concerned about those who have already travelled here, and the influence it will, and is having on The Good People of both your village, and of Daniel's village, and in particular Daniel's."

"But, Father, what about Daniel's father and little White Swan? How are they to return to their home?" argued, Tijus-Keha.

"It is unfortunate my son, but they are adapting well to their place within the village, are they not?"

"Yes Father, but they do not belong here; they do not understand our ways."

"I shall not allow the portal to again open, my son."

Further arguments between Tijus-Keha and his father did not change the situation. The portal remained closed.

Tijus-Keha returned to the East Colossus Village and went immediately to see Daniel. After the usual pleasantries he offered his condolences over the death of Running Fawn. "Daniel, my brother, I too am saddened by the death of Running Fawn. But, believe me when I say, it was meant to happen. Both my father and I knew she was destined to do something of great importance for The Good People."

Daniel, shocked by what Tijus-Keha had just told him, blurted out, "You knew she was going to die and you didn't do anything to prevent it? How could you? What kind of brother are you?"

Tijus-Keha was a bit shocked by Daniel's tone of voice. He was not accustomed to mere mortals addressing him in such a manner, but he held his displeasure. "Daniel, you must understand, my father and I were powerless to prevent it from happening. We knew she was destined to do something of great importance, but even we did not know what she was to do. That part of destiny

is determined by the actions of the individual. It was Running Fawn who made that choice. But, I say, if my father or I knew what was going to happen, we would have done nothing to prevent it. It was meant to be. Please find comfort in the fact that her great sacrifice saved countless lives, and most probably your life too."

Daniel nodded his agreement. "I understand, my brother. Please forgive me. What you say helps, but it does not make me feel much better. I miss her so very much."

"I too feel a great loss, and no, I do not believe it makes it easier. But I hear that Ahawi has been helping you in your wigwam."

"Yes, she is doing a great job of getting me to keep my place tidy and warm. But that's all," he added quickly.

Tijus-Keha smiled. "I hear she is a good cook too."

Daniel said nothing, just smiled and patted his stomach.

"A great battle you commanded and an overwhelming victory against the Wendowa and Wakemsui war party when they attacked. You had some different ways of doing battle."

"Yes, luck was in our favour, but everyone said it was Kitchi-Manitou who smiled on us that day."

"That may be true, but it was your ideas that won the battle."

Daniel was noticeably pleased at the praise from one who was held in such high esteem by all The People.

"But now, Daniel, we must honour Running Fawn in our way. Have you made the arrangements and has her body been cleansed?"

"Yes," replied Daniel. "I cleansed Holly's body yesterday." He shuddered at the memory. It had been necessary for him to divorce himself from the gruesome task and forget that this body had been Holly. That was not so difficult because it no longer looked like the Holly he remembered.

"You cleansed her body?" asked Tijus-Keha.

"Yes. The elders allowed it because Holly did not belong to a clan and that I was in fact as close as anyone to a blood relative, they gave their permission for me to do the cleansing."

"That is good. However, we must talk about the burial arrangements, Daniel. My father has a great honour he wishes to bestow upon Running Fawn, and to do so, certain arrangements must be made. I will tell you what must be done."

"It will be so," replied Daniel after Tijus-Keha told him.

While the village people were making the arrangements as instructed by Daniel, Kizhok and Coyote Song journeyed to the mouth of the Michi-Zeebee and brought back Zoong's body so The People could honour him in a

similar way as they were to honour Running Fawn.

At Running Fawn's burial ceremony Tijus-Keha stood beside Daniel and Ebony. It was a solemn ceremony to honour the dead. "Be wise my brother," said Tijus-Keha. "It is necessary to show strength in front of The People. Do not let your emotions rule your countenance. Remember Running Fawn as she was - strong and free."

Daniel nodded his agreement, but his eyes welled up when Holly's body was finally laid to rest on top of a platform not far from the village across the marshes to the north alongside other departed village members.

Zoong's body was buried in a shallow grave not far from Holly's platform.

Anthony was confused over the difference between the two burials.

After the ceremony, Daniel explained to his father. "It was Tijus-Keha's suggestion. He wants to return Holly's body to her time, but of course we cannot since the portal has been closed by his father. He believes the need to return Holly to her own time will convince his father to re-open the portal. It will be easier to remove her body if it is on a platform rather than buried in the ground. And, once the portal has been opened again, it'll be much quicker for us to move her without the village knowing."

"Any idea of when that might happen?" asked Anthony.

"No, but at times of great celebration, he said his father is sometimes moved to grant wishes more often than at other times."

The planned meeting with the elders of Daniel's village in the council chambers, the meeting that was cancelled when the village had been attacked, took place a few days following the burial ceremony. Daniel struggled to remain focused on the changes he wanted to suggest.

Once the elders had gathered, Daniel stood at the front and asked for silence. He began introducing his ideas. "As leader of the village, most responsibility for the well being of The People rests with me. I want to share my responsibilities with the council. Already each clan has a Matron chosen by the clan members. It is the Matron's responsibility to chose two members from her clan, one to sit in the general council meetings as the clan representative to put forth his clan's opinions on matters of village concern. The second clan member chosen by the Matron of each clan is in matters of war, to act as the clan war-leader to represent the clan on the war council. Until now, once the decisions are made by each of the two councils, it has been necessary to bring these decisions to me and I either approve them, or reject them. From this day forth, it will no longer be necessary to bring these decisions to me. I wish still to be consulted and I will add my opinions on proposed changes and rulings, but it will be the council who has the final say, not me. If it is the will of The People, then their choice will ultimately overrule mine. The only change I wish to see within the clan is that the member chosen by the clan Matron to repre-

sent the clan in the general council does not always have to be a warrior. If a squaw is better suited for the position then a squaw will be chosen. But on the war-council, I still believe it should be a warrior who is chosen.

The idea of a central council that governed the growth and politics of The People was not a totally new idea as it was already practised within each clan. However, decisions pertaining to village rules and directions had always been under the direct control of Tawis-Karong and then Daniel. It had been that way for so long it was unthinkable for The People to be able to make decisions that affected the direction of the entire village without the village leader's approval or rejection. Daniel reminded the council members that Tijus-Keha's West Wolf Village was ruled by such an arrangement during his absence for so long. And since his return his many duties and responsibilities prevented him from resuming his previous role as outright leader of the West Wolf Village, consequently, democratic rule within the village council continued.

A great murmur went up among the council members. The concept of a democratic government, one that ruled in favour of the majority, was an unknown concept to the East Colossus Village, but one they were willing to try, as long as Daniel was there to help govern during an initial trial period. But there were many objections to having women sit in as clan representatives. Most men considered women a lesser people good only for doing menial chores like cooking, gathering and cleaning.

Makadewaa stood and asked why Daniel thought squaws should serve on the council?

Daniel was waiting for this question and already had a prepared answer. "It is a wise question, my friend. I will explain my thoughts. It is the women of this village who are the peacemakers. It is the women who are the least likely to go to war. It is the squaws of the village whose first priority is the welfare of the children of the village. And it is the children who are the future of the East Colossus Village. For those reasons, I would like to see the interests of the women of this village heard."

"Your ideas are sound, Daniel," commented Makadewaa. "But it is already the Matron of each clan who instructs the clan representative on what he should say at the council meetings. We feel squaws are properly represented in this way."

The decision not to allow squaws on the general council was unanimous. On this issue it seemed Daniel had to concede to the majority. However, Daniel had another option he discussed with the council.

"Now it is only the men of the council who speak on various issues being considered," he said. "But I wish to allow anyone who wishes, not only council members, but any of The People, both warriors and squaws, to have the right to speak in the general council meetings and to voice their opinions and ideas. However, I would suggest that anyone wishing to present an idea for discussion at a council meeting must first receive approval to do so from

the clan Matron. But the final vote on issues will still remain restricted to the council representatives."

Again the council was divided over allowing anyone to speak at general council meetings.

Coyote Song stood, raised his hand and asked to be heard.

"Speak my brother," motioned Daniel.

Coyote Song looked down at his feet then cleared his throat, not sure how he was going to say what was on his mind. Long ingrained fears of reprisal by the East Colossus Village leader of the past caused him to hesitate, but Daniel's earlier words gave him courage. "I, um, am reluctant to agree to your ideas of allowing women so much say in how the village should be run. Next you will be suggesting women will go out and hunt and defend the village against our enemies. And then next you'll be asking the men to stay in the wigwams and cook the large pots of food and tend to the papooses. And then you'll be asking men to clean up after the little ones."

The council members laughed and cheered Coyote Song.

"I assure you Coyote Song," smiled Daniel, "the men will still do the

hunting and fishing, will still protect the village from our enemies and will make the decisions to go to war. Women will still gather our food, prepare the food for clan members, make our clothing and look after the family unit, especially the papooses."

After a long discussion concerning Daniel's latest proposal, no decision was made, but again they agreed to try it for a trial period.

Daniel then introduced another idea he wanted to try. "We are gathered here inside our new council chambers. I would like to suggest building more larger wigwams, like this one, and gather all family members in a clan together to all live in the one large wigwam."

The elders were confused and said that The People had lived in individual wigwams for many lives and wondered why they should change?

"The clans are made up of family members, husbands, wives, children, grandchildren, grandparents, aunts, uncles, nephews and nieces, and many suffer greatly in the cold season. Some starve to death in their little wigwams even when they are within a few man lengths of another wigwam. With all family members living together they would pool their resources for the good of all. It would be warmer, fewer people would go hungry. I wish to make this suggestion only at this time. But if the council will agree in principle then let us begin building the first long wigwam and try it, and if The People don't like the idea,

we can always use the long wigwam for food storage."

This arrangement seemed the easiest to implement, but there was still some dissension among the elders about such changes.

Daniel paused at that moment and sat down to allow the council members to think about what he had just said. A few moments later he stood again, and all went silent.

"There are two other ideas I wish to suggest. One is in matters of war. I no longer wish to be the war leader.

"And who will be our war leader," someone shouted.

"It will not be me," replied Daniel. "It would be for the war council to decide. All members of the war council have a voice. It would be the council who will choose a leader, but the council must pick the warrior who is the best at making decisions of war."

There was silence for a few moments before Coyote Song stood. "But, Daniel, after our latest victory, we might chose you as the best person to lead us in matters of war. What them?" The council burst into laughter.

Daniel too smiled, but he continued on with his last suggestion. "I have one last idea to suggest at this time. I want to appoint some of The People who are best at making drawings to record on birch-bark scrolls a written account of our history so that people many generations from now will better understand what is happening here, in our time, with our way of life."

"But, we do that now with our songs, and our story telling around our winter campfires," commented Kizhok.

"Yes, I know. But, after the story or song is repeated many times, things get changed, and before long it is not the same story or song anymore. I suggest we have a permanent history of our Nation so that in many, many summers from now, The People can look at our scrolls and know precisely how we lived and why."

This last suggestion was met with more opposition than Daniel had expected. He thought perhaps he had asked too much, too soon. He stood again and spoke. "Maybe I have talked about too many things. There is much to think about. I will say no more now; we will gather again next moon to talk more."

The People broke up into little discussion groups as they left the meeting. Many lingered long after others had left just to talk amongst themselves.

Daniel had been translating into English bits of what he had said, so Anthony would understand what was going on.

"Good idea to give them time to think about things. What other ideas do you have in mind?" asked Anthony.

"A lot more, but I want what we have talked about today to be accepted first, and in place, and working. Once that's been accomplished, then I'd like

to talk about the farming, and maybe the idea about building more permanent structures than these wood and bark buildings. Winter will be upon us soon. And it is in winter that we do most of our talking around the campfire, where we tell stories, sing songs, and discuss the future. And, when food is scarce, it is the best time to talk about changes so that in the future none of The People go hungry. It's not going to be easy to sell my ideas about farming, and building a stone house is going to be even more difficult."

"Well, don't rush it. You've already gained The People's trust in many ways. The problem is they've been living their way of life successfully for generations. Don't mess too much with a proven system."

"Yeah, make haste, slowly, so to speak," chuckled Daniel.

"Yeah, right," confirmed Anthony, smiling.

It had been nearly two months since Jennifer had last seen Anthony and Brittany when they had left to deliver the boat load of goods to Daniel.

"First Daniel, now the rest of my family, it's not fair," Jennifer shouted to the empty house. "I can accept the loss of Daniel. I understand he made that choice, but not Anthony and Brittany. And Holly too has not returned. I will not give them up without a fight. Ebony, Big Black, Tijus-Keha, you owe me." But, her shouts of anguish went unanswered, as always, and as always she collapsed onto the chesterfield and sobbed, her despair heightened by the emptiness of her home.

"I am not sure what I can do, Jennifer," said Sharon, when Jennifer voiced her concerns during a visit with her friend. "Not many of my people believe what you claim has happened to your family. And even fewer are willing to acknowledge the possibility that there is a portal leading to the ancient village site, to Daniel, and to a time when Kitchi-Manitou's two sons walked the earth. You must agree that it is hard to believe. You know it does exist, and I believe it is true, but that does not make it true in the eyes of everyone."

"Yes, I hear you, but I don't know what to do? I'm getting desperate. There's no white authority who believes any of it, not even Tom at the Ontario Provincial Police."

"Okay, okay," sighed Sharon. "Let me think about it. I'll talk to the elders, and I'll let you know if we can do anything. Give me a day or so."

Two days later, Sharon called Jennifer.

"I gathered the clan council last night to tell them I'd had a vision in a dream."

"Oh, yeah, did you really have a dream, Sharon?"

"No! But many still have strong feelings for dreams. I thought it would,

how you say, grab their attention."

Jennifer laughed. "And, did it?"

"Oh yes, they were very interested. I told them how strong my vision was and that I had seen Holly, Brittany and Anthony in my vision. I told them of some of the honourable things they have done for the Anishinabe People. I told them what these deeds were and the importance of these deeds to The People. I said they must be honoured in the traditional Anishinabe way. And, because Holly, Anthony and Brittany have all gone together from our presence, the village has to honour them all together and in the same way. I suggested having an ancient Ojibwa Feast of the Dead celebration on the old village site. We've scheduled it for two week from next Sunday, if that's okay?"

"A Feast of the Dead, but they're not dead," declared Jennifer. "I don't like the idea of pretending they're dead."

"It is the only way. You must do as I say, Jennifer."

"Okay, okay. Damn, you've been so quick to anger these last few weeks. What's wrong?"

"Nothing is wrong. You must not question my decisions."

"Well, when it comes to my family, I will question whoever I want." Now Jennifer was showing anger.

"Yes, I am sorry, Jennifer. I don't know what has gotten into me the last few months. There has been a strange side of me that is so angry all the time. It is all I can do sometimes to stop from hitting people."

"I guess we're all a bit edgy these days." Jennifer took a deep breath. "Exactly what is a Feast of the Dead? Please explain."

"A long time ago," began Sharon. "The Anishinabe people had their own way of dealing with those who had died. Of course, we now bury our dead the same way the whites do. But, back before the white people came, the normal way to honour the dead was to leave the body for a period of time in either a shallow grave or on top of a platform to allow all their worldly appearances to decay and return to the earth."

"Worldly appearances, what's that?"

"It means for the skin and outer layer tissues to decay so only the bones are left and maybe some muscle tissue."

"Oh!" was all Jennifer replied.

Sharon went on. "Then The People would gather up the skeletal bones, and during a celebration of life called, the Feast of the Dead, the bones would be placed together with other family members, or specially honoured members of the band in an ossuary or large mound."

"I don't know, Sharon. Not sure I like the idea. I don't believe they are dead, and I'm not about to pretend they are."

"Jennifer, please. Let me explain the rest of my idea."

"Okay, okay, sorry."

"Well, the plan is to have this feast with dancing, drumming, and singing. We have not had a Feast of the Dead ever in the lifetime of anyone in the band. Most of the oldest elders really like the idea, only because it will show the young people of the band how we used to honour our dead in celebration, not in mourning. The only parts of a Feast of the Dead my generation has seen or heard are from drawings in books, pictures painted on walls, or told in stories.

What appeals most to the elders is the celebration. It is really a celebration of life, not a celebration of death."

"Maybe you should change the name to Feast of Life then?"

Sharon half smiled, but continued. "Songs are sung about the departed. Their great deeds are told in story. And, the tradition begins a new line of stories to hand down to future generations. The Feast of the Dead is in name only, to help Holly's parents, to help you, and to help us all appreciate how fragile life can be. It will also help to remind us that the lives of those no longer with us, and their intimate memories, are not forgotten. It will be in name only. We have no skeletal remains to re-bury. This is the story I told the elders. In truth, I am hoping someone else will be listening during the feast."

"Someone else? What do you mean?"

"Those of the Departed Spirits," replied Sharon.

"Departed Spirits?" Jennifer,confused with Sharon's last comment, but did not question it further, thinking she may have meant someone or something from the other side might hear it.

A large flotilla of canoes, a few motorized row boats and one large motorized pontoon fishing boat carrying another dozen people and all the equipment set sail for the east end of the little lake. Within minutes of arriving at the old village site, the drums had been set up and began their rhythmic beat. The women had fires going and the great quantities of food and tea were being prepared. About eighty Ojibwa people, Jennifer, her parents, Heidi and Jason Davis, Jennifer's sister Ashley and husband Doug, and Holly's parents had gathered for the celebration.

All the participants sat in a large circle. In the centre of the circle sat all the elders of the Manitoulin Island First Nations People. Black Sky stood and called for silence. "We are gathered here today to honour those friends and loved ones who are recently gone from us. It is an old tradition for the Anishinabe Peoples to honour our band members in a celebration of life called A Feast of the Dead. Gone from us are Daniel, Anthony and Brittany Santos, and Holly Kanipiswet." Black Sky inviting anyone who wished to tell a story to come forward and speak. Sharon was the first to walk to the centre of the

circle. She welcomed everyone and then told a story about Holly and how she was given her name, Running Fawn. Then she went on a bit about Anthony, and talked about his many contributions to the Ojibwa First Nations people as a member of the Ontario Ministry of Natural Resources. Of course she could not leave out his and Jennifer's contribution to the native community with the Wolf Education and Research Centre.

Everyone shouted the acclaim of Anthony's victories in a battle of a different nature, but no less of a triumph.

Others, too, stood and proclaimed the good deeds of both Holly and Anthony.

Then the dancing began, and it went on endlessly, and the singing, all to the beat of the drum. Some dancers stopped for food and water, while others joined in, many dressed in their finest native regalia.

It was almost too much for Jennifer. She endured the constant reminders of what she had lost especially at this place, the old village site, where her family last set foot in the 21st Century. Tears filled her eyes frequently, but she had managed to keep them in check most of the day. With so many songs, so many stories told about her husband and daughter, and Holly, all in the past tense, it felt to her like an acceptance of their deaths.

Jennifer's emotions, so controlled for the entire afternoon, reached a breaking point. She stood, hesitated then ran to the centre of the ring of dancing and singing Indians. "No," she screamed, and fell to her knees. She raised her arms to the sky and shouted. "They are not dead. Do not let it be true. Ebony, you owe me."

All dancing stopped and a hushed silence hung in the air. Everyone stood looking at Jennifer; her great sorrow felt by everyone present.

"Ebony, Kitchi-Manitou," she shouted towards the silenced audience. She raised her arms to the sky. "Return my family to me, please, I beg you." She laid her head in her hands and openly wept and repeated their names again and again. The silence was almost deafening; the names Ebony and Kitchi-Manitou echoed in the distance.

Sharon and Jason helped Jennifer to her feet then led her back to the blanket where she had been sitting.

The dancers all seemed in need of water, tea or food. So were the

drummers. There was silence, save the low murmur of whispered voices in conversation.

"I am sorry, Jennifer. I did not stop to think how this feast would affect you. Maybe it was not such a good idea."

"No, no, it's okay. I'll be all right. Just let me sit here for a while."

"Would you like some tea or something?" asked Heidi.

"Yes please, tea would be nice."

Sharon stood to help Heidi get the tea. "Jennifer," she said, pointing to the far side of the clearing. "What's that over there?"

"Where?" asked Jennifer, turning to look in the direction Sharon pointed.

"Over there, beyond the tent where the tea and sausages are being prepared. There in the bushes at the edge of the lake."

"I don't know. Looks like a dog. Did anyone bring a dog?"

"No not that I know of, certainly not a black dog. It looks more like a wo...." Sharon paused. "Jennifer, that's Ebony."

"Ebony, are you sure? What's he doing here? Why doesn't he come over?"

"I don't know. Maybe he wants you to go to him? Come on. I'll help you."

Jennifer wiped her tear stained face on the back of her hand and she and Sharon slowly walked over towards the black canine.

Many of the people turned and watched as Jennifer and Sharon walked around the corner of the tea tent.

The black dog turned and walked slowly back into the bushes and bullrushes. Jennifer and Sharon followed still not sure it was Ebony, not until they were out of sight of all the people and were suddenly surrounded by a yellow light.

A drummer began to beat out a single note on the drum and a lone singer began chanting a song. Another drummer began and another singer, and before long all the dancers were in the ring all singing and shouting in celebration of the Feast of the Dead.

Chapter 22
The Legacy

Sharon materialized at one end of the council chambers; Jennifer and Ebony at the other end. Like the smoke from a burning cigarette, a faint, almost imperceptible mist curled upwards from Sharon. She was too excited about being in the actual village of Daniel's dream to notice the mist, or more importantly, the emotional weight its absence lifted from her.

The mist floated around the council chambers, drifted outside, hesitated for a moment and entered a wigwam next to the council chambers. It floated around the inside perimeter of the bark structure, circled two clay pots standing near one wall, and flowed over the sleeping robes on the platform. It circled the dying embers of a fire in the centre of the structure and dipped down under the hide flap used as a door covering. Outside, a slight breeze gathered it up and pushed it down towards the lake shore and there it found grandfather Makadewaa sitting on a rock watching the children at play in the water. The mist circled above Makadewaa, then dropped engulfing his body and mind.

Makadewaa sat up straight startled by the sudden chill. "Oh," he said. "What was that?" And he shivered in the heat of the sun. "I am cold," he said to himself, but at the same time he felt a strange feeling of energy from within. He stood up to walk down to the water's edge and was surprised; his aching bones and joints no longer troubled him. He could walk as he did when a young man. "What has happened?" he asked himself, wondering about the physical change.

Tijus-Keha, still in the guise of Ebony, also felt something strangely familiar, something he did not like. He looked around, but saw nothing untoward that might be cause for concern. With more pressing matter that needed his immediate attention, he shrugged off the negative feelings.

Like everyone else before her, Sharon was overwhelmed by the experience of her journey through time from the ruins of the old village site to the actual village in its prime thousands of years before the appearance of any European explorers.

She too marvelled at the workmanship in the construction of the building. "It is so simple a design," she said to Jennifer who had walked over to join her. "I have seen recreations of village longhouses and wigwams, but never

expected the real ones to be so beautiful."

Daniel, Anthony and Brittany appeared at the doorway.

"Mom," shouted Brittany and she ran into Jennifer's outstretched arms.

Tears welled up in Jennifer's eyes. She wiped them away as best she could with Brittany tightly wrapped around her.

Anthony walked over and placed his arms around the two of them.

Jennifer's emotions overflowed openly weeping tears of both joy and relief. All those long days and nights alone and all that pent-up anger were released in total peace once again reunited with her entire family. She sniffled then looked over at Daniel.

"You wouldn't happen to have a tissue, I guess?" she asked with a smile.

Everyone laughed.

"Oh, how I've missed you, Daniel," she said reaching out a hand. "My you look great. Life must be agreeing with you. How are you?"

"I'm much better now for seeing you," he replied, taking her hand. "I've missed you so much too. It was nice having Dad and Brittany here for so long, though."

"How about me, great warrior," said Sharon touching Daniel's arm.

"Hi Sharon, it is great to see you again. Now you know I was not possessed by a Windego and that all I said was true."

"Yes, it is amazing," she replied. "I did believe you, but there was always a small bit of doubt."

"I have thought about you so many times in the last year or so. I could have used some of your wisdom and knowledge of Anishinabe customs now and again. I am so happy Kitchi-Manitou has allowed the portal to open again and that you and Mom are able to visit."

"Where's Holly?" asked Jennifer. "I thought she'd be here to meet us." She looked around but not seeing her, she looked questioningly at Daniel, sensing something wrong.

Daniel looked awkward and turned away from his mother's questing eyes.

"What's happened?" Jennifer reached out and touched Daniel's arm.

It took Daniel a few moments to gather his emotions, and with Anthony's help, explained what happened.

It saddened Jennifer to learn of Holly's death, but she was deeply moved by her sacrifice. "Tijus-Keha did say that she was destined to do some-

thing of great importance for her people. I see now just how important it was. Could he not have prevented her death?"

"No," replied Daniel. "Kitchi-Mantou no longer controls the destiny of The People. Neither Tijus-Keha nor his father knew what it was she was going to do."

Wanting to change the subject, Jennifer asked if she and Sharon could have a look around the village.

"We do not have much time. Tijus-Keha said the portal will not stay open for long, so we must hurry. Tijus-Keha said his father promised that you will be allowed to visit another time and we will be able to talk more then. Come, we must go. We have important things to do." He turned and picked up two fur robes neatly folded on the ground and handed one to Jennifer. "Please wrap this around yourself. It will hide your modern clothing. The extra robe we'll need where we are going. Ebony will lead the way. We will walk through the village so you will get to see a bit of it at least."

Ebony and Daniel led the way closely followed by Brittany, Sharon, Jennifer and Anthony, who had his arm around his wife. They slowly walked, but had gone no more than a few metres when they ran into Coyote Song.

"Daniel," I ah, wanted to speak with you." He looked at Anthony with his arm around Jennifer. "This is Anthony's squaw?" he asked. She is your mother?"

"Yes. Coyote Song, this is my mother, Jennifer," he said hesitantly, beginning the introductions.

Jennifer smiled and said hello in Ojibwa, but had difficulties pronouncing his name in the Indian language.

"And this is Little Fox," said Daniel introducing Sharon, who had no difficulty pronouncing Coyote Song's name.

"The decorations on your moccasins and the design on your dress are wonderful," Coyote Song said to Sharon.

Sharon smiled.

"You have such beautiful bead-work in your dress. Where did you get such tiny beads?"

Not knowing what to say, she elected to tell the truth. "Wal-Mart," answered Sharon and smiled.

Coyote Song tried to pronounce Wal-Mart but failed.

"We must go Coyote Song," said Daniel. "I will speak with you later. There is something I must discuss with you."

"Yes Daniel, of course." He gave a short bow of respect and let them pass.

Daniel sighed. "Oh, well," he said, and continued walking through the

village. Daniel greeted and waved at many people all of whom were busy with their normal daily chores. Everyone stared at the visitors, but seeing strange people was becoming normal village activities now, and The People just accepted it as a quirk of their white-skinned leader.

At the back of the village, Daniel lifted a log across a small gate in the palisade, opened the gate and directed everyone to step through. Once outside the palisade, he closed the gate. To his right he grabbed a lever in the wall and pulled it. The log on the inside behind the door could be heard falling into place and the gate was once again locked. "Neat, eh," Daniel smiled.

To everyone's immediate right were two long logs standing upright that were laced together with vines and bits of rawhide. Daniel reached up and untied a vine rope, and with the use of a series of crude wooden pulleys he lowered the two logs to the ground. The logs became a bridge that ran from the firm ground at the base of the palisade wall across the marsh to a pathway of more logs lying about fifteen metres away.

"I'm particularly proud of this thing," he said to Jennifer and Sharon. "Dad helped me build it. The People were really impressed when they first saw it. The logs form a bridge to the mainland. It's about 200 metres through the bull-rushes. All the village people said it couldn't be done, but when I showed them how it works with the use of various pulleys, they were amazed. They don't question my ideas as much anymore."

The party walked across the bridge to the mainland, and Daniel explained what they were about to do.

"Dad and I are going to enter the sacred burial ground. Once we enter, we cannot speak to each other or touch anything other than Running Fawn's platform. It's over there," he said pointing through the trees. "What we must do is place the extra robe over top of Running Fawn's remains. Once we have

covered her body, Dad and I will take hold of the handles at each end of the platform and bring her back here. Ebony will wait here with you and when we come back with Running Fawn we'll all go back to your time. Any questions?"

"Are you going to bring the whole platform?" ask Brittany.

"No, silly, when we constructed the platform we made a small stretcher on top with handles so we could lift it easily. We planned ahead for this moment. Okay?"

Brittany nodded yes.

"Good, let's go then," said Daniel who lifting his index finger to his lips. "Now, everyone be quiet."

While Daniel and Anthony were retrieving Holly's stretcher, Ahawi came across the bridge and stood staring at Sharon's and Jennifer's clothing.

"Hello, I am Ahawi. I heard Daniel's mother was here and I wanted to meet her," she said without taking her eyes off Sharon's dress. "Coyote Song said your dress was beautiful, but I did not think it would be so wonderful."

Sharon tried to distract Ahawi by suggesting she should be quiet.

At that moment Ahawi saw Daniel and Anthony walking back with Holly's stretcher. She gasped, but said nothing.

Daniel too was silent; to say anything would have shown great disrespect to Holly. He held up his hand for Ahawi to step back.

Ahawi stepped back a few metres to the edge of the bridge.

The original group all stood together beside Holly's stretcher, Ebony stepped close and soon everyone was surrounded by a yellow glow, including Ahawi. A moment later, they all disappeared.

At that precise moment, Makadewaa, standing by the wall at the back of the village not far from the little gate, raised his arms and whispered, "I, Tawis-Karong, first-born son of Kitchi-Manitou, has returned."

Out of sight from the dancers at the old village site, a yellow glow appeared behind some trees in back of the tea tent. From out of the glow stepped Jennifer, Sharon and Ebony, and carrying the platform with Holly's remains, Anthony and Daniel.

Unknown to the first group, another less evident glow appeared behind some bushes a few metres away in the trees. From out of the second glow stepped Ahawi.

Brittany walked out from behind the tea tent followed by Jennifer and Sharon. Immediately behind them walked Daniel and Anthony carrying the stretcher and behind Anthony came Ebony.

The procession walked to the centre of the ring of dancers. Daniel and Anthony placed the stretcher on the ground. All dancing, drumming and singing abruptly stopped and everyone stared at the new arrivals.

Jennifer walked over to Holly's parents, quietly took them by the hand and led them to the centre of the circle. She hugged each of them.

Ebony looked at Holly's parents and they at him. There was a transfer of information from Ebony's mind to Holly's parents. At first startled by the intrusion into their private thoughts, once they realized from who it came, they nodded their acceptance of the information and confirmed they understood. What he told them was essentially how Running Fawn had died and what a great deed and personal sacrifice she had made for so many of The People.

Holly's parents were heartbroken over the loss of their daughter, but felt an inner pride they could not explain.

Jennifer had previously confided in Holly's parents after Tijus-Kehas had visited her to help Holly when she lay in hospital. She had told them what Tijus-Keha had told her, that Holly was destined to do something of great significance for The Good People. They bowed their heads towards the black wolf and both conveyed their gratitude.

Holly's mother put her arms around her husband and cried. Holly's father spoke quietly to Ebony. "We are saddened by Holly's death," he said. "But we are greatly warmed by your words of praise for our daughter. She was a very special person. We are very proud of her. Thank you for sharing her story with us."

Ebony walked over to the stretcher lying on the ground near the drum. He bowed his head. A bright yellow glow surrounded him. His form grew in stature within the glow, and a moment later there was Tijus-Keha standing beside Ebony.

There was an audible gasp from the circle of people watching intently. "Here lies Running Fawn," shouted Tijus-Keha in English then repeated his words in his own language, his voice pure and unspoiled. "She is to be specially honoured in traditional Anishinabe fashion. I am Tijus-Keha, first-born son of Kitchi-Manitou. Hear my words and obey for they are the same as if The Great Mystery, Kitchi-Manitou himself, spoke them."

He told the story of what Holly had done, how she guided the enemy war party over the falls to their death, thereby saving the entire East Colossus Village from possible annihilation, the village that once existed on these very grounds, and in so doing sacrificed her life to save The People.

"In honour of Running Fawn's sacrifice, it has been decreed by my father, Kitchi-Manitou, that her spirit shall forever exist within the falls on the Michi-Zeebee to the east. When the sun has just past its highest point in the sky on each day, Running Fawn will again come to life. Viewed from the

resting rock, she will be seen in the mists at the base of the falls, and, from the falling waters will come the cries of the enemy warriors as they plunge to their deaths." He paused for a moment.

There was much talking among the people gathered around the circle.

Taking a deep breath, Tijus-Keha continued. "Do not forget the name of Running Fawn, or the sacrifice she made for all our People for all time. Tell her story around the campfires in winter, and sing her song of praise."

There was silence within the gatherers. All eyes watched Tijus-Keha as the first-born bowed his head and spread his arms out over Holly's remains.

"My father has spoken," he said. "Let it be so."

A slight yellow glow engulfed the stretcher and as Tijus-Keha lowered his arms the glow subsided. "It has been done," he said, and he smiled. He put out his arm to Daniel and Ebony to join him beside the stretcher. A yellow glow surrounded them and they were gone. All was as it had been.

Ahawi had watched from her hiding place behind the bushes. She had listened to Tijus-Keha's words, but many of his words she found strange, like the words often spoken by Daniel, White Swan and their father Anthony. *Is this their home?* Ahawi wondered. She looked around and found the terrain strangely familiar. *There is the point of land where the warriors from my village waited to attack from behind,* she thought. *And over there is the entrance to the river, and there is the big rock over on that side of the little lake where I often go to swim and bathe.* What she saw confused her. "If this is my lake, where is my village, where are my people?" she whispered. Ahawi watched the activity in the clearing, and especially she watched White Swan and Anthony, the only two people she recognized, other than the two new strangers she had met just before coming here, Daniel's mother, Jennifer and Little Fox.

Ahawi stayed hidden watching the people standing around the ceremonial circle. She watched with interest and wondered about their strange clothing and funny head-wear. Some were dressed like her, but even their clothing did not look right, like Little Fox's dress.

A lone drummer began a slow beat, soon followed by a singer who sang the praise of Running Fawn, relating as closely as she could the words just spoken by Tijus-Keha. Soon others joined in and before long all the dancers were dancing and singing the praise of Running Fawn.

Ahawi stepped out from her hiding place and walked over towards the dancers to get a better look at people. She moved cautiously, very unsure of herself and very confused as to where she was, because everything was so strange.

It was Brittany who saw her first. "Sharon, look," she said. "Isn't that Ahawi?"

"Where?" asked Sharon.

"Over there watching the drummers."

"Yes, it sure looks like her. How did she get here? If that is her she must be really scared. Come, we must go and rescue her. How are we ever going to explain to her where she is so she will understand?"

Brittany walked casually around behind all the people surrounding the ceremonial circle, came up behind Ahawi, reached out and took her hand.

Ahawi jumped back, startled. "White Swan," she said in her own language.

Brittany motioned for her to follow. Reluctantly, she allowed Brittany to walk her over to where Sharon sat.

"Ahawi, please sit," said Sharon. "You remember my name is Little Fox?"

Ahawi knelt down on the soft blanket and ran her hands over the strange wool material. "Where am I?" she asked. "And who are all these strange people? This is my lake and my village, but my village is not here. I do not understand."

Sharon tried to explain. Ahawi seemed to grasp the concept that she was many summers in the future, but there was no way she could fully understand just how much time there was between her village and where she was now. She seemed so forlorn sitting there totally out of step with time.

Anthony and Jennifer had been listening, but understood little. Anthony spoke a bit of Ahawi's language but not enough to carry a conversation.

"What are we going to do with her?" asked Jennifer.

"We can't leave her here, and with all the people here we can't try to contact Ebony or Daniel. She'll have to return home with us and we can come back tomorrow and try to contact the other side when no one's around."

"Ahawi," said Sharon. "You are going to go back to Jennifer's and Anthony's home with,,," she hesitated and turned to Brittany. "What's your new name, Brittany?"

"It's White Swan," replied Brittany, sticking her chest out in pride.

Turning back to Ahawi, she put her hand on Ahawi's arm and continued. "You will go home with White Swan to her wigwam for the night. It is important that you trust her totally." Sharon hesitated then continued. "I,,, I am not sure how to tell you this, but I must advise you that you will see many strange things when you leave here. You must totally believe White Swan when she says there is nothing to fear. She is your friend and she would not do anything to harm you. Please believe me when I say this."

Ahawi hesitantly nodded her agreement.

Eventually, the dancing and singing stopped and the people were packing up to return to their homes.

Holly's remains were put on the pontoon boat to be taken to the Ojibwa village at Gore Bay. It was decided the village people would have a very quiet normal funeral service for her with no information being leaked to any authorities that would require an investigation to determine the cause of her death. The official reports would remain that Holly was missing.

Sharon, Brittany and Ahawi shared a canoe on the paddle back to the western end of the lake. Sharon kept talking to Ahawi pointing to various landmarks around the lake, landmarks that Ahawi mostly recognized. But, when she saw the docks, the few cottages that surrounded the east end of the lake, the road and all the automobiles parked beside the road, she was speechless and ready to flee. Sharon continued to talk to her in her language to calm her. On the dock, Brittany took her hand and they walked up to a black pickup truck. Brittany touched it, then slapped her hand on the front fender.

Ahawi reached out a cautious hand and gently touched the truck. "It is cold and hard like a rock," she said, and smiled. She too slapped the fender, then laughed as had Brittany.

At that moment, one of the other vehicles' engines was started. Ahawi quickly withdrew her hand and jumped back so quickly she knocked Sharon to the ground.

"It's okay Ahawi. It's okay," said Brittany. "It won't hurt you," and she took Ahawi's hand and led her over to her mom's red Tracker. Brittany opened the door, got in the back seat first then patted the seat beside her for Ahawi to get in too. After much coaxing she did, but experienced claustrophobia when the door was closed.

"Watch this," said Jennifer.

Sharon translated Jennifer's words.

Jennifer opened all the electric windows then closed them again and once more opened them.

Ahawi began to laugh along with everyone else in the truck.

When Jennifer started the engine of the Tracker, Ahawi stiffened, but Brittany took her hand and held it tight and Ahawi relaxed. The drive home was equally as amazing for Ahawi. She was beginning to trust her friends and was more willing to accept all these strange things as normal for the people here. But still it was incredible to her, such magic.

Sharon tried to explain how some of the things worked, which made it all seem less magical to Ahawi. If she thought the truck was magic, the house and all its conveniences was impossible to accept; it was all just incredible. Nothing else at her level of awareness could explain electric light bulbs, mirrors, electric appliances, hot and cold running water, the house itself and all the material in it, television, radio, music, DVD players, digital cameras and photographs, metal pots and pans, microwave ovens, stairs, walls separating

rooms, computers, a toilet, furniture, telephones, stove-top heating elements, and everything else 21st Century people take for granted.

Jennifer was in the kitchen preparing dinner. Brittany, Sharon and Ahawi were in the front room talking and Anthony was outside putting away his garden tools and cleaning up his workshop a bit. Jennifer poked her head around the corner into the living room. "Excuse me, Sharon. "I was thinking it might be best if you stayed the night just in case Ahawi has problems and we are unable to communicate with her."

"Yes, I too was going to suggest that."

"Oh, good, um, we can put Ahawi in the spare bed in your room Brittany. It's at least an hour before dinner. Why don't you two take Ahawi upstairs and show her where she will sleep tonight, and maybe run a bath for her. She might like to clean-up before we eat."

"Yeah, sure Mom," replied Brittany. "This should be fun," she said, turning to Ahawi, "Come on." She took Ahawi's hand and headed for the stairs, dragging the reluctant time traveller behind her. "You sleep here," said Brittany in Ahawi's language.

Ahawi looked puzzled. "No, sleep here," she replied pointing to the floor.

"More comfortable here," argued Brittany patting the mattress. "Try it."

Ahawi cautiously sat on the mattress, and smiled.

"Lie back," suggested Sharon.

She did. "Too soft, here is okay," and she again pointed at the floor.

"Okay," shrugged, Brittany.

"Okay?" Ahawi repeated in English.

"You learn quickly," replied Brittany also in English.

"Come," said Brittany in English and curled her finger for Ahawi to follow.

"Come," repeated Ahawi as they walked down the hall to the bathroom.

Brittany pointed to the tub. "Bath."

"Bat'." repeated Ahawi.

Brittany turned on the taps and began filling the tub, checking to be sure the water was not too hot. When the water level was high enough she motioned for Ahawi to take her clothes off and get in the tub but Ahawi was confused.

"It is for you to bathe," said Sharon, and then further explained what Brittany was asking her to do.

In the meantime, Brittany went to the cupboard and took down a large bath towel and handed it to Ahawi.

Again Sharon explained the purpose of the towel and that they were going to leave her to bathe herself. Ahawi hesitated and asked if Sharon would stay with her. "I am how you say, a bit nervous."

Sharon smiled, "No problem."

Ahawi stripped down and stepped cautiously into the tub.

"Your body is beautiful, Ahawi," she said. "But you have so many scars and bruises. What happened?"

Ahawi felt a little embarrassed and wrapped her arms across her breasts. "The gauntlet," she said without offering further explanation.

Jennifer tried to make a meal that would not be unlike what Ahawi might eat at her home - boiled rice, a mixture of beans and squash, and meat with berries and gravy. Not having wild animal meat, Jennifer substituted stewing beef. She made a vegetable burrito for herself and an extra one in case Ahawi might like to try one.

Sitting down to a table seemed an odd way of eating a meal to Ahawi, but remembering the table Daniel made, she said. "Oh, now I know why Daniel made his eating platform."

Sharon translated her words to the family and everyone laughed.

Jason opened a bottle of wine, but Ahawi did not like the taste and preferred peppermint tea instead. The cutlery was totally foreign to Ahawi who ate most of her meal with her fingers, but she picked up the plate and used the spoon to shovel the rice into her mouth.

For dessert Jennifer made apple crisp with ice cream, both flavours totally new to their guest. Ahawi had seconds of dessert and asked for more, but unfortunately it was all gone. "I'll give you some apples to take home with you," she said, and suggested she could take some of the seedlings she had growing in the greenhouse, and a package of apple seeds. "You could plant them and grow your own apples. It would take a number of years for the trees to mature, and even longer for the seeds to produce fruit, though. Daniel will know what to do."

Sharon had difficulty translating the word mature, but Ahawi got the idea and said she would try.

"When will I go home?" she asked Sharon.

"We will return to the village site tomorrow and try calling for Ebony. By now Daniel will have realize you are missing and he probably assumes that you accidentally came here. That will make it easier for Tijus-Keha to convince his father to open the portal to let you return home. That's what we are

going to try."

"What if the 'port' will not open?" asked Ahawi, struggling with the strange word.

"Good question. I do not know. We will try first," assured Sharon.

Ahawi spent a restless night on the floor of Brittany's room, twice during the night calling out. Both times Sharon came to her to calm her down. Each time she had said she was confused and a little frightened. Morning finally came along with the light, much to the relief of the three girls.

Jennifer prepared oat meal porridge and scrambled eggs on toast with sliced apples on the side for breakfast. Sharon translated Jennifer's words about how much Tijus-Keha liked the porridge when he visited their home.

After breakfast they were getting ready to leave, but a cool wind blew from the north and heavy rain began from a leaden sky. "We should give it a couple of hours and see if the rain stops," said Jennifer.

About 1:00 PM the rain did stop and a weak sun peaked out from behind the thinning cloud cover. "Let's go," Jennifer shouted. "Oh, hang on a minute. I have to get the seedlings out of the shed."

Ahawi had no trouble getting in and out of the Tracker for the drive to the docks. She stood on the dock and gave Jennifer a hug. "Miigwech," she said. "Daniel, omaamaa an gaye baabaa ozizhishiwag."

Jennifer looked over to Sharon for the translation. Sharon smiled. "She said thank you, and that she thinks Daniel has a wonderful mother and father."

Jennifer smiled. "Oh, don't forget your apples." Jennifer handed Ahawi a plastic bag full of Macintosh apples. "And here are the little apple trees. There are eight of them. I hope you can manage all of this stuff. If you plant these, you will have apples about two years sooner than planting the seeds."

Sharon translated what Jennifer said so Ahawi understood.

"T'ank-u," replied Ahawi trying to form the words in English.

Reluctantly, Awahi let go of Jennifer's hands. A tear had trickled down the side of her nose; she wiped it away, smiled and stepped into the canoe between Sharon and Brittany. She turned and waved as they pushed off from the shore.

Jennifer waved back. She watched the canoe glide out into the lake and disappear around the far point of land. "Bye and good luck" she whispered. "Daniel is a lucky man to have such a lovely woman. Hope he appreciates you."

At the far end of the lake Brittany was first to jump out of the canoe followed by Ahawi and Sharon.

"Well, here goes; hope he's listening," said Brittany as she looked

around to ensure no one else was watching them. "Ebony, Ebony," she shouted. "It's me White Swan calling. Ahawi is here. Please open the portal so she can go home." Twice more Brittany repeated her message. Finally, a now familiar faint yellow glow appeared and grew brighter and larger, and out of the centre stepped Ebony.

"Ebony," Brittany shouted, and put her arms around him.

Ebony planted a message in Brittany's and Sharon's minds. "Thank you," the message said. "We were wondering where she had gone." Another message he planted in Ahawi's mind for her to stand beside him with all her things. She did so and was immediately surrounded by a yellow glow. Ahawi turned and waved, and she and Ebony disappeared.

"I like her," commented Brittany.

"Me too," agreed Sharon. "I would like to have spent more time with her to get to known her better; maybe another time."

"Yeah, but in whose time?" asked Brittany.

"Too confusing. Come on let us get back. Your mom will be waiting."

A great deal of scepticism remained among the First Nations people on Manitoulin Island who had witnessed the Feast of the Dead, but few spoke of what they had seen for fear of showing disrespect to the miracle many said happened.

During the next few weeks, life around the Santos' household returned to some semblance of normal. Business at the Wolf Education and Research Centre continued to be brisk with a full season of school groups booked for the winter. The first fall of snow had already dropped a few centimetres on the ground.

Jennifer and Anthony were sitting around the fire one evening shortly into the New Year. "I wonder how Daniel's doing." Anthony asked again, as he often did.

"Probably just fine, but I wish we'd had more time to speak with Ahawi. She seems like a lovely young woman, and she is definitely very fond of Daniel. Do you think she is keeping his bed warm?"

Anthony laughed. "I wouldn't be surprised, but last fall Daniel was still too upset over Holly's death to get too serious with another woman. Give it time."

Both sat in silence for a moment. "Oh, by the way," said Anthony. "Your father mentioned the other day that Jim Kirby has been fired from Sudbury television."

"Oh, really, that's too bad," Jennifer replied, and giggled.

Spring arrived reluctantly around the Santos homestead. Most of the snow had gone except from north facing rocks and hills, and the ground around the place was a quagmire of mud and rivulets of running water. The first Sunday morning in early May dawned bright, clear and breathless. Anthony, Jennifer and Brittany drove into Little Current where they rented a motorboat from the marina and headed along the North Channel, under the swing-bridge and then north-east to Killarney. Following the coast along the top of Georgian Bay, they arrived at the mouth of the French River. They pulled up to the dock at the campsite, climbed out of their small craft, tied their boat to the anchor rings, and walked the short distance up river to the base of the falls.

They spent an hour or so walking around the base of the falls and the groomed lands trying to envision what had taken place there so long ago, and wondered how different the area might have been back then.

"That must be the rock over there that Tijus-Keha mentioned where Holly came to rest," said Anthony, pointing.

"Yes. It's the only natural rock around that looks like a bench," replied Jennifer.

Brittany looked at her watch. "It's just coming up to 12:00 o'clock now. Come on. We don't want to miss it."

They all sat down on the rock bench and watched the mists curl up from the base of the falls. The view was spectacular.

Brittany sat in quiet solitude. Holding onto her mother's and father's hands, she imagined the Wakemsui canoes full of warriors cresting the top of the falls and crashing down the wall of water in front of her. Suddenly, the mists began to coagulate and form a denser mass in the middle just above the rocks and cries of anguish could be heard from the falling waters.

"Look Mom. There's Holly, and she's smiling at us."

"Yes, Brittany, it really is her. Isn't it wonderful?"

Brittany and her parents waved and they too smiled. Then as quickly as it had appeared, Running Fawn's image faded back into the mists of the falling water.

"Bye," whispered Brittany.

The adventures of Daniel, Ebony, Ahawi, Jennifer and Anthony continue in the fourth novel in the series about the black wolf. Soon to be released.

The Legendary Fortress

Chapter One
Lame Beaver's Vision

The two great rivers merged into one where two valleys of an important crossroad met. The swirling waters breached their banks flooding inland many metres beyond their normal paths and threatened a large village built high on the rocks on a flat field overlooking the tortured scene. It had been a particularly cold winter with an abundance of snow and now with the sudden rise in temperature the additional spring run-off added considerably more strength to the liquid rush.

The village site in the field high on the rocks had been chosen carefully to provide a fortification against attacking enemy forces, for easy transportation to and from hunting grounds, along with convenient access to the fresh water of the rivers for food, drinking, cooking and washing.

A gusting wind blew from the direction of the one Star Child who did not move in the sky and brought an instant chill to the air around. Standing on the hill just outside the village gates overlooking the swirling torrents, Skyaq shivered in the cold wind, pulled his elk hide cloak tight around his shoulders and tucked his hands under his armpits. He watched the fast-running waters eat away at the river bank that supported a large tamarack pine where he had frequently played as a child swinging out over the usually peaceful waters on a long vine and flying into the water. He marvelled at the strength of the tamarack as it stood high and proud against the onslaught of the growing tide. But unseen beneath the surface of the waters the raging torrents ate away at the earth supporting the very root of this mighty tree. As Skyaq watched, the tree shook slightly then began a slow motion roll forward and fell into the bubbling foam. The

water pulled and tugged at the root system swinging the heavy tree around in its angry boiling mass. The tree clung to the river bank; suddenly the roots planted so firmly in Mother Earth snapped free and within seconds the tree disappeared beneath the seething water.

"Father Winter always leaves with such vengeance," Skyaq said to himself. "I will miss that tree. It was a good friend." Shaking his head to clear his mind, he said. "I must speak with Oweznee. We have enough warriors to succeed with my plan. And this time of year all our enemies are weak from the hardships of winter and in no mood for battle. It is the right time to strike." He turned and walked in through the village gates.

"Uncle, are you home; may I speak with you?" asked Skyaq at the doorway to his uncle's lodge.

"I am. Please enter."

Skyaq stooped down and pushed back the animal hide that hung down across the low entranceway. It took a moment for his eyes to adjust to the low light of the fire-lit interior. "Now is the time, Uncle," demanded Skyaq. "The On-Da People are weak, their warriors lack courage and they have many children. We must rebuild our ranks. We too are weak, but many of our warriors have survived the winter well. Our sacred rivers gave us a good supply of winter food. If we attack the On-Da now, we can capture many children and in a few summers we will once again be strong and greatly feared by our enemies. We must act now or it will be too late."

Qweznee turned to Skyaq, "Do you have any idea of what you are asking?"

"Of course, if we do not act now, as a Nation we will die."

"You are so young; how do you know? Not one major honour of war hangs from your lodge poles. How dare you come to me and demand we take up arms against the On-Da. You are too impulsive, just like your father. And look where that got him and many of our best warriors who blindly followed him."

"Do not insult me or my father with your lame talk of honour or prizes of war as being necessary prerequisites of a good war-chief. What have you done in the last few summers to show your courage as our war-leader? Under your leadership the Wakemsui have grown weak and no longer feared by our neighbours."

Oweznee had to stop and think. "Yes, I agree that the Wakemsui are not as powerful as in our glorious past. And yes we lack only strength of numbers to regain our feared status." He also realized that this brazen young man standing in front of him was becoming a respected warrior amongst the youth of the village. Many of the young warriors who had

recently come of age looked up to him and came to him for advice on matters of war. Among other anxieties with all the young warriors, they wanted to prove their newly acquired manhood. Without trophies of war how could any of them win the approval of a young squaw's Matron.

"Young Skyaq, please, we must be careful not to lose more of our numbers in frivolous battles. The On-Da Nation is not as weak as you suggest. And above all, they cherish their children and will go to extreme measures to protect them. All Peoples will be hunting for fresh game to rebuild lean bodies from Father Winter's challenges. Your idea is risky, but I agree times like now demand extreme measures. Your idea has merit. Let us bring it to the council meeting in three sun turns. If it is agreed, then it will be so."

Skyaq grunted his agreement.

Whew, thought Oweznee after Skyaq had left, *I am glad I was able to temper young Skyaq's anxiety to fight. This will give me time to think of a plan to present to the council meeting. I must be careful not to give too much power to this hot headed young warrior. Like his father, he'll lead us all to death.*

Skyaq's father, Kwa-Erha, had been one of the Wakemsui's finest war chiefs. In a battle many summers ago he and all his warriors had been slain by a mysterious foe, a foe many said was the Great Kitchi-Manitou himself, and their bodies, along with his father's, had been left where they'd fallen to rot and be eaten by scavengers. His father's remains had not been honoured in normal Wakemsui tradition. And then, a few moons later what had remained of the Wakemsui's most respected warriors had joined forces with the Wendowa Nation in a battle for revenge, but all had been wiped out attacking their most feared enemy with the white skinned leader. This defeat of their finest warriors had left the Wakemsui and Wendowa peoples seriously short of young men to protect their village and to strike fear in their enemy's hearts. In the years between, what few warriors remained had begun systematic raids on neighbouring Nations to steal fertile squaws to become slaves and to bear children that would be adopted into Wakemsui families. It was a slow process to increase village population, but was also a common solution practised by the Wakemsui for generations. It had also been decreed by village elders that each eligible warrior would take three squaws, a decision that had gone against normal village beliefs, but a decree that all agreed had to be made if the village was to multiply. These children would be raised in the Wakemsui way and would be just as eager as any Wakemsui warrior for honours of war.

§

Near an inland village many kilometres away, the Holy Man of the On-Da Nation, Lame Beaver, supported by Oak Leaf, stepped carefully into his canoe.

"Go carefully, my husband," remarked Oak Leaf. "Our people are relying on you to find the answers to our difficulties."

"I will, my love, and thank you. Call the elders together for a meeting at first light one sun turn from now. I shall return."

Lame Beaver paddled his canoe out into the mists of the great lake upon which his people had lived in harmony for so many generations. But this year the great lake did not surrender its bounty to the hungry people of the On-Da Nation. No village elder could ever remember a time when the lake had not supplied fish for their winter needs, or a time when game in the forests had been so scarce.

Out in the middle of the lake, Lame Beaver stopped paddling and let his small craft float lazily on the gentle currents. He raised his arms to the sky. "Oh Great Eagle," Lame Beaver prayed. "Bring me the answers. I have fasted for three days in the traditional manner of the On-Da People. No vision came to me last night in the sweat lodge. I have no answers to guide the People. I ask you in the name of the On-Da Nation to guide me and show me the light. With no fish from the lake, no animals from the forests, my People are in great need. The Big River the other side of the mountains runs too swiftly for our canoes and is filled with many dangers this time of the season. We cannot paddle out to fish from its waters. Our many children are starving. Many of the old, my mother included, have already gone from the village to find their way to the Land Beyond so they will no longer be a burden to the young. It is a sad time for us, Great Eagle. I ask you; please bring me your vision."

Lame Beaver sat back on his seat, closed his eyes and let out a deep sigh. He felt more exhausted than he could ever remember. His concerns for the people of the On-Da Nation were taking their toll on the aging shaman. Floating lazily on the tranquil waters of the great lake, his mind thought about many things then touched on the day he had inherited his new name, the day he startled a large beaver many jumps from the lake. He smiled at the thought. With no easy escape route, to protect itself the beaver had lunged at the Indian's leg and bitten deep into flesh and muscle and tore a big chunk away. Lame Beaver was a much younger man then, a man on the verge of exploring his own emerging powers as a respected dreamer. He'd stumbled back to the village with his somewhat embarrassing tale of woe. The elders laughed that a man of such respect should be so injured by a normally benign and friendly creature. In the

following days, the wound had festered and Lame Beaver had remained bed ridden. Had it not been for the knowledge of healing herbs and teas possessed by his squaw, Oak Leaf, he might have died, but he eventually did heal. However, the remaining scars had left him with a permanent limp and from then on he had been known as Lame Beaver.

Weakened by the sparse diet of the last winter and by his three-day fast, Lame Beaver's eyes grew heavy, his head slumped and he dozed in the quiet of the early morning sunshine. He shook his head to clear his thoughts and waited for the vision that had always come, but this time seemed to elude his demands. He slumped forward again mumbling to himself. Again he vainly tried to jerk upright, but a deep sleep overcame him.

A new image began to form, that of a large feathered head in front of him that bobbed from side to side. His hands clung desperately to the feathers all around. To either side, large wings flapped. Up and up he flew.

Far below, rolling hills and green forests with open meadows spread before him. Patches of white dotted the hills all around. A great ridge of mountains, mountains he recognized, ran the full length of the horizon over which set Evening Sun. Straight towards the yellow orb they flew. He closed his eyes from the bright light and burrowed his body deep into the feathers for warmth. A cold wind blew. Many moments later, cresting the mountain ridge, far below, bathed in a golden hue, a village surrounded by stone walls appeared in a vast field. Within the village walls were many people. Squaws and children tended three large gardens of growing vegetables or scraped at hides on the ground. Many warriors walked between the buildings within, some carrying animal carcasses while others played games. Never had Lame Beaver seen such a huge village fortified in this way and with so many growing fields within. It must be truly a mighty Nation to have such a village. Three of the larger structures in the centre of the village ringed what looked like a huge meeting place where many people could gather for celebration or for talks. From his height above the village it appeared to be an important meeting place where many warriors could meet in council.

The large bird swooped down low over the meeting place, but strangely no one within the village seemed to see them. A large fire burned in the middle and the aroma of cooking food filtered up from racks built over the fire, racks laden with raw meat and fish.

They flew on into the bright light and came to where the two boiling rivers merged into one. A village surrounded by a palisade of tree trucks planted in the ground overlooked the rivers. A fire burned in the centre of the village tended by a number of squaws and children. The

scene below began to fade and Lame Beaver felt himself falling. A moment later he stood on the ground inside the village's wooden palisade walls. His vision once again blurred and was replaced by a new scene inside a long bark lodge. He was sitting in council across a small fire with many warriors. These warriors were from Nations not far from his village and seemed to be in council. Many were in heated debate and many others were shouting a strange word, 'confederacy', while still others were eating, drinking and laughing in quiet conversation.

The warrior immediately across from Lame Beaver stared at him. His long beak-like nose was the predominant feature of his lean and long face. His chiselled chin gave his expression a ferocity that was cold and demanding. His head was clean shaven save a narrow strip of hair across the top of his head from the front all the way down to the nape of his neck. A single grey feather with a white tip hung over his shoulder attached to a leather thong sewn into a small braid of hair that hung down his back. The warrior pulled his arm out from within the elk hide he wore and raised his hand in a peace sign. Lame Beaver found himself giving the same sign, then the image faded and he awoke in his canoe.

He shivered; a cold breeze had come up. The morning mists had gone. He looked around and realized his canoe had been blown many lengths down the lake and was beached on the small island in the middle. How long he had been there was unclear, but Father Sun had already travelled across the sky and now hovered just above the trees on the far hills on the opposite side. "Have I slept so long?" he asked himself.

Excited and confused at the vision he'd been given, and still unclear of its true meaning, Lame Beaver grabbed his paddle and began the journey back to his village.

Michelle

In the house by the lake

you have woven a dream,

a victory, all the squares

and rounds fused in a

subtlety you never imagined.

In the darker shades of recall

animal soft reached to comfort

and sustain, your dearest reward

being simplicity.

In the house by the lake

you have woven a dream,

the stars being of your own keeping.

Merci Fournier

Michelle Duff

Michelle was born in 1939 in Toronto, Ontario, Canada. She has lived most of her life in Toronto, although in the 1960s she spent eight years travelling parts of Europe and one year in California, USA. In 2000 she moved from Toronto north to the wilds of Central Ontario and the town of Coldwater. She lives in a small winterized cottage on two acres of rocks, trees, bugs and bears, 100 metres from Lake Otter where she has a dock and a canoe. She is often seen swimming in the lake or canoeing around the gentle waters in summer or cross country skiing or skating across the ice in winter. She shares her life with two dogs and three cats, and whatever other wild creatures are in need of company. When weather permits she sits outside on her deck, laptop at the ready and adds copy to a novel or a magazine article in company of her cats or dogs and numerous birds and other furry critters stealing bird seed from her bird feeders.

Since her early teen years she has had many magazine articles published on a variety of topics, but only recently has she taken the craft of writing more seriously. Running Fawn's Legacy is Michelle's sixth book to be published, the third in the series about the black wolf. Four, maybe five, novels in total are planned in the life of the black wolf.

Michelle is also a talented nature photographer.